A Divided Duty

A sequel to *My Painful Duty*

Ben Vizard

Best wishes

Ben V...

Published by Independent Publishing Network

Cover design by BespokeBookCovers

Printed in Great Britain

Although every precaution has been taken in the preparation of this book, the publisher and author assume no responsibility for errors or omissions. Neither is any liability assumed for damages resulting from the use of information contained herein.

ISBN 978-1-80352-906-6

Acknowledgements

I'd like to record my great thanks and appreciation to my principal editor, and probably the greatest nitpicker in the world, Lottie Fyfe, whose sensitivity and perception have immeasurably improved this story. Also to Eleanor Smith, who took forensic care in checking the final draft was correct in every way. And Peter at Bespoke Covers for his great cover design.

I'd also like to thank my friend Victoria Wood-Matthews for reading and commenting on an early draft. And all the people who read and enjoyed my first book and encouraged me to inflict another story on the world!

And finally, this book is in memory of my dad, Michael Vizard, whose rich life provided, and will always provide, an inspiration to me.

Part One

1939

Chapter 1

There was a shimmer on the ceiling. A distorted echo of the bright sun which glistened on the water. Hansen felt the warmth of it on the side of his face and stretched out in the bath. He felt light-headed, in the way that a few glasses of wine could once achieve. Pleasant, but a little out of control. Tension seeped away into the water. It was replaced by a heaviness in his limbs. He allowed his head to rest against the enamelled rim.

An incongruous smile shaped briefly across his lips. Absurd, in light of recent events. He had hoped to ease the memories away too, but the warmth of the water and the quiet of the bathroom, interrupted only by the occasional drip from the tap, gave his mind free rein. When had it all started? Six months ago? No, it was longer than that. Time had begun to stretch, and he had stopped counting days.

Events that had surely been only weeks ago felt like months or years, and vice-versa. The last time he'd felt anything like this was more than twenty years ago, during the war. The Great War, as they had known it then, though a greater one was now in prospect. The war to end all wars had singularly failed.

Almost like a magic spell, the thought opened a Pandora's Box of emotion which he feared he could not control. He curled his toes and tried to force the memory away. The dreams had returned, with a vengeance, and the shaking too. He put his hand to his forehead and felt the warmth of the water and a steady pulse against his skin. He was intent on keeping those demons from reawakening, whatever the cost.

It seemed insane now to think that he had tried to go back. But he had. February, was it? Or January? There had been a cold wind that bit into his joints, especially his knee. His damaged knee, scarred and shattered as it was. The ground crunched with ice as he made his way heavily to the recruiting office. A hope, though a forlorn one, that he might recapture something of the person he had been.

Sitting in front of the recruiting sergeant, he'd felt like a schoolboy again. The raw innocent whose legs had gone from underneath him when he had first taken command of a company of men on the Western Front, after seeing his commanding officer blown to atoms in front of him.

He had stripped for the doctor and been prodded and poked, and then he had waited.

Emily had frowned when he had told her. More of a half-frown really, her bottom lip jutting out and her brown eyes looking up at him in a mix of sadness and frustration.

'Why would you put us…' She had stopped. 'Why would you put yourself through that again?'

It was not said with anger, but with what appeared to be a genuine bewilderment. And he had not known how to answer her. The truth was simple: commanding a unit was the one thing he knew he could do. With no conceit, he had undoubtedly been a good officer. And, though he could barely admit it to himself – let alone his wife – he had enjoyed it.

There was something in being needed, in being important, that made the experience as thrilling as it was terrifying. He had known then that another war was imminent, and the thought of being needed again, to be in control again, was compelling.

He caught a glimpse of himself in the mirror above the basin, his face just visible above the bath rim. His blonde hair was greying now and thinning. His eyes heavy and lined, the blue faded. Haggard and weary. It was hardly his face at all. A stranger. Had it been a stranger, he would have asked if they were quite well.

Emily had tried to convince him not to go, but it had been impossible. He was set on it, and she had realised it soon enough. At the last she had voiced the thought that had obviously been in her mind from the outset:

'If there's another war,' she had said, and stopped there, turning away to hide the glint of a tear in her eye.

'If there is,' he had replied, 'then I shall at least have a purpose again.'

He had surprised himself with his own bitterness. Seeing her about to cry had prompted a flash of anger, though he didn't know why. He had reached out to take her hands in apology.

Emily had not reciprocated or replied. She had walked into the garden and taken up her usual thinking place by the laurel bushes, watching the fish in the pond. It was the first thing she had suggested they build when they had moved in, shortly after their marriage, though he'd never known why it meant so much to her. Even in the bitter cold, she had sat there for at least an hour. When she returned, she had simply embraced him and said softly:

'I understand, my love.'

Not that any of it mattered. The arguments and the anxiety were for nothing when the recruiting sergeant had simply told him, two weeks later, that he was not fit for service.

'I served in the last war,' he had remonstrated.

'I can see that, Mr Hansen. I have the information here. Major Richard Hansen, Devonshire Regiment. It's a distinguished record, without doubt. But the doctor said he was surprised you went back after your last wound. You're certainly not fit for service now, in peacetime, especially at your age.

'I'm sorry, sir,' he had added, in a sympathetic tone that riled Hansen.

'You won't be so picky if there's a war,' he'd replied petulantly.

'Even then, sir, the doc tells me he'd pass you at best C3. Only fit for desk work, he said.'

Hansen barely remembered the hours after that. He had a vague memory of finding himself in Christ Church Meadow, beside the Isis. He had looked at the river then as he looked at the bathwater around him now.

Emily had always been clever. So very insightful and curious, and it had taken her to places that neither of them could have imagined. Curating exhibits at the Ashmolean. Respected, even revered, by her peers, while he had only floundered. It shouldn't matter, but it did.

Emily loved his writing, but she was seemingly the only one. Scratching a living as a freelance journalist would hardly pay the bills, and there was little satisfaction or recognition in it for him. When he'd chucked it in to return to the law, she had supported him. But now he was practising in a profession for which he had little proficiency and even less passion.

He had pushed her to begin with, proud of her every accomplishment, but increasingly he felt resentful. That she should fly while he had never found his wings. Did she sense it? He couldn't be sure, but he hated himself for it all the same, and buried it deep. Those unworthy feelings.

The short day had ended as he sat thinking in Christ Church Meadow, and with the darkness closing around him, he had found himself not heading for home, but instead sitting in The Bear. A glass of whisky placed in front of him, he cradled it in his hands for a time, and enjoyed the dance of the log fire, filtered through the gold in his glass. He raised it to his lips and allowed it to burn there for a moment, inhaling the sweet, peaty aroma.

Distracted, he had not noticed a figure approach and stand in front of him, until they coughed delicately to gain his attention.

'You're not going to drink that, are you?'

There was something more to the question than a simple enquiry, and he had looked up to find a familiar round face staring back at him, his head tilted to one side.

'Good God!'

'He is indeed.'

'Ernie!'

'Do you know how many pubs there are in Oxford, Richard? I believe I have been in all of them this afternoon. And it's rude, of course, not to enjoy something of the landlord's hospitality, having entered a place. So if you don't mind, I shall sit down for a moment and gather myself.'

The little man looked so much older. But of course, it had been nearly twenty years since he had last seen his old padre, Ernest Crosse. He was so genuinely astounded he could not have been more surprised had a unicorn trotted into the bar and ordered a pint. It took him some moments to pick up his thoughts and accept the hand that Crosse had extended. His old friend dropped heavily into the chair opposite, and there was the momentary awkwardness of seeing an old friend for the first time in a long while. Neither of them knew quite how to begin.

'You were in New Zealand!' he had exclaimed at last, as if that fact made it impossible for Crosse to be there.

'I was that,' said Crosse, taking off his glasses and wiping them in the way Hansen remembered so well. It broke all awkwardness.

'I started hankering for the old country, you know? And the school went bust, which was unfortunate…'

He stopped his cleaning and leaned across, wagging his finger. 'Don't say I told you so!'

Hansen just shrugged and smiled.

'I've been here a few months now. Working part-time with the regiment.'

'Oh.'

'Oh indeed, Richard.'

'I'd rather not talk about it.'

Crosse folded his arms and nodded gently. He stretched out his legs to warm them by the fire.

'So, you didn't answer my question. Are you going to drink that?'

In reply, Hansen had pushed the glass towards his old friend, keen to be rid of the temptation.

'I thought so. You don't mind?'

Hansen waved his hand in assent. Crosse sipped appreciatively and gave a low grumble of satisfaction.

'Mmm. It seems helping you to keep your promise to Emily is to my benefit. Speaking of whom, she is well, I trust?'

There'd been something shifty in his face as he'd said it. Crosse had always been an open book. He omitted things certainly. But rarely lied, and always badly.

'I suspect you know already, Ernie. You've seen her, haven't you?' said Hansen.

Crosse began to stammer a reply, but he cut him off abruptly.

'And—'

'Richard—'

'And… she sent you to find me, didn't she?'

Crosse placed the glass down deliberately and took his spectacles off once again.

'Emily was worried. Can you blame her?'

'And you told her I failed the medical?'

'I would never do such a thing, but she's your wife. It doesn't take a genius to understand that a man who struggled to walk when I last saw him might find it difficult to be accepted back into active service. And now you're...'

'Old?'

'Hardly that, yet. Unlike me. But... you're what, forty-five now?'

'Forty-four, actually.'

As if the year made all the difference.

'In your prime, it could be said. In any other walk of life. But in the army...

'Look, you don't have to explain to me. We both know another war is likely, and you want to do your duty. That's who you are. It's noble, in a blinkered kind of way. But it's for a new generation to fight this time, God help them. Not you. And especially not me.'

Crosse had taken a swig of whisky and twisted his face as he swallowed.

Hansen bowed his head and couldn't look his friend in the eye. He couldn't bring himself to admit just how much he really did need it. The uniform had gone to the back of the wardrobe, but he had never really taken it off. He had never felt as valued or as purposeful in the years since, however much he had tried. And he had tried.

'Well, you know all this,' continued Crosse. 'I won't labour the point. Like your old service revolver, that experience is best kept locked away, in the attic, out of sight, but to hand if ever, God forbid, it should be needed.'

'The madman in the attic,' said Hansen. It was intended to be a joke, but neither of them smiled.

Hansen sighed deeply and fell back into the leather padding on the booth. Crosse raised a curious eyebrow.

'But I am delighted to see you again, old chap,' he continued, changing the subject with little subtlety. 'Tell me about things. How long have you been in Oxford?'

Hansen had made an effort to smile and be gracious. They had chatted away for several hours. He explained all that Emily had accomplished and was surprised at the pride that came into his voice as he did so. Crosse had given him the knowing half-smile that he remembered so well.

He described the travelling they had done, to all the places they'd both dreamed of seeing. They had ventured across America, explored the Mediterranean, and even made it as far as India, where Emily had insisted on riding an elephant. He chuckled at the memory of his attempts to mount one, and how his pride had taken as much of a beating as his backside. He hadn't found it as funny at the time, but Emily had never let him forget it, and he smiled even more at the memory of her gentle teasing.

Crosse had had plenty to tell as well. As predicted, being a headmaster in New Zealand hadn't been quite what he had planned, but he had made the most of his time there, and he described the country with great affection. He had married too and brought his wife back with him. They were happily settled in London, but he was regularly in Oxford, he said, on business. As well as seeming to travel a great deal.

'Perhaps the four of us could have dinner sometime?'

'I should like that very much,' said Hansen. Once before he had likened his old friend's timely arrival to being thrown a lifebuoy, and so it seemed again now.

'And do you get back to Devon often?'

The question took him aback a little, and Crosse picked up on his discomfort.

'I'm sorry… sensitive subject?'

'No,' he lied.

Crosse saw through it and nodded sympathetically.

'Your parents never accepted your marriage, I take it?'

'My father did. My mother – well, you know how she was… not until her dying day, and not even then.'

As he spoke he could feel his voice cracking. He stopped abruptly, and more than ever he wanted the comfort, false though it might be, of a first drink in twenty years.

'Has something happened?' asked Crosse, his eyes searching out Hansen's expression.

'There was a telegram a few days ago…' he began. Crosse handed him a glass of water and he took a gulp.

'My father passed away. It was a stroke.'

He said it in the most matter-of-fact way he could manage, as if he were talking about an acquaintance. Saying it out loud did not make it any more real.

'I'm sorry,' said Crosse.

Hansen batted away the platitude and ploughed on.

'Now they want me to return to Exeter and take up my father's business.

'We hadn't been close in these last years. I always thought he was a little disappointed in me. Or at least that was the sense I had. But I feel an obligation, you know? Even if I can't aspire to what he accomplished. It would be something.'

As he said it to Crosse, he had realised in his own mind the significance of this part of it. He had expected to feel the loss of his father, though it had hardly been sudden. (Did that make it better or worse?) But that wasn't it entirely. His hometown was scarcely a place of happy memories, and he'd been quick enough to quit it before. Nevertheless, there was a feeling of unfinished business.

'And what does Emily think?'

He shifted uncomfortably and took another sip of water.

'You have asked her?' asked Crosse, his face wrinkled in agitation, breaking his usual phlegmatic calm.

'Have you told her at all?'

Hansen shook his head. Crosse sighed and knocked his pipe out onto the table with a loud crack.

'You don't change, Richard. She won't break. She's stronger than you realise.'

He'd tilted his head a little in thought as he opened his pouch of tobacco.

'You're worried she won't want to go?'

'Would you? If you were her? That house has nothing but bad memories for her. I can't ask her to do that. But at the same time... it's my father's legacy. He built a life there from nothing when he came to this country. Everything he achieved is there. I can't just let it go.'

'No.'

Crosse refilled his pipe slowly. As he put it to his mouth and lit it, he looked over his glasses at Hansen.

'And what happened today – how does that fit?'

'It has nothing to do with it,' Hansen had replied sharply.

Crosse had frowned and turned his pipe in his mouth. He could sense the lie like a bloodhound.

'Alright, damn you,' said Hansen. 'Perhaps I'm less worried that she won't want to go, and more worried that *I* don't. When I last saw my father, he virtually begged me. He knew he was dying, and I made him a promise. It's his life's work. But I thought if I had another purpose, a greater duty, I might… I might…'

'Have a reason not to go?'

Hansen brought his hands together tightly in front of him, almost as if in prayer. He nodded reluctantly.

'And you want to keep all your promises,' added Crosse, tapping the now-empty whisky glass. 'You know that's not always possible. We all have to make choices. And you need to tell her.'

'Yes.'

'Is that a "Yes, you're right, as usual, Crosse, and I will", or a "Shut up, I don't want to hear it" yes?'

'What do you think?'

Crosse tilted his head to one side and gave one of his little lopsided smiles. 'She will understand.'

'Yes… Yes, she always does,' he said sadly.

'Well, then I shall conclude my mentorly advice for today,' said Crosse. 'Whether you appreciate it now or simply come to appreciate it later, I will leave to you.

'"Train a child in the way he should go, and when he is old he will not turn from it."'

'Don't start quoting from Proverbs, Ernie,' said Hansen, rubbing his temples.

'You always enjoyed a good quotation, I seem to remember? I see you haven't lost your gift for attribution either. How about this one: "Sons are a heritage for the Lord; children a reward from him."'

Hansen had looked up sharply at this.

'What do you mean by that?'

Crosse seemed genuinely shocked for once.

'It's just a quotation, Richard. It happened to come to mind…'

Hansen narrowed his eyes. Nothing Crosse said had ever been just happenstance. Hansen looked quickly at his watch. 'I hadn't realised the time. Emily will be waiting.'

He picked himself up, keeping his eyes away from Crosse's scrutiny, worried at what he might see there.

'But thank you. You do have a knack for appearing at the right time though, you know? Almost as if it were ordained.'

'You can blame my boss,' said Crosse, pointing skywards.

They had shaken hands and he'd left the pub in a hurry. As he walked, something in what Crosse had said about promises took hold in his mind. Could he break one promise to satisfy another?

In time, he'd reached their home and as he pushed open the door, Emily had hurried down the hall towards him. The words 'Where have you been?' seemed to be on her lips, but before she could say anything, he interrupted.

'I ran into Ernie.'

'Oh,' she said awkwardly. 'That's good. How is he?'

He had put his finger gently to her lips and stopped her.

'It's alright. I know he was here. I didn't mean to worry you, I'm sorry. Before you say anything, there's something I need to tell you.'

Now she did look worried. Her face had gone ashen, and she pushed her dark hair back behind her ears, something she did when she was nervous. He had always found it endearing.

'The telegram that came a few days ago...'

'Yes?' She stepped forward and touched his arm gently. Telegrams were not so common now, and of course she had wondered.

'My father has passed away.'

It took a moment for the news to sink in before a flash of anger passed across her face.

'Your father died, and you didn't tell me?'

Just as quickly, the anger seemed to pass, and her face softened again in sorrow. 'I'm sorry.'

She embraced him and held him tightly.

'I didn't mean to get angry. It's just I... He was...'

There seemed to be something more she wanted to say, but she held back. 'Never mind.'

They had stood there together for some time. It had once been so usual to hold her like this. He breathed in the warm scent of her hair, felt her soft skin against his rough cheek, and allowed a tear to roll silently down his face. She didn't seem to want to let go, and he felt her shiver with emotion. He was content just to feel her closeness.

Eventually, she lifted her head, and he hurriedly wiped his eyes and projected a cheerful expression.

'Are you alright?' she asked.

'Fine. It was his time. You know he'd been ill. It is how it is. These things happen.'

'Richard!'

'What?'

'Please talk to me.'

'People die.'

'It's not "people". He was your father. And in many ways, he was…'

She stopped herself again.

'He was what?'

'A good man,' she said. Though it was clear that that was not what she had intended to say. 'A man who should be honoured and remembered.'

'He was, I know,' he said quietly. He hardly needed to be reminded.

The weight he felt was intense. A need. Not just the idea that he would never see him again, but that something would forever be missing. That he could succeed him but, in so many ways, could never replace him.

As he had studied Emily's face, Hansen discerned a deep sadness. The same sadness he had seen before, on the steps of the hospital. Then, he had felt impotent, unable to help. And surrounded, suffocated, by his own grief. He'd had the sense that if he opened himself to her, he would be overcome by it. Weak, when she needed his strength. He had experienced an overpowering urge to run away, to find a place to hide, to find air, to find himself again.

'Please stay,' she said, sensing his movement. 'I can't bear it when you pull away.'

He had felt crushed by guilt. For his father. For her. But it was too much.

'I can't. I just can't...'

He found himself holding his breath with the tension of each memory. Sliding down further into the bathwater, he rhythmically opened and closed his hands to try to relax them.

The distance between them had seemed to grow by the day. The longer things were left unsaid, the harder it became.

In the end, he had had to broach the idea of returning to Exeter for the funeral, and, perhaps, for longer. Would she consider moving, at least for a time, back to Devon?

He thought he had learned to read her every expression in the years they had been together, but this time he couldn't be sure. He imagined he sensed fear, but if that was what it was, she had sought to hide it quickly. She had asked for time to think about it, and over the days that followed, she had spent much of her time in her thinking place in the garden.

Then, as they were getting ready for bed one night, she had sat down on the mattress and held out her hand to him. She pulled him next to her and held his hand in hers, as she had many times before. It still sent a little shiver through him.

'I've thought about what you said,' she began. 'And I know it matters to you to protect your father's legacy. It matters to me, too. But it matters more that you are happy. So… I think we should go.'

He could feel she was holding something back, but at the same time, there was huge relief in hearing her say it.

'I promise it won't be for long,' he had heard himself saying. 'Just until we can sell the house and secure the business. It's not that I *want* to be a solicitor – you know that.'

'I know,' she said, smiling. 'You told me that a long time ago. But if you feel we need to go… that will make you happy, won't it?'

'Yes… I'm sure of it.' He tried to keep the doubt out of his voice. 'At least, I think it would have made him happy, and so that must make me happy, mustn't it?'

She nodded. A reluctant half-nod.

'And your work?' he asked.

'I'll ask for a leave of absence, I suppose.'

She smiled, but it was not a complete smile. Her eyes told a different story and there was a tension in her hands as she held him tightly.

She caressed his face and kissed him tenderly on the lips. They lay down together and she guided his hand to her thigh, pushing her nightdress up. He could feel passion building as he kissed her more deeply. Her breathing shallowed and she began to open his shirt, button by button, as her other hand stroked his hair. But as she pressed her hand onto the scars on his chest, a feeling like an electric shock passed through him, and he pulled back.

'We shouldn't,' he said, buttoning his shirt again.

'Please…' she said.

'It's late. And I know you haven't been sleeping these last few nights. I'll sleep in the guest room.'

As he'd lain there that night, he had felt cold, in every sense of the word. But there had been no choice. He had told himself then, and he told himself again now, as a new chill came over him despite the steam still rising from the bathwater. He might have given in to his passion, the craving for closeness, the desperation to hold her, but then what? Joy again. Expectation again. Loss again? Every choice he made was because he wanted the best for her. For them both. Wasn't it? He had told himself that, even as he had heard her crying in the next room.

Chapter 2

'Why did you do that?' said a voice. Distant, almost whispered. Hansen strained to hear. He opened his tired eyes and searched the room. A figure stood in the lengthening shadows as the gold of a late summer sunset filled the bathroom. How long had he been lying in the water, thinking, remembering?

'Who is that?' he asked.

'Why did you do that?' repeated the voice, clearer this time. The figure moved closer now and Hansen could see from his outline that he was wearing an army uniform, though his features still seemed indistinct. Whether it was the dying light or his eyesight, he couldn't be sure, but it was a familiar figure, and a familiar voice.

'Duncan?' he asked plaintively.

He would swear that the figure resembled his erstwhile best friend. A friend who had done more for him than anyone else had, or ever could. But a friend who couldn't possibly be there. Captain Duncan Martin.

'Why did you do that?' repeated the figure for a third time, his voice steady and patient.

'Why did I do what?'

'You left her.'

'I had to.'

'She was crying.'

'Yes. She was cold, she was alone, on the step...'

He stopped. His memories were mixed up.

'But you couldn't know that, Duncan... you never knew Emily. You were... you weren't there.'

'You talked about her – I remember that. You talked about how you couldn't bear to see her upset like that. When you first met?'

Hansen strained to lift himself. His mind was foggy now. Too tired to focus.

'Yes, she was cold, scrubbing the step. Her hands were red raw. Then, when she turned around, I could see she had been crying. She was so small, so vulnerable. I wanted to protect her.'

Why this memory? So long ago now. More than twenty-five years. But it persisted.

'So you warmed her hands?'

'Yes. I tried to reassure her it would be alright. That there would be other chances.'

'Other chances?'

'When she was crying, on the steps of the hospital. No, not then… on the front step…'

'You're confused.'

'I can't think. It's too much.'

'She was crying when you met her twenty-six years ago? A child.'

'A child. Yes.'

'And at the hospital?'

'Yes… no. That wasn't then. That was a different time. I can't think…'

He took a moment, and suddenly the memory became clear and distinct.

'Last year. God, it was only last year. And before. How many times she went through it… She cried, and I couldn't help her. I didn't know what to say. I never knew what to say. She was braver than I could ever be.'

'And you left her?'

'I didn't want to.'

'But you left her.'

'I couldn't let her go through that again!'

He rolled his head away and his vision swam. 'I don't want to talk about it.'

'You can't tell me anything I don't already know,' said the figure. 'Where I go, you must follow.'

Hansen rested his head back again. His memories were whirling like leaves caught in the wind and his forehead creased as he tried to focus.

'How is it you are here?'

Martin sat on the edge of the bath, or at least he appeared to. Hansen couldn't help thinking that for a ghost he looked healthier than should be expected. The situation was so absurd he couldn't help laughing. The real Martin would have enjoyed it too. He was sure of that.

'You went back to Devon?'

'Yes, we went.'

That first day back in Devon, they had reached the door of the house they both knew so well. Where they had both, in their different ways, grown up. He had joked with her on the front step. The step where he had met her for the first time, aged only thirteen, his family's new housemaid, in need of protection. And the same step when he had returned from the war, and saw her fully for the first time, as an adult, an equal. Not fallen in love. That would come later, by degrees, such that he hardly knew when to call it by that name. But then it had been something else.

'Do you remember when I came home from the war, and you hugged me?' he'd asked, as he unlocked the house. The now empty house.

'I remember being as embarrassed as I've ever been in my life,' she replied, smiling sheepishly. 'But it didn't stop me doing it. And neither did you – stop me, that is – if I remember?'

He had taken his wife around the waist then and they had walked in together. She had shivered visibly as they entered the hall. Everything – every flower on the wallpaper, every scuff on the skirting board, every tasteless ornament – had seemed unchanged. As if they had stepped back into their shared youth. And, like frightened children, they had looked into every door in their exploration, as if expecting to find someone there.

As Emily had looked down the stairs that led to the kitchen, where she had spent so many unhappy hours, she seemed to stiffen. She had talked at speed, trying to fill the silence and the emptiness of the house. She summoned every happy moment, every joke told, and every confidence shared, as if to drown out the other memories.

'And then you knocked down the painting in the parlour with your cricket bat,' she stammered, trying to smile. 'And you tried to hide the tear with the curtain.'

But as she had turned, she had noticed his changed expression.

'That wasn't me. That was Sebastian.'

He had felt her regret from across the room, but the house had them both out of sorts, and as he turned to walk out, Emily called after him.

'You can talk about him, you know? I wish you would. Otherwise it's as if he never existed.'

The minutes that followed had been a blur, a whirl of unwanted images and intense feelings. But when Hansen had recovered himself, Emily had been holding his hand and offering him a glass of water.

'We should never have come back,' she had whispered, though he hadn't known if she had meant for him to hear.

The days and weeks that followed did little to contradict her assertion that it had been a mistake. It would have been better to sell everything and be done with it. But he had allowed himself to be talked into taking his father's place as senior partner – at first only for a short time, but the weeks lengthened to months, and he began to enjoy the feeling of having others defer to him again. The work had little to commend it, but there was a satisfaction in seeing the practice run efficiently.

One evening he had returned late to find Emily sitting in the parlour, reading a book by the fast-diminishing May twilight.

'You'll strain your eyes,' he had said, but she only turned away and impatiently remarked that it was fine. She seemed to be hiding the book from him, so he had sought to reveal the cover.

'What are you reading?'

'Nothing.'

She had moved to hide it again, but he had, in an attempt at playfulness, caught her hand and turned the cover towards him. He saw that it was *Three Men in a Boat*. Her book. The only one she had owned as a child. The one her mother had read to her, and which embodied for her all those feelings of love and comfort. She had gifted it to him so many years ago and he had carried it, close to his heart, to Germany, when he had told his aunt and uncle of Sebastian's death. It was a book that she had left on the shelf in all the years since.

'Your favourite. Why didn't you want me to see?'

She had taken it back from him and walked to the door, hiding her face from him all the while.

'You said this would be temporary,' she snapped.

'It is. But the business needs me. You can see that, can't you? I can't leave yet. I have a duty.'

He could see her visibly deflate at the word.

'And what about Oxford?' she asked. 'I have a life there.'

'And you don't have one here? With me?'

'My life here is everything it was before,' she replied quietly. 'Everything of the nothing it was.'

She refused to respond when Hansen called after her, and she spent the rest of the night locked in her room.

The next day she had made a great show of being the caring wife, but it did not bear close scrutiny. Behind her eyes, he could see the fire that had once burned so fiercely was starting to flicker. Guttering and starved of fuel, as if it might go out.

'You saw all of this, and you did nothing? You stayed in the house she hated?' cut in Martin's voice, dragging him all at once back to the present. Hansen waited, as if expecting some corner of his mind or some flash of divine inspiration to explain it, for he had no answer. Instead he found himself remembering the first day of the Somme, more than twenty years ago, when Martin had gone in his place into Mansell Copse, to be cut down in the barbed wire, while he had only watched. How many times in his life had he allowed someone else – everyone else – to sacrifice themselves for him? Emily most of all.

'It was a duty,' he said meekly, 'to my father's legacy.'

'Something you cared nothing for while he lived,' said Martin. 'Why were you fighting so hard to maintain it?'

His lips touched the water, bitter to taste, as he allowed his head to hang. At that moment it came to mind how Emily had often talked about a passage from *Jane Eyre* that had meant so much to her:

'I have a strange feeling with regard to you. As if I had a string somewhere under my left ribs, tightly knotted to a similar string in you. And if you were to leave I'm afraid that cord of communion would snap. And I have a notion that I'd take to bleeding inwardly. As for you, you'd forget me.'

He had often wondered which of them would be which. Although now, he thought, it seemed to be already decided, and she must – if she were to have everything that she deserved – be the one to forget.

Chapter 3

Other times and other places might be muddled, but that weekend... That July weekend was indelibly marked, for good or bad. Or perhaps both for good and bad. Though he could no longer tell the one from the other.

Emily had kept her distance for much of the previous month, following the book incident. They had gone onto separate tracks, passing, but never meeting. He working all the daylight hours, she spending her evenings more often than not at a library she had found that was open at all hours. He worried about her returning in the evening and at first went to meet her and walk her home, but the gesture had not been welcomed.

That weekend, that Friday evening, he had returned to find her unexpectedly at home. When he opened the door, she had come to meet him, her eyes wild and wide. She paced and smoothed her hair and he had instinctively put his arms around her. It was a surprise to him that she did not resist. She had relaxed and put her head to his chest. It was a moment of intimacy to be savoured, but it was short-lived. She lifted her head and whispered:

'There's someone here.'

'Who?'

She had taken a moment to gather herself and then she shot out all the words at once.

'He says he is my brother.'

Hansen believed he had misheard, but before he could respond, she continued:

'I don't know if I believe him. But why should he lie? And he does look…'

She trailed off and returned to pacing. As far as Hansen knew, she had never had a brother. It had only ever been her mother and her. And her father, who had left when she was a newborn. He had been Italian and, from Emily's depiction, a bounder and a wretch who had abandoned all of his responsibilities. It was unforgiveable.

'Well,' he had said at last. 'May I meet him? And then perhaps I can get a feel for whether he is telling the truth. One thing a lawyer knows is how to spot a liar.'

'Or how to spot another like himself,' she said, with just a little too much barb for it to feel like an affectionate tease.

As Hansen entered the parlour, a well-dressed man stood up. Of taller stature than Hansen, he had jet-black hair, brylcreemed over his ears, a tanned complexion and a pencil moustache like Clark Gable. He carried a trilby in his hands. His eyes were dark like Emily's, and his face had a similar, agreeable shape about it. But all the same, there was something indefinably cocksure and brash in the way he looked that rankled immediately.

'Signore,' said the man, bowing slightly.

'Emily tells me you claim to be her brother.'

'That is so, signore. I realise it is a little…' He searched for the English word and pronounced it carefully, '…unorthodox… to make your acquaintance in this way.'

Hansen narrowed his eyes and viewed him with suspicion. He signalled for the man to sit down again, and he took a seat himself.

'What is your name, sir?'

'I am Salvatore. Salvatore Portinari.'

'Richard Hansen,' he returned curtly. It was peculiar how this man had got under his skin so quickly, despite being all easy charm and courtesy. He looked across at Emily as she smoothed her hair back behind her ears and then repeated the gesture while he watched. He imagined closing the gap between them and reaching out to her in reassurance, but he left his hands where they were – knit tightly together in his lap.

'Can you prove that you are my wife's brother?'

Emily had frowned at him from across the room and tilted her head in an enquiring way, as if to ask why he was being so cold.

'I'm sorry… sir,' she cut in, not knowing what to call the man. 'We don't mean to be ungracious, but it is a shock.'

'I realise,' said Salvatore. 'I understand, of course, and I would not presume, except that I am here because the matter is urgent.'

Hansen nodded for him to continue.

'My father – our father – he is a sick man. He may not live for much longer. And you understand he wants to atone for all the wrong he has done before it is too late. It is our way. He tasked me with finding his lost daughter… finding you… though we expected it would be difficult.'

'How on earth *did* you find me?' asked Emily.

'He told me your name, and that of your mother – Catherine?'

Emily nodded and smiled at the mention of her. It was pleasing to see, Hansen thought.

'I found where she had lived in Wales and made my way to the place where she was. The "workhouse", you call it? They told me that she had died…' He looked to Emily in sympathy. 'But also where you had been sent as a child. Though I did not expect to find you here after so long.'

He had looked from one to the other of them, not wishing to ask the question that was clearly in his mind. Hansen did not wish to explain it to him. Almost as if, in that moment, he were ashamed of it. Ashamed that Emily had once been maid to his family? Or ashamed of still being in the same house, with the same lives as they had had before?

'And you would wish Emily to go to Italy with you?' he asked, frowning despite his best efforts to be pleasant.

'It is my *father's* wish. Though he has no expectation that Emily would desire to know him. It is a request…' He turned back to Emily. 'A chance to know you. We live in a place called San Nicolo, in the Veneto region.'

Hansen looked up sharply.

'You know it, signore?'

'I do. I was stationed near there for a time during the last war.'

'Then you know it is a most beautiful place.'

'I can't say I noticed the scenery. I was too concerned with defending your country.'

Emily had shot him another stern glance before turning back to her brother and smiling.

'We have seen Venice. Such a beautiful city. We travelled a lot when we were first married.' She cast a quick glance to Hansen. 'It is strange to think that you were so close by then and I didn't know.' Salvatore smiled sadly. 'Will you allow me time to think?'

'Of course, signora. Or should I call you sister?'

Hansen stood up abruptly.

'A pleasure to meet you, Mr Portinari. Perhaps you will call again in a few days?'

'Nonsense!' interrupted Emily. 'You should have dinner with us, and you can stay too, if you wish? I will make up a room for you.'

The Italian had nodded graciously, and Emily spent some time fussing around him and showing him to a guest room. When she descended the stairs again, it was with an expression of thunder.

'I've never heard you speak to someone like that before. What on earth did you think you were doing? He's not a witness in court!'

'You believe he's your brother, I take it?'

'My half-brother. But yes, I can't think otherwise.'

Hansen hemmed and hawed. He could see the joy and sparkle in her eyes when she talked. He was filled with warmth seeing it in her again, but he had sighed when he wondered if he could still bring her that same happiness.

'You don't believe him then?' she said.

'I can't consider that it's been proven beyond reasonable doubt.'

Emily shook her head in disbelief.

'And what evidence would you require, "your honour?"' She laughed a little in bewilderment. 'I can't understand why you're being so cold.'

'And I can't understand why you are so certain. It's not like you to be so… impetuous. You can't just dash across Europe for someone you hardly know. I don't want you to regret it.'

'I did for you,' she said simply. 'Should I regret that?'

Her eyes pleaded for the answer she wanted to hear. For himself, he could never regret that. Never. But for her…

'It was a long time ago,' he said at last.

Her head dropped and she looked to the floor. She almost seemed to shrink. To become as small and meek as she had been twenty years before. Her words caught for a moment, and then she cleared her throat.

'I… I haven't decided if I'll go yet, though. Or… if *we* should go?'

She looked at him enquiringly.

'We'll talk about it later,' he replied.

She had clasped her hands together in frustration and put her face into them.

'Don't be like this, Richard, please,' she said quietly. 'I know things have changed, but you know how much this means to me. You know I never knew my father. He was only ever the charming Italian who swept my mother off her feet, who took her away from her family, took away her reputation, and then abandoned me… abandoned us. How it is that you can miss someone you've never known, I can't say, but I did. I always wanted to know why I looked different. I wanted to feel like I was not alone, like I belonged. And you know how I wished my father could have been there, on our wedding day, to walk me down the aisle?'

'I know it wasn't how you wanted it to be,' he replied. 'I'm sorry for that.'

'I could have a whole family I never knew about. I never had a family, like you had. Wouldn't *you* want to meet them? To understand why? I need to understand.'

Her expression had been filled with hope and excitement as it had not been for years, and, above all, determination. Though he fought to empathise with her, he failed, his heart filled with the very opposite.

'It's too dangerous,' he had said weakly.

'Then come with me.'

She had reached for his hand.

'I have to go back to the office,' he replied, backing away. 'Something I forgot to do. We'll talk later.'

He hadn't looked back and had walked the streets trying to fathom his own feelings and hers. It was unusual to see her so passionate. Emily's early life in the workhouse and as a maid had taught her to be circumspect, to hold back her true feelings and do what she needed to do to survive. Even when it meant setting aside her dreams. She had tried to leave it behind, and he had encouraged her, but it was still ingrained. When she felt vulnerable she would still retreat to protect herself. He had seen her do it. He had made her do it. So to be so forthright now could only signal how important this was to her. A new family to care for her and love her, when his were all but gone – the end of a line of Hansens stretching back generations, who had all made something of their lives. He envied what she would have but was eager for her to have it just the same, though it might leave him all alone.

As he walked, he remembered their wedding, or more precisely, the wedding she had wanted.

It had been in the days following their meeting in Germany, where she had followed him. He had let go of all doubts at that point. She had known everything about him, even his darkest secret, and still she had been there. What more reassurance could he need that she loved him and would not give up on him?

They had gone on to Paris. He had wanted to bring some joy to her life again, and he had enjoyed the city when he spent leave there during the war. They roamed around, wrapped as much in each other as in the beauty of the place. It had truly been the best week of his life. A week of complete perfection, in which he could fulfil every dream of hers. Seeing the art she had only read about, walking in the steps of her favourite authors – and all for the first time. The perfect week was capped with the perfect moment when the city had opened out before them from Sacré-Cœur and he had finally taken the ring from his pocket. The sunset of sunsets glowed on her face as she had accepted him. Even his malfunctioning knee had complied with his wishes, and he stood again and kissed her.

Later, as they sat at the table of a café, where Emily scrutinised the faces of those around them, searching out possible artists, writers, poets, they had agreed on the perfection of the moment. He was eager to know what she wanted to do next. Where life might take them now.

'Why must we think beyond this?' she had said. 'I just want to enjoy being here, with you, in this moment.'

'I'm just interested,' he had said. 'You could do anything you want. If this is a perfect week, what is a perfect life?'

She had laughed and poked him playfully with one finger.

'It's not like you to be so philosophical. What's brought this on?'

'It must be Paris,' he had said. 'And seeing you so happy. Makes me regret everything before.'

She had shaken her head.

'I won't allow it. No regrets. We are thinking to the future, not the past. We agreed.'

'Alright. Humour me, then. If we're thinking of a perfect future, at least tell me what our perfect wedding will look like.'

She had wrinkled her nose and given him a cheeky pout.

'If you really want to know... And I'm not admitting that I have given this much thought.' She smiled. 'If you ask me on oath, I will deny it. But...'

She had proceeded to describe the day in elaborate and specific detail, from the colour of the flowers to the style of the church (it had to be a church), and even that the wedding breakfast should be served either on, or next to, the river (she hadn't been completely decided on this). And the dress, which, as she pictured it, sounded like something only a princess could expect to wear.

'And of course, it would be the very perfect wedding if my father could walk me down the aisle,' she had said.

This had soured the moment somewhat, so she had made light of it.

'It's all a silly fantasy, though, of course. That most of all.'

'Well,' he said, trying to cheer her. 'I may not be able to guarantee the last, but in every other particular I want you to have your dream.'

She took his hands in hers and smiled.

'I didn't tell you about the last part of my perfect wedding day, though, did I?'

'The last part?'

'Yes. But you'll have to wait for that,' she said with a twinkle.

Over the coming weeks he had moved heaven and earth to make her wishes a reality. But it proved impossible, as their means were limited, and neither of them had very many friends to include in the invitation. His mother had resisted all entreaties to put aside her suspicions and had refused to attend. His father had showed every indication of following his mother's wishes.

Crosse had come up trumps by not only agreeing to marry them, but also by finding a suitable church in Oxford, where they had decided to settle so that he could finish his deferred degree, and Emily would have opportunities to pursue her interests.

Many of those they had met on their travels in Cornwall had been there. Emily had quickly bonded with Gertrude Harvey. She would be a bridesmaid, as well as providing suitable flowers from her garden. Sybil Cairns had agreed to make Emily's dress and was there too, alongside her brother-in-law Robert. Hannah Allen and even her husband William had been persuaded to attend, although he scratched at his stiff shirt collar and looked supremely uncomfortable throughout.

In the end, it was far from the perfect day that she had imagined or that he would have wished for her. But it was the most he could manage. As he waited nervously for Emily to arrive, he regretted most that she would have to walk down the aisle alone. But, at the last moment, his own father had stepped out of a cab and trotted up the path towards the church. As he reached the door, out of breath and perspiring, he had looked his son frankly in the eye.

'I'm not too late, I hope?'

'Perfect timing, Papa.'

He had embraced his son for the first time since he was a child, and it seemed that there might be another reason why fate had intervened to bring his father to the church at the last possible moment. He had decided to take a chance, for Emily's sake.

'I wonder if you might do us a great honour, Papa? Would you be willing to walk Emily down the aisle?'

His father had simply smiled and nodded.

'I have often wondered if that was the right thing,' said Hansen to Martin. 'But she looked so beautiful... so beautiful...' With a pleasant feeling of light-headedness coming over him, Hansen found himself smiling broadly at the memory, then in turn giggling uncontrollably like a foolish drunk.

'"There's more of gravy than of grave about you, whatever you are!"' he said.

'Dickens, you know? Scrooge... Scrooge. He was selfish too... and alone.'

His vision started to blur, but memories were still vivid as he struggled to regain his focus.

'Emily barely knew my father. But it was the best I could do. The day was so far... so *far* from what I knew she wanted. A handful of people in what was little more than a rowing boat. A picture Jerome K Jerome could have conjured. Hardly the reception she described to me. It must have been a great disappointment to her... a great disappointment. But she never showed it. Much like with everything that followed in our life.'

'So you wanted to leave her?'

'No. I never wanted that. But a part of me thought it would be for the best. I remember thinking, before we were together, that she should never be tied to someone like me, and I think I was right.'

On the Saturday after Salvatore Portinari had arrived, he decided to confront the man. Emily's father had abandoned her – could her supposed brother be so very different? He needed to understand who it was that had come into his home… their home. Even if it was to understand that he had misjudged him.

He climbed the stairs a little before dinnertime and was about to tap on Salvatore's door when he realised that it was slightly ajar. He heard the Italian's voice from inside. At first he thought he might be speaking to Emily. He thought about bursting in to berate her for being alone with Salvatore. The same room where she had spent the night alone with him once upon a time. But he stopped when he realised the language was not English. It seemed to be whispered, rhythmic, urgent. And when he drew nearer, he realised it was not Italian either. It was a language he'd never heard before. Perhaps a dialect? He knew there were such things in the Italian Alps. But his sixth sense, so honed during the war, prickled. He pushed forcefully at the door, and it swung open with a bang. Salvatore sprang back from his kneeling position and retreated briskly to the window.

'I didn't mean to surprise you,' said Hansen, watching him closely. Salvatore stuffed something into his jacket pocket and straightened his clothes.

'Dinner will be ready shortly. If you'd care to join us?'

'Thank you, signore.'

Hansen looked around the room.

'I thought someone was here with you…?'

'No… I was…' His eyes seemed to narrow a little. '…thinking aloud.'

'I see. Well, I'm sorry to disturb you.'

After that he made his mind up to tell Emily he didn't think she should go to Italy. That it was too dangerous and that this man claiming to be her brother was not to be trusted. He had known, of course, that she would react badly. That she was independent enough to leave without him. But even so, her anger had taken him by surprise, as had the suitcase she carried down the stairs. An ultimatum of sorts.

'I've given up everything to come back here to Devon with you!' she had almost shouted, her anger barely contained between taut lips. 'Where I have nothing. Where I *am* nothing. And when I ask you to support me in this – in finding my lost family – you just say no?'

Her eyes were wide, circled with sadness as well as indignation.

'I've told you why.'

'You really haven't.'

'It's a feeling,' he said in a hushed tone, conscious of her brother waiting in the parlour.

'*You* have a feeling?' She snorted.

'He was speaking in a language I didn't understand.'

'I never thought *you* would be suspicious of someone because they're a foreigner. I don't understand it. And I don't believe it. Worse, I don't understand *you* any longer. We've been abroad many times. It's not the place, is it? And you won't do this? You won't do this for *me*?'

'I am doing this for you.'

She shook her head, in sadness and incomprehension.

'I have to go.'

'And I have to stay.'

'So that's it?'

He could see her eyes shining, but she was fighting it, fury winning out over sadness. She opened the door to the parlour and guided her brother towards the front door and out onto the street. She turned back and picked up the case, holding it up to Hansen. A sign of her intent. For a moment she looked like she wanted to say goodbye – to kiss him or embrace him. But instead she remained at the door, balancing on the step, rocking between inside and outside. Looking down at the floor.

'You could write to me, if you want. I'll tell you where I am. If you don't, then…'

She looked up shyly. He nodded slowly. He wondered if he would be able to bear to read her writing. To feel the distance between them magnified with every line.

'You should go,' he said. 'You don't want to miss your train.'

Don't go, he longed to say.

'I hope you find what you're looking for.'

And find a better life without me holding you back, he thought.

She searched his face once again, and once again he strained to hold an impassive expression. She turned away slowly and stood with her back to him.

'I love you,' she said, so softly it was almost a whisper. He began to form the words to reply but stopped himself. For so long he had felt cocooned from feeling, trapped in a suffocating malaise. But now, just as he needed his resolution the most, he was overcome. In a despair of tortured regret, he understood just how deeply his feelings for Emily still ran. He would have given all he had to wind the clock back to 1919 and save her all of this. To protect her again, but this time from the pain he had brought her. But he took the cowardly decision – to pretend he had not heard what she had said.

'Take care,' he replied.

Though he had told himself she was only crouching to pick up the case, she seemed as well to crumple and collapse. But after a few moments' pause, with a sudden jolt she seized the case firmly and strode decisively away towards the cab where Salvatore waited.

Hansen didn't want to watch her go. So he closed the door and found himself gripping it tightly with his hands out wide in supplication and his cheek resting on the wooden panelling.

'Goodbye,' he said out loud.

It felt final. More final than either of them had allowed themselves to speak about.

'And you didn't write?' said Martin.

'She wired, but there was no address. Just to say she was well. Almost as if she didn't want to ask the question.'

'And what would you have said?'

'I would have said, I love you. But I think I love you too much.'

'But not enough to try?' said Martin. 'It's not too late, even now.'

'I think you know it is. When I heard the wireless today – the Prime Minister – I knew I couldn't face another war. Not alone.'

'So you'll leave her?'

'It's too late,' he said, pushing his heavy arm up the side of the bath, blood streaming down the side and into the water, now stained a deep crimson red.

'All you have to do is cry out for help,' said Martin. 'Think of all the people, like me, who gave their lives for you. Including Emily. If there's one thing you could always do, it's fight. It's time to fight.

'The maid is downstairs. Just shout.'

Chapter 4

As they descended the steps and into the waiting cab, Emily could feel her whole body shivering. She was leaving behind everything that her life had been, for a future that was unknown and, perhaps, unwise.

In the back of the taxi, she could no longer contain it, and she let out a strangled gasp as tears streamed down her face. She felt paralysed; she was shaking, though she tried to stop, finding each breath more and more difficult. Her brother looked on, concern building in him.

Sweat trickled down her back and all she could hear was the thumping of her heart in her chest, echoing around her skull. It seemed like it might explode through her ribs, and her throat tightened as she tried to speak. She began to worry that she would run out of air entirely, and all she could think was that she was dying. In books she had read about heroines succumbing to a broken heart, but she had always dismissed it as melodramatic nonsense. Now, if that was what this was, it felt utterly real.

Her brother took her hands, and he gently turned her face towards him.

'Listen to me,' he said. 'Listen to my voice. Count with me... ten...'

'Ten,' she mouthed, hardly able to gather breath.

'Nine.'

'Nine.'

'Eight.'

'Eight,' she responded, more easily now.

'Seven.'

'Seven.'

As they counted down, she regained a measure of calm. She felt cold, and a little faint, but she could breathe again. In time she recovered enough to gather her thoughts.

'Thank you,' she said.

He nodded graciously.

'My sister,' he said. 'My other – younger – sister. She has had such *experiences* before. This seems to help. It has a calming effect when she is agitated.'

'I see.'

There was discomfort in being so vulnerable in front of this new brother, barely an acquaintance. She dabbed her face with a handkerchief and sought to change the subject.

'You have another sister?' she asked.

'Yes. That is, *we* have a sister,' said Salvatore.

'Yes, of course.' She shuffled uneasily. 'Will you tell me about her, Salvatore? I'd like to know what she's like.'

'Of course. It would give me great pleasure. But, you know, only the priest in our village and my mother, God rest her soul, ever called me Salvatore. To my family, I am Toto.'

He paused a moment, as if waiting for her to understand that he meant she should call him likewise, and then continued.

'My sister, Mira, she is somewhat younger than myself. She is but seventeen years old. Sadly my mother, she died in the birth.'

'I'm sorry,' said Emily. 'You must have been very young yourself?'

'I was thirteen,' said Toto.

'I was the same age,' she said.

Emily dropped her head. She remembered well the child she had been when her own mother had died of cancer in the workhouse. She had cared for her for so long, though she hardly knew what it was to care for herself, but it had been to no avail. Nothing she could do could prevent it. Her entire world had fallen in upon itself. She had never, before or since, felt so alone and fragile. Or not until now.

Toto seemed to be reflecting, too, on bitter memories, and closed his eyes briefly. He shook his head a little and went on.

'She is full of life, my sister. She has her eyes wide to the world, if you understand me? But our father, he does not allow her to go away from the farm, so she has not seen how it is now, in our country, with Mussolini. She wants to be a doctor. But I don't think it will be possible.'

'You've told her that?'

'No. I dare not. She is so sure that it is what she will do. But she can see what is happening.'

'Things may change. We have come so far. When I think what things were like here when I was her age…'

'Perhaps.'

They fell into an uneasy silence, and she did all she could to distract herself from a heaviness inside that seemed to be consuming her. As if, were she to give in to the sadness, she would be lost to it.

'Tell me about the place where you live,' she said.

He looked up into space, as if trying to picture things more precisely.

'There is nothing special about it,' he said. 'At least, to anyone else there is nothing special. But a place that is home, it means so much more, does it not? It is a simple farm. Olives, sheep, some small vineyards. We are not rich, but one does not need money when you belong. Do you agree?'

It was not what she had expected him to say. Somehow it did not match the opinion she had formed of him so far, and instinctively she distrusted such a simple worldview. Sentimental even, she told herself. But she checked her own cynicism. He seemed sincere, and there was an appeal in his honest conviction.

He must have noticed her frown in thought, for he raised a questioning eyebrow and smiled sheepishly.

'I know I must seem very… simple… to you. I have never lived in a city such as this.'

She worried that she had hurt his feelings, but at the same time the idea of Exeter being a cosmopolitan city like Rome or Venice made her smile.

'I don't think anything like that,' she returned. 'I love the way you speak. You really shouldn't think that this city is anything so special. And as for education, I had precious little of that myself.'

The question seemed to be on the tip of his lips once more. A question that would lead to others that she did not wish to answer at that moment. So she moved to distract him again. 'And have you always lived there?'

'Yes. For myself, I was born in San Nicolo, and it has always been my home. My father, of course, travelled for many years before he settled there.'

She nodded in understanding, but the mention of her father prickled every nerve. This time she would not give away her thoughts so easily, however, and she breezed on as if everything were perfectly normal.

'And does anyone else live there? You, your sister...'

'For now, it is the three of us. But soon there will be, I hope, my wife.'

'You are married?'

'Soon, I think. Her name is Gabriella.'

'Congratulations.'

He bowed again, graciously.

'Perhaps... Perhaps you will be there at my wedding? I should like that very much.'

'Perhaps,' she replied.

She let her head rest back in the cushioned seat. There seemed no safe place to go in this conversation that did not trigger memories of pain. She could not avoid now thinking of her own wedding, and the hope and promise that had filled her heart on that day. But no. Although she did not wish to think of it now, it could never be a painful memory. There had been few moments in her life until that point that could be called joyful, but on that day, and in the days before, that's what she had felt. Their time in Paris, which had been the most perfect of her life – and when he had finally asked her, there were no words needed but the one that mattered.

The day itself had been all she had wanted. It had been simple, to be sure, but Richard had taken such care in everything, and it had been shared with all the people who mattered to her. Her only regret had been that her father would not be there to give her away. Though when she had walked into the church, all had been made well. For Richard's father, Thaddeus, had been there, unexpected though it was. He had greeted her with the words that she would never forget:

'Would you do me the honour of allowing me to walk you down the aisle… my daughter?'

He and Richard had disagreed on so much, but Thaddeus had never wanted to lose touch with either of them. So she had met with him often in the years that followed, and often without Richard. He understood his son better than Richard had ever given him credit for, and she had missed him in those last months. More than she had ever admitted to Richard. He had, in a way, been the father she had needed.

He had often wished for grandchildren, and each time there had been such hope and expectation in his eyes. If only, she began to think. If only…

But she wrenched herself away from that thought as a tear formed in the corner of her eye and she roughly wiped it away. Nothing was to be achieved by finishing that train of thought. There was nothing she could do; it was in the past. A past that they had agreed to bury, but which nevertheless tried to reach out to pull them back at every turn. Now she must find a way to live without Richard, for now or forever. It wasn't clear which.

'Do you regret coming with me?' asked Toto.

'Regret? No…'

As she said it, she vacillated. She had not yet brought the jumble of her thoughts and feelings to any resolution. But there were so many questions about her past that remained unanswered. When she had followed Richard to Germany, she had broken off the sensible, pragmatic engagement with Colonel Dawes, all to follow her heart. It was so unlike her. And yet here she was once again, making another journey of the heart.

'But you have left behind your life here?' continued Toto.

She did her best to gather herself and present a positive façade.

'I can honestly say this is one of the few recent decisions I have made that I do not regret.'

She was being at least as honest with him as she was with herself.

'I'm glad to hear it,' he said, smiling. 'My father likes to always tell us a proverb: "One is not old until regrets take the place of dreams."'

Time passed slowly as they made their way from train to ship and ship to train. Toto told her more about their life in Italy, which sounded more idyllic with every hour. Idyllic because it was, or because she fervently needed it to be, given all she had risked to experience it? Ever and again she revisited the decisions she had made and the things she had said. It was a thought loop that reached no end and exhausted her with each repeat.

As the train rattled away into the Swiss Alps, Emily breathed in the cold, clear air through the open carriage window. The landscape was the most perfect orderly farmscape, such as she had imagined could only exist in paintings or children's books. Her brother came to sit down opposite, smoking his foul-smelling cigarettes.

'I have told you everything about our life in Italy,' he said. 'But you have not asked me about our father.'

Hearing Toto call him 'our father' rankled, and the smoke from his cigarette billowing across her face did not help her mood. It seemed like an honorific that should be earned, not given away so easily. Others had deserved it more than this man who was no more than a caricature to her.

'Why should I?' she replied curtly.

'I just thought that, as you are here, you must be curious? Shall I tell you something about him?'

'If you wish.'

She listened politely. In a way she would prefer that the caricature remain, roughly drawn and grotesque. But she would listen.

'He was never a farmer, my father, but my mother told me when he married her that he was determined to do something worthwhile. He bought our farm, which was a wasteland, and he turned it into something. He worked so hard.'

'Did he?' she said, keeping all signs of interest from her tone.

'Oh yes. When I was old enough, he started to teach me what he had learned. Now I want to continue to grow what he has created.'

'He sounds like the ideal father,' she said, with little attempt to hide the bitterness in her voice.

'I know—' he began. But she cut him off.

'No, you don't.'

She had never been someone who hated easily. Rather, she had always sought to understand, to know why. But at that moment her heart was so blackened by anger, so coated and dripping in rage that it weighed her down like a sickness, leaving her empty and tired. The feeling had been building steadily, it seemed, and it was exhausting to go through it again and again. Old thoughts, which had been with her since she was a child and conscious of what it meant to grow up without a father in her life. And new feelings that were confusing, uncertain. How was it that finding her father, finally, at the age of thirty-nine, felt more like a loss? The loss of a life that might have been. Her life as a daughter, loved and protected. Or was it the loss of a life as a wife and mother that was at the root of this? In her mind, her 'father' had been a monster. The callous, uncaring wastrel who had panicked and run. Panicked and run as she had just done, she thought ruefully.

She took the book from her bag, the book that had once meant comfort to her, and smoothed the paper under her fingers, reaching for that certainty and security. But as she read the words again that had meant so much to her and to Richard, and which he had written onto the flyleaf – *Someone to love, and someone to love you* – the anger bubbled up once more, and she threw the book down. There was no longer comfort there. Just betrayal. And lost years. Wasted years.

She grieved for her lost family and feared for what she might find in Italy. But most of all she wished to be stronger. A stronger person would not have failed in her marriage. A stronger person wouldn't feel this vulnerable and uncertain. And a stronger person would not give in to anger and fear. When she caught sight of her reflection in the window, she hated the person she had become.

* * *

Toto helped her out of the taxi, holding her hand and watching her intently, as if she might shatter at the smallest wrong step. The Italian sun bore down intensely, and she regretted having no hat. She had packed in such a frenzy, convinced that it would only be a bluff to bring Richard on the journey, that she had hardly thought about where she was going. The air was warm, and filled with the scent of lavender, which at home lined the drawers in the bedroom and had given all her clothes a faint smell that reminded her of her mother. And of home.

'I hope you will like it here,' said Toto.

She tried to smile back at him. He was trying so hard to make everything perfect for her, to the extent that it put her on edge.

'I may not stay,' she said.

He knitted his brows and mouthed to ask why.

'I have enjoyed spending time with you,' she continued. 'But this is all so... so...'

She petered out, unable to explain.

'All so...' he replied, understanding her meaning.

'Don't take it amiss if it doesn't work out,' she said. 'Dreams aren't always as powerful as regrets.'

He made a little bow once again, as was his habit. She had come to enjoy the gesture.

As they made their way through a grove of orange trees towards the farmhouse, a young woman raced out and bounded down the steps, two or even three at a time. There was a wide grin across her face and a mass of dark curly hair swayed this way and that behind her as she ran. This could only be Toto's sister, Mira.

As she reached them she went immediately to Emily and threw her arms around her, wrapping her in the kind of unrestrained embrace that normally only children give.

'I'm sorry,' she said, pulling away nervously. 'I could not help myself. Are you alright?'

She had noticed that Emily had closed her eyes and was taking in a long deep breath.

'Yes,' said Emily. Her mind was full of the memory of another unrestrained embrace, in another time and place.

'I'm pleased to meet you, Mira.'

'You guessed who I am?'

'Of course she did,' said Toto. 'I have told her about you, Mira, and there can't be anyone else like you, can there?'

She giggled and cuddled up to him, and they continued arm-in-arm towards the house.

'You speak very good English, Mira,' said Emily. 'You both do.'

'Our father taught us,' she replied. 'He thought it would be useful to know, and of course he learned it from his time in England.

'I always dreamed that I would have a sister. I am so glad you are here. Did you have a sister in England?'

'Mira!' said her brother sharply. 'I know you are curious, but Emily did not know who we were a few days ago. Be kind.'

'I'm sorry, Emily,' said Mira. 'I get carried away. Forgive me?'

Emily couldn't help but take to her new sister, who was so full of verve and vigour. Had she grown up here, would she have been so very different at Mira's age?

'There's nothing to forgive,' said Emily. 'To answer your question: I never had a sister. Nor family, really. It was only my mother and me. And later my husband.'

Mira seemed to want to ask more, but she held back this time and simply smiled sideways at Emily as they walked. She was so open it made Emily smile herself.

As they reached the door to the house, it was flung open by a stout, sturdy woman who looked like she could uproot trees with her bare hands. Her demeanour was stern but softened immediately when she saw Toto.

'You must be Toto's new sister?' asked the woman, with an intensity that was not to be questioned.

'Yes,' said Toto. 'This is Emily. Emily, this is my wife-to-be – Gabriella.'

Gabriella took her hand and shook it robustly, before pulling Emily in and kissing her on both cheeks.

'This is the Italian way,' she said, by way of explanation. 'I know you English don't like it.'

'I-I wouldn't say that,' said Emily, stuttering. 'It's just not, um…' She trailed off.

'Relax here,' said Toto to the two of them. 'We will fetch some wine.' He and Mira disappeared into the house and left Emily alone with her sister-in-law-to-be.

'You will come to our wedding, yes?' asked Gabriella.

'If you would like me to?' asked Emily diffidently. Gabriella seemed to be such a force of nature that denying her would be impossible.

'Of course,' she said. 'Except, I must know… are you a communist?'

'I'm sorry?' said Emily, not quite understanding the direction of the conversation.

'You are a communist?' repeated Gabriella. 'Like me?'

'Oh. No, although I did vote for the Labour party candidate at the last election, if that makes a difference?' replied Emily, feeling faintly absurd as she said it. Gabriella's eyes drilled into her and made her feel rather self-conscious. The gaze was abruptly broken, and Gabriella grinned and kissed her once again on both cheeks.

'I joke,' she said, not altogether reassuringly. 'Come and sit down.'

She guided Emily to a table in a little garden where jasmine curled around the trellis and roses, pink and red, lined the border.

As they sat down, Emily noticed for the first time Gabriella's rounded belly, and she in turn noticed Emily's attention.

'We must marry soon,' said Gabriella.

'Oh, I see.'

'But Toto's father, he does not like me, I think. I want to marry Toto,' she said, 'but I want to fight the fascists too. Now everything is difficult.'

'I see,' said Emily again. 'You don't want to have a child?'

'No. I do not choose it,' she said matter-of-factly.

Mira and Toto brought out wine, bread and olives to the table. The green fruit was new to Emily, and she found it bitter on first taste. The wine was good, though, and soon she was feeling the effect of it. Time passed pleasantly, but at last her brother turned to her with a look of seriousness.

'Would you like to meet your father?'

It seemed like such a small, everyday thing expressed in that way. But these simple words had a whole life encapsulated in them. She nodded slowly, perhaps buoyed by the wine, though she still had no conception of what she would say.

Toto guided her through the house and into a little hallway with a staircase climbing steeply upwards.

The creaking stairs seemed to narrow and twist with each step she took. Her heart raced and every speech she had prepared, every diatribe, every barrage of righteous anger that she had imagined delivering to this man, if he were worth the word, seemed to fly away. As the door to the bedroom opened before her, she saw instead a small, shrivelled figure, huddled in his bedclothes, and she couldn't formulate a thought. Instead she stood and she stared.

'Emily?' said a weak voice, from somewhere in the sheets.

'She's here, Papa,' said Toto. He turned back to Emily and touched her on the arm. 'I will leave you.'

She made contact with the pale, yellow eyes that looked back at her. He was breathing hard, a crackle on the lungs evident with every gasp. Something made her want to turn and walk away, but she didn't.

'You hate me,' he said.

Every part of her wished it were so. That would have been easy.

'I don't know,' she answered honestly. 'I came here because I think I want to understand why... why...' She found herself almost unable to complete the question. 'Why... didn't you want me?'

He dropped his eyes for a moment. He must have expected the question, but perhaps he had no answer.

'As you stand before me,' he said slowly, 'every explanation seems insufficient. Would you believe me if I told you that I was too young? That I was scared? I wanted to be the perfect father for you. But...' He held his hands out wide, as if to say he knew he would never be adequate to the task.

'It never had to be perfect!' she protested. She surprised herself with the vehemence of her feelings, which rose like a wave to crash all around her. So much emotion had been building inside her since they had left England and now she couldn't help but let it spill out. And in this moment, perhaps unfairly, it was focused on him. 'I just needed you. I needed you to hold me. I didn't want to be alone!' She was shaking now, tears streaming down her face.

'You had a family that I never had. Why now? Why look for me now?'

The old man, so tiny, so unlike the person she had seen in her mind's eye for so long, was reaching for her, his arms outstretched.

'I wanted your forgiveness. Before it is too late. I always loved you, my daughter.'

His words only served to remind her of his absence from the most important day of her life.

'It's not enough,' she said, wiping away her tears. 'I never felt it from you, the way they have.'

He bowed his head into the covers.

'It was so easy for you, wasn't it?' she cried. 'To fail as a father and then just start all over again? So easy!'

She fell onto the end of the bed and lunged forcefully towards the prone figure.

'You had a chance I never had. How I wanted what you have; how many times I tried. You think you can tell me how it feels to lose a child?'

It was too much. She turned and ran from the room, vaulting down the stairs and out into the warm evening air. She ran and ran until her legs went from beneath her and she found herself under an olive tree looking up at the stars beginning to appear in the twilight sky.

She trembled, sick in a sea of emotion. Among the waves of thoughts, one memory emerged. A remembrance of a summer night, like this one, but in Paris. A warm embrace. A profound sensation of reassurance and love. She had wanted him to hold her like this when she had stood on the steps of the hospital, cold, alone and grieving, and she wanted it even more now.

Part Two

1940

Chapter 5

May

Gas. A morbid green. Rolling in waves over the ground and seeping into shell holes like the spray from a polluted sea. As he looked left and right, the figures of his own men seemed to be swallowed by it. One moment walking steadily forward, the next all gone.

He tried to turn away, but his feet were heavy, locked in deep mud. Each movement to pull his boot out took all his effort, and each time it was pulled down again.

The cloud came closer. Ever closer. And suddenly he was alone, his comrades faded into the mist, and the silent bank of gas came on, surrounding him. He reached up to touch his mask, only to realise he had no mask.

He could taste the gas on his tongue, tingling and acrid. His eyes burned and throat closed. He lifted his gun, but it became heavy in his hand. Too heavy to hold, and, dropping it, he looked down to see his hands red, as if burned by fire. He was drowning, gasping for every shallow breath, his throat sharp like glass, as the fog closed around him and all he could see through darkening eyes was the billowing gas, stinking and sinful...

Hansen jolted awake, his hands sweaty, gripping the bed sheets as his thumping heart gradually began to slow.

He screwed up his eyes against the bright sunshine that was reflecting from the mirror on the wardrobe, lifting his hand to shield them as he groped his way across to the bedside table and reached for the glass of water there. He drank deeply, his mouth dry, his forehead hot to the touch and his head throbbing.

The door opened and his nurse, Lucy, came in. Unlike the others, she smiled readily, and seemed to always have time for him. It was, perhaps, because she had lost both her own father and her elder brother to the trenches. She put a hand to his forehead now and he flinched.

'Sorry, cold hands. You shouldn't be lying here in this heat, Major. You're dehydrated.'

She poured him some more water. He wasn't sure whether he liked being addressed by his old rank or not. When she had discovered his service, she had dropped the 'Mister' straight away. It was well-intentioned, he was sure.

'Cold hands, warm heart,' he croaked.

'Charmer! Well, someone has to look after you lot, when you won't do it yourselves.'

She fluffed the pillows to allow him to sit up.

'Now, will you come outside for some tea? Everyone else is sitting on the lawn.'

'Perhaps later. In any case, isn't this your afternoon off? Your brother is home on leave, is he not?'

'Kind of you to remember,' she said, turning her back to him to tidy his things on the dresser. 'But we are short-handed today. And my brother isn't coming after all. All leave cancelled.'

'I'm sorry. I know you were looking forward to seeing him.'

'It is what it is.' She shrugged. 'The war…' She smiled sadly at him as if to say, 'You know.'

'You'll see him again.'

'Don't say that,' she said fiercely. 'I don't like to expect anything. In case…' Her expression softened again. 'Here's your fine James Cagney hat. Why don't you wear that on the lawn?'

'I look like a mobster in it.'

She pulled on the hat, although it fell down to her eyebrows.

'"You dirty rat!"' she joked.

'Is that your best James Cagney impression?'

'What did you think?'

'It's almost as if he's in the room.'

She chuckled and skimmed the hat across the bed to him.

'It doesn't fit me, anyway. Come on, Major Bighead. Tea, outside, now.'

'Yes, sergeant!'

She took his arm as they went out into the corridor. He no longer needed help; he hadn't for some time. But he didn't let go.

'So where did you get your Cagney hat?' she asked.

'In New York, as it happens.'

'You were in New York?' she squealed, grabbing his arm more tightly.

'Steady on!'

'Sorry! I've just always wanted to go to America. You must tell me everything. When did you go?'

'A few years ago. We went over on the *Queen Mary* and took a tour right across.'

'We?' There was a pause. 'As in, you and your wife, whom we don't talk about?'

'I never said that.'

'Your face does. Or you always change the subject.'

'Do you want to hear about America or not?'

'Of course, Major,' she replied, winking.

They made their way out onto the lawn, and Hansen took a wicker chair under the shade of a tree. As he looked around him, a man in his sixties, in a world of his own, dribbled his tea from one side of his mouth as a nurse tried to feed it to him. Another, younger man was walking in circles around a tree and still another cried out in distress as his nurses took his empty cup from him.

Hansen looked up, anywhere but at the people around him. A Spitfire flew overhead. A brave pilot on his way to do his duty. He dropped his head once more and pulled his hat down to cover his eyes. As penances went, this place was more than he deserved.

'Lie down, if you prefer,' said Maberly, who was waiting, his legs crossed, in an overstuffed leather chair. He signalled for Hansen to go to a chaise longue.

'I'm fine sitting, thank you.'

'As you wish.'

Maberly pulled out a folder with a collection of notes and licked his fingertips before flicking through them. Hansen noticed once again the combination of mothballs and peppermint as he sat opposite the man. It was a smell redolent of schooldays, and a particular master who had tormented him.

'So,' he began. 'You have been having the nightmares again, yes?'

Hansen rolled his eyes.

'Lucy told you?'

'It is in your notes. There's no blame attached. She is here to help you, as we all are. Why hide it?'

'They're only dreams.'

'Some would say those dreams mean something though. Would you not agree? They may help us to understand what it is that you are dealing with.'

'If you say so.'

'When did the dreams first occur?'

Hansen got up and began to pace around the room, absent-mindedly studying the books on the shelves.

'You've read all of these?'

'Of course. Mr Hansen, you are avoiding the issue. Please tell me about your dreams.'

'To what end?'

'So that you may start to get better.'

'I feel fine.'

Maberly made a note in his book and turned a quizzical eye on Hansen, watching him move to and fro.

'You no longer have suicidal thoughts?'

Hansen frowned and made for the door, which he found locked.

'You're locking me in?'

Maberly stood slowly and placed his notes back on the table. He moved to the door and gently removed Hansen's fingers from the handle. He took a key out of his pocket, unlocked the door and held it open.

'We are just talking, Mr Hansen. We should talk again when you are ready.'

Time passed, almost without notice. When he'd arrived, he'd fallen into certain habits quickly and easily: a walk in the grounds after breakfast, sessions with Maberly, painting (badly), conversations with Lucy, more meals, and early to bed. Now, some months later – he couldn't remember how long exactly – after following his usual routine, Hansen was sitting in his chair after breakfast. He was putting on his shoes, ready for his walk, when Lucy came in and told him he had a visitor. He tried to imagine who might know he was there, and at first he was inclined to tell whoever it was to leave. He resented the interruption to his day, and it made him anxious.

'Who is it?' he asked.

'He won't give me a name,' said Lucy. 'He just said to tell you he is a friend of Peterhausen.'

'Peterhausen? He definitely said that?'

'Yes. Who's Peterhausen?'

Hansen left the question unanswered, and let Lucy guide him to the office where the visitor had been asked to wait.

A small man lounged in a chair. As they entered the room, he stayed seated. His hair was close-cropped and mousy, and he had a five o'clock shadow though it was only nine in the morning. He held a stubby cigarette between a yellow thumb and forefinger and drew on it slowly while his penetrating grey eyes studied Hansen in what seemed to be microscopic detail.

All of a sudden the man leaped up, as if stung by a bee or a jolt of electricity, and proffered his hand.

'Major Richard Hansen?' he asked, with a roll of his 'r's that gave away a gentle Scottish accent.

'I am.'

'Sit down, old man.'

'Making yourself at home?' asked Lucy.

'As always,' he shot back, and slumped back into his chair, the surge of energy having expired. 'We'll call if we need anything, my girl. Thanks ever so. TTFN.'

He waved her away absently and Hansen could hear Lucy sigh heavily behind him. She left, muttering and slamming the door with noticeable force.

The man snorted with laughter and patted the chair opposite him. As Hansen took the seat, the man flicked open a cigarette case and offered it, but swiftly pulled it away again.

'No, of course – you don't, do you?'

Hansen shook his head slowly.

'You have me at a disadvantage, Mr…?'

'Yes, I do. It's Captain, actually. Royal Navy. Not that I go in for ranks and such all that much, but I do like to get things right.'

His eyes fell to Hansen's wrist, and Hansen pulled down his jacket sleeve self-consciously to conceal the scars.

'My name is Thurso. Anthony Thurso.'

'Which ship?'

'Well, that's a bit complicated. We'll come to that in time. But I must say, first off, that you're not quite what I expected.'

'How is it that you expected anything at all? And how is it that you know Peterhausen?'

He snorted again with a kind of rasping chuckle. He took another suck on his cigarette and looked around for something to drop the ash into.

Finding nothing suitable, he tapped it on the side of his teacup instead.

'Oh, I get around. To Germany occasionally, though never Peterhausen. Not yet anyway. I never was much for tea either. Unlike a mutual friend, who speaks very highly of you. One Ernest Crosse.'

'Ah,' said Hansen.

'Indeed. He got to hear about how you're fixed here, and he asked me to come and look you up.'

Or look you up and down, he might have said, from the way he was studying Hansen's every move and every pore. Crosse's unerring ability to be in the right place at the right time had struck again. Now it all made sense. Although Thurso was not your conventional military type – the stiff bearing and the clipped style of speech that one might normally associate with his rank did not hold true, and nor was he in uniform. His pinstriped suit instead gave him the air of an insurance salesman.

'How is Ernie?'

'Inscrutable as ever. I call him the Sphinx. He has some useful qualities though, as you know.

Not least of which is knowing everyone there is to know, and everything there is to know about them.'

'You work with him, then? Same line of work?'

Thurso flicked a curious glance at him for half a second, long enough for Hansen to register his evidently growing interest, before looking down again and picking a piece of lint from his trouser leg.

'Which is what, do you suppose?'

'Military intelligence – correct?'

Thurso grinned.

'I see; he was right. You *are* sharper than the regular cannon-fodder types. I don't like to beat around bushes, or any other sort of plant. He's been helping us with some recruitment, and he reckoned I should talk to you. That your – *interesting* – background might be useful to us.'

'In what way?'

'Well. My outfit is called Section 6. The plaque on our door says: "Minimax Fire Extinguisher Company", but you'll understand the only fires we put out are metaphorical. And given that, by all accounts, you're about as British as

Prince Albert, you could be useful to us… "Over There", as the old song would have it. You know the language, you know the country. And better that than the alternative – ending up as a Category A prisoner in an internment camp.'

He gave a sickly smirk and bore down with another intense glare, but it was clearly flim-flam. A test, perhaps?

'I was born here. I have a British passport. I'm a solicitor, but even if I weren't, I'd know that trying to scare me with talk of internment is ludicrous. You really don't know me as well as you thought.'

This time Thurso dunked his cigarette into his cup with a hiss and set it aside. He took out a notebook and began to leaf through the pages.

'No. I know you don't scare easily. Three promotions in as many years, a Distinguished Service Order, wounded three times. Took a machine gun post at Piave in somewhat vague circumstances according to your own report, but which others tell me was undertaken virtually single-handed.' He looked up again, with something of a twinkle this time. 'No, I can't doubt your courage.'

Thurso got to his feet in a second sudden burst of energy, shook Hansen by the hand, and was at the door in a flash. 'I'll see you again soon, Major. We'll talk more. I needn't remind you to keep this between us, need I?'

'I'm not sure what I should hide, given you've told me so little.'

'Call it a prelude to a tap on the shoulder.'

In the days that followed, Hansen found it hard not to keep going back to his strange encounter with Thurso. He'd always considered military intelligence to be somehow underhand. Ungentlemanly. Even un-British. But he had to smile at the irony that it might very well be his own un-Britishness that they sought.

As he pottered around the garden, he considered whether what Thurso had really seen in him was fear. The Scot had had a penetrating gaze that seemed to burn through all artifice. Had he seen into the corners of his thoughts, where he wondered whether he could ever enter society again? Whether he even wished to? It was more than the general feeling, that many surely had now with France about to fall, that their very way of life was threatened for the first time. It was guilt, too. To be sitting idly while others were at risk. One in particular.

'I'd like you to tell me more about your dreams, Mr Hansen,' said Maberly. 'Are they always the same?'

'I'm not sure. Some things are always the same.'

'And which things are those?'

'Gas. There is always poison gas. And usually a gun.'

Maberly nodded and made a note in his book. The act of his writing always made Hansen nervous.

'Describe it to me. What form does it take in your dream?'

'It's a revolver. My service revolver. I'm holding it, but it becomes hot to the touch, painful, and I drop it, even though I need it to defend myself.'

'Interesting,' said Maberly, sucking on his pen. 'The revolver may be a representation of your power, or your… potency.'

Hansen sighed and rolled his eyes.

'And sometimes, Doctor, a gun is just a gun.'

Maberly smiled, for perhaps the first time.

'Mock me if you wish, Mr Hansen, but you should not discount these ideas. What does a gun represent to you? Power, yes? Violence? It could be that, in being unable to use this weapon in your dream, you are expressing your fear of your own power to do harm. Or your wish not to bring harm to others. Metaphorically, of course.'

Hansen stood and went to the window, from where he could see the towers of the cathedral in the distance. The view he had often seen from his bedroom in the family home.

'Tell me when you first had dreams like this,' said Maberly.

Hansen sat back down heavily on the chaise.

'After the war.'

'You served in France, yes?' He consulted more of his copious notes. 'And Italy as well?'

'Yes. I'm sure I'm not unique in that.'

'No, indeed. And you are not alone in the symptoms you have had. I have seen many who served in the last war. The dreams went away, though, before?'

'For a time.'

'How long a time?'

'Some years.'

'And then your symptoms returned?'

'Yes.'

'What do you think prompted that?'

'I'm not sure,' Hansen said doubtfully.

Maberly narrowed his eyes.

'What else was happening in your life at the time?'

Hansen was disoriented for a moment. An image reared up, unbidden. The steps of the hospital. Cold. Tears.

'Mr Hansen? Shall we stop?'

'I'm fine.'

Maberly looked sceptical but persisted.

'What form did these symptoms take?'

'I slept poorly. I was on edge the whole time. Anxious. And I was seeing things that weren't there.'

'A recurrent memory?'

Hansen nodded. It was too small a description for an experience which often left him uncertain of reality and fearful of the next time it would happen.

'And did you tell anyone? Your wife?'

A shiver ran through him.

'No. I didn't want to worry her.'

'Wouldn't she have wanted to know?'

'Everything had been so good. And then…'

'Then?'

'Being with her was enough for me. But I failed her. Entirely failed her. She should never have married me.'

His hand had begun to tremble visibly, and he drew his legs up onto the seat and clutched them tightly to steady himself.

'You are safe, Mr Hansen. No harm can come to you while you are here.'

Later, on his own, he considered what Maberly had said. Lying on his bed, his arms folded behind his head, his eyes went absently to his DSO medal, which Lucy had carefully pinned to his pyjama jacket, though it embarrassed him.

Power. The power to do good or do harm. It was something his father had impressed upon him when he was young – the responsibility of their rank and privilege. He was clear that it carried obligations as well as rights. He'd come from nothing, his father had said. He said it so often that it had almost become a joke. *He* understood what it meant to have what they had, because he had come from nothing. *He* would have appreciated the education, the money, that his son took for granted, because he had come from nothing. Hansen had smiled and nodded and agreed. Now he was sorry that he had taken it so meanly.

There had been a moment, as a child, when he had put on his new school uniform for the first time. The symbol of an expensive, private, education. On the steps of the house, he had cast a glance at a boy he knew slightly. Fourteen, like himself, but who, unlike him, was on his way to work. As children do, he had revelled in the moment and teased the other boy.

'Wear it lightly,' his father had told him.

He had not known what his father had meant then and resented him more than a little for spoiling his moment of triumph. But the war had made it plain. Money, education, breeding: none of these things changed the facts of death.

It had been a point of pride of his father's to hold his hand out to help those who needed it. It was his nature. Even when the hand was slapped away because they heard his accent or sneered at his lack of culture. Then there was disappointment. But only ever for a moment. And afterwards, the hand would be offered again. Perhaps it was naïve of him to be this way, but he admired the English. It was his life's ambition to be considered a gentleman, and all that meant in his eyes. So he endeavoured to lose the German accent, to fit in. In anyone else it might have seemed an ostentation, but he valued these virtues as seriously as others valued the trappings of power. His father had been the exemplar of those qualities, while Hansen could only see his own shortcomings in the same.

There was a gentle rap on the door and Lucy entered, carrying the evening paper. She set it down on the dresser, seeming caught in her own thoughts. Her usual smile was not there, and he missed seeing it.

'Thank you, miss,' he called. And when no smart remark was forthcoming, he sat up.

'Is something wrong, Lucy?'

She shook her head vigorously, as if to displace the thought, and there was the twitch of a smile, but no more.

'Of course not. I'm tickety-boo.'

She turned to go out, but almost immediately spun on the spot and came back.

'Can I ask you a question?' she said.

'You just have,' he replied. When he realised she had not risen to this either, he smiled warmly and patted the bed next to him. She sat down. There was silence for some moments, and she consulted her watch repeatedly, displacing her nervous energy as she decided on her opening.

'I wanted to ask you about war.'

'I know no more than you. What's in the papers, on the wireless…'

'No, I mean… what it's like.'

He looked at her sharply and narrowed his eyes.

'Have you been talking to Maberly about me?'

'No, never,' she said. 'He never discusses what you talk about.'

She registered the look of suspicion on his face and got up.

'I'm sorry,' she said. 'I didn't mean to bother you. It's nothing to do with you.'

He imagined what his father would do and heard his voice clearly. He relaxed his posture and found himself waving at her to come back.

'Wait! What did you want to ask?' he said, patting the bed again and giving her a reassuring smile.

She slowly took a seat.

'I just can't help thinking of my brother,' she said. 'And I thought it might help to understand what it is that he might be facing. That it might be reassuring in some way.'

'It wouldn't be that,' he said sternly. 'Not if I were to tell you truthfully. I'm not sure it would be a good idea.'

She turned to face him and looked directly into his eyes, holding his gaze until it became uncomfortable.

'I'm not afraid to hear the truth,' she said. 'It can't be worse than I have imagined.'

Maberly had told him it would be therapeutic to talk more about his experiences. In their sessions he'd given voice to things that had, until now, been hidden in the dark places of his mind. Those places were unguarded now.

'If you really wish to hear it, unvarnished?'

'Unvarnished.'

Hansen took a long breath and looked down at his feet, unwilling to meet her gaze or read her expression.

'Imagine noise,' he said slowly. 'Louder than you've ever experienced. That vibrates through your whole body, and continues, day and night.

Imagine that you never feel completely clean, dirt in every pore. Cold. Wet. Lice that itch your skin, rats that crawl over you. Soldiers whose feet turn black and rot away with the constant wet.

'Imagine that you crouch wherever you go, not because you need to, but because you are terrified that a bullet will burst your skull, like the man you called a friend as he stood next to you, whose blood you could never remove from your tunic.

'Imagine being afraid to sleep, because you might wake choking, with gas all around you, or a bayonet in your chest.

'Imagine taking someone else's life, as easily as you flick a switch, because otherwise it would be you. And hoping that the next enemy you meet will have his back to you or his trousers around his ankles, because he'll be easier to kill that way.

'And imagine your comrades, closer than brothers. Bleeding, cut in half, without a face, or worse, blown to nothing while you watch, powerless. Men drowned in mud, bodies eaten by animals or used to prop up trenches. They die calling for their mother, while you, in shame, can only be glad it's not you.

'Imagine all that, and you'll know only the half of it.'

Lucy looked at him, unmoving, tears streaming down her face. His father had tried to teach him what it meant to be a gentleman. He had often quoted Matthew Henry: 'Be careful if you make a woman cry, because God counts her tears.' Now he felt as far from a gentleman as he had ever been. A selfish brute who had backed away from all his obligations. Cared for, not caring. Weak.

She ran from the room and didn't turn back. Hansen ripped the medal from his chest and threw it across the room. No more of this. No more introspection. No more watching and waiting and doing nothing.

When Thurso returned, he suggested that they walk outside this time. He brandished his cigarette once again, though he seemed distracted by the nature around him, which seemed to bother him immensely.

'I'm a city boy.' He smiled, flicking away a bothersome bee. 'Give me a street brawl or an overcrowded tenement building, and I'm you're man. But I don't know what to do with fresh air and exercise.'

'I know you value directness,' said Hansen, changing the subject. 'So I'll level with you. I need to do something.'

Thurso looked at him intently before nodding to himself.

'My superiors have had their doubts about you. One of them quoted Charlemagne to me, which is one of his more peculiar habits. "To have another language is to possess a second soul," he said. An odd thing to say, but they seem to think this "second soul" of yours – this German soul – may make you... unreliable.'

Hansen rounded on him, cheeks aflame.

'No one has ever doubted where my loyalty lies,' he snarled.

'But you have doubted others, haven't you?' said Thurso calmly, his thin smile provoking further fury in Hansen. Thurso let the ash on his cigarette burn down as he watched him intently, looking for a reaction.

'Your cousin – Sebastian – for instance?'

With no more than a second's hesitation, Hansen punched Thurso full across the face. His hand stung with the impact, throbbing as the other man sprawled on the grass, blood streaming from his nose. His teeth were coated in it too, sticky and scarlet, as he grinned back at Hansen.

'You punch hard for a dead man,' said Thurso, picking himself up and pinching his nose gingerly to stem the blood flow.

'I won't play your games,' said Hansen, and he began to walk away.

'I'm not playing,' said Thurso, scurrying after him now. 'I wanted to see whether the man before me has nothing to live for, or nothing to lose. Because the former is no good to me. But the latter; that's exactly what I need. It's what this country needs, because, let's face it, there's precious little else standing between us and oblivion.'

'I couldn't help you, even if I wanted to,' said Hansen bitterly. He extended his arms wide and gestured at everything around him – the buildings, the nurses and the patients – and then down at his own dressing gown. He walked calmly back into the building and Thurso did not follow.

As he returned to his room, Lucy was there waiting, with all his bags packed.

'Doctor Maberly has ordered your release,' she said, all attempted ease, but badly hidden. 'That's good news, isn't it?'

He nodded, not knowing what else to do. Thurso had clearly arranged all of it.

He could still say no. There had to be some end, even to duty. Some limit he could not cross. He wondered where Thurso might lead him, wondered whether he might be required to kill again. Something he would not – could not – do.

'I've telephoned for a taxi,' continued Lucy.

'Where will I go?' he asked innocently.

'Home?'

He scanned the room around him, touching objects and committing it all into memory. Nine months in this place, away from life. Or nine months that would begin a new life?

'Don't forget these,' she said. She picked up his American hat and a small folding photo frame from the dresser that had remained closed since his arrival there.

'In case you want to talk about her sometime,' she said, handing him the frame.

'Thank you. I think you should keep the hat, though. It always suited you better... Jimmy.'

'Don't change the subject,' she said, smiling. 'But thanks.'

'I'm sorry,' he said. 'For what I told you before. It was unnecessary.'

'No, it *was* necessary,' she said.

'I didn't mean to scare you...'

She gently touched him on the arm.

'And I'm sorry. We will be here, you know, if you need us again. It's the least we can do.'

She leaned in and kissed him gently on the cheek. She handed him his case and tipped her new hat at him as he left.

In less than half an hour, he was back at the family house in Exeter. He took a deep breath as he climbed the steps, remembering well his emotions when he had returned in 1919, and who had been there to greet him. He felt lost then – alone and uncertain. For others the war had taken their lives. For him, it was his life force. Emily's welcome had been one of simple warmth and love. How he had needed it then. How he still needed it. Now there was no one to provide such a reception.

He pushed past a mound of post on the doormat as he opened the door and gathered it all up. He dropped everything onto the table in the parlour and sat back in the chair, breathing in the still, stale air. The house was completely silent. Even the ever-present ticking of the hall clock was missing, with no one to wind it.

Absent-mindedly, he began sorting through the letters. Mostly bills or flyers of one sort or another. Then he came upon a pale blue envelope. The address was written in a hand he recognised better than his own. He opened it and read the short note that Emily had written:

Dearest Richard,

So many times I have sat down to write but found I could not until now. I'm sorry if it has caused you to worry in the meantime.

When I think back on the way we said goodbye, it is with such sadness. It is obvious to me now that the love we once shared is no longer something we both feel. Perhaps it is for the best that you go your way

*now, and fulfil what your father wished for you, and
for me to remain here for now, to see where things
will lead.*

*I only wanted you to know that if things change, you
would be welcome here. But if Christmas arrives and
I have not heard from you, then we will both know
how it is between us.*

With no regrets.

*Love always,
Emily*

The letter was dated September of the
previous year. Only a week after he had been
admitted to hospital. Christmas had come and gone,
and she had waited, with no way of knowing. He
ached with remorse. How many tears must now be
counted, and how many more would there be?

The ring of the doorbell shook him out of his
thoughts and when he went to answer it, Thurso
stood on the front step.

'Home again?' he asked.

'As you see,' said Hansen.

'You have heard, I suppose, that Mussolini
declared war on France and Britain yesterday?'

Hansen almost staggered back in shock, his head swimming.

'It makes a trip to Italy rather difficult, doesn't it?' Thurso smirked knowingly.

Hansen considered him. 'You knew!' he shouted. 'And you never said anything. What kind of a man are you?'

'It is what we do, Major,' said Thurso. 'We do what is necessary.'

'Get out!'

'If you wish. But I will strike you a bargain right here and now. You can stay here in comfort and see out the war at your leisure, or you can be the person you ought to be. The man who serves his country and does what others will not. A man who does his duty. A man who fulfils his obligations.

'We need you, Major Hansen, or even Lieutenant-Colonel Hansen, if that has a better ring to it. If you help me by giving us that second soul of yours, in Germany, then I promise, if the opportunity arises, I will help you find Emily. You know she's in danger. It's the only way to protect her now, and you'll be a sight closer to her there than you will be here.'

'And if the Nazis discover who and what I am?'

'Then you know what will happen.' Thurso drew his finger slowly across his throat. 'But that's only if you fail. And you won't.'

'That's all you have to offer?'

'Nothing but blood, toil, tears and sweat. But a chance, all the same.'

Hansen looked down at the letter, grasped in his sweating hands.

'Blood and tears are old friends,' said Hansen. 'And as you say, I have nothing left to lose.'

Chapter 6

June

A gentle breeze blew through the cypress trees as Emily brushed her hand through the stalks of lavender in the pot beside her. She half-closed her eyes and listened blissfully to the rustling in the branches and the buzzing of bees. She dipped a finger into her glass and sucked a little wine off it, letting the tannins coat her lips and the warm taste of blackcurrant, or cherries, tickle her tongue. The gentle warmth of the setting sun played on her face, and she thought back to younger days, when she had had the time to appreciate these small sensations that life provides. She wondered how often she had taken that time more recently. Too rarely, she decided.

'Are you with us, sister?' asked Toto.

She opened her eyes and realised everyone at the table was looking at her.

'I'm sorry?'

'Head in the clouds, as usual,' said Gabriella, smirking behind her wine glass.

'And what is so very wrong in that?' said Mira. 'Dreams are important.'

'And actions more so,' said Gabriella pointedly, spoiling for a fight.

'Quiet, you two,' said Toto. 'Enough debate for this evening. Emily, I was saying that on such a special occasion, I'd like to share a few words about you.'

Emily blushed a little and smoothed her hair back behind her ear.

'I think,' said Toto, 'I speak for all of us, Emily, when I say how much we have all valued having you here this last year. I know it was not easy for you in the beginning. But you have, I think, found something here too. In coming to us you knew nothing of who we were, but you have embraced our language, our way of life, and I am grateful for that.'

'We all are!' said Mira, taking her hand.

'Thank you,' said Emily. 'For my part I had never known what it was to have family before I came here. What was it you said then about regrets? In some ways I may still regret leaving, and the reason for coming, but I cannot regret arriving here. You have helped to make this feel almost like home.'

'Almost?' said Toto.

'Almost,' she confirmed, and offered a crooked smile. Toto understood and began to raise his glass in a toast. Mira swivelled in her chair and touched her brother on the arm, signalling something to him by raising her eyebrows high.

'What is it, Mira?' he said.

'Shouldn't we…' she began, before raising her eyebrows again.

'Shouldn't we what?'

'You know…' She paused meaningfully but seemed frustrated when her brother failed to take her meaning. 'Give a blessing…'

Toto seemed embarrassed suddenly, while Gabriella frowned.

'Oh, there's no need,' said Emily, playing peacemaker. 'But I didn't know you were religious?'

'We're not,' said Gabriella determinedly.

'Not really,' said Toto mildly. 'But it is a special occasion. That's what you meant, isn't it, Mira?'

'Yes,' she replied. 'I suppose it is.'

Toto raised his glass once more.

'To you, Emily, and the years to come we have to share, not the ones we've missed.'

They all raised a toast and, though she would normally expect to feel self-conscious being so much the centre of attention, here, in this place, and at this time, there was simple contentment. How often had it been this way? No falsity, no need to hide any part of herself. Was it selfish to want to keep it? To remain a little longer in a place that seemed idyllic? Except that something in her dissented. There was always the suspicion that the ideal was only ideal because it was incomplete. Only when something or someone was fully whole and fully known could it be real, and then it must come, as all things do, with its imperfections and its pain.

The wind freshened and flocks of birds spotted the skies, racing away from grey clouds in the far distance. There was rain on the way for sure.

'At least this infernal heat will break,' said Gabriella, ever the pragmatist. 'And the crops will be thankful too. We should take everything inside…'

'Ah, we have time yet,' said Toto. 'Besides, I'm enjoying the breeze, aren't you?'

'You're going soft,' teased Gabriella. 'I'll serve the lamb. Help yourselves to the bread.'

As they ate, Mira leaned in to Emily and whispered conspiratorially.

'Will you test me again later, Emmy?'

'Of course. What is the subject now?'

'Pharmacology.'

'Ah, so you've moved on from pathology?'

'No, I'm reading up on both, but I can't find enough books.'

'Toto might be able to help you?'

Mira curled her bottom lip over her top lip and scowled in a childish show of temper. She didn't need to say anything further to make her feelings clear.

'Fine,' said Emily. 'But you need to realise that all of this work may not go anywhere. Be realistic.'

'Were you?' countered Mira.

'Touché. But you know it's not the same.'

'No. You had someone who believed in you.'

There was the scowl again, but immediately Mira turned away in regret.

'I'm sorry, Emmy. I didn't mean that.'

'It's alright. And it's true. I did always have that. But you have me, and I believe in you. But you know how it is here—'

'Yes, I know,' said Mira, interrupting. 'If you're a woman and you're not content to be a wife and mother, you're not wanted.'

Emily swallowed hard to hear it stated so starkly.

'What about in England?' continued Mira. 'Do you think I could be a doctor in England?'

Emily placed her hand over Mira's and stroked it reassuringly.

'I'm sure you could. One day.'

'I'm not a child,' said Mira.

Emily took a sip of wine. Not for the first time, she noted more than a little of her younger self in Mira. She had been eager to show the world what she could be as well, though never with the certainty that her sister possessed. Mira's father – it was still odd to think of him as her father too – had in large part been the source of this confidence, Mira had told her. He had always encouraged her to reach further, and when her teachers had told her she couldn't join a science class and should instead learn cookery, her father had confronted the headmaster and got him to change his decision. It continued to be difficult to hear good things said about him. She could have laid all the blame at his door for leaving her as a baby if he were a rogue, but what did it mean if he were actually a good man all along?

It was still a source of regret that she had allowed her resentment and bitterness to prevent any rapprochement with her father when she had first arrived. He had held on, it seemed, for her arrival, but died soon after, with so much remaining unsaid between them. Even now she spent time constructing the right words, but there was no longer anyone to hear them.

She watched Toto and Gabriella bickering over something insignificant. It was a curious relationship to be sure, and she wondered what each had seen in the other. As they broke off arguing for a moment, a high-pitched shriek from baby Beatrice, until this point contentedly asleep in her cot in the house, caught Toto's attention. Gabriella seemed more concerned with figuring out her next point and looked irritated at the interruption.

'Darling, the baby is crying.'

'I can hear, Toto. Can I not have one meal in peace? I don't suppose you'll pick up your own daughter, will you?'

Eager to prevent another argument from breaking out, Emily stood up and went towards the house.

'I'll see to her.'

Gabriella avoided eye contact with her as she took her leave. Meanwhile Toto had pushed his chair out and was sitting in a sulk.

Emily went to the cot and peered in at little Beatrice, who stopped whimpering at the sight of her and offered a cheeky smile.

'Did you just want some attention, young lady? Is that it? Yes, I think it is,' she cooed.

She picked Beatrice up and cradled her close to her chest so she could hear her heartbeat. As she held her, the baby relaxed and rubbed her eyes sleepily. Though she tried not to allow it, it was a natural feeling, a sensation of closeness that she had longed for for so long. She rocked her gently.

'Sleep well, little one,' she murmured.

Now that she held the baby, she didn't want to put her down, and she took a chair by the stove and smoothed her dark hair as little Beatrice wriggled and found contentment in her dreams. But she began to regret her offer. The warmth spreading through her was met with a colder emotion, something that she might identify as guilt. Or shame. Or envy.

'She looks well with her aunt,' said Toto, who had entered the room without her noticing. Emily started a little and went to return Beatrice to her crib, before Toto raised a hand to stop her.

'She's happy with you. Why don't you hold her a little longer?'

'If you don't mind,' she said.

There was a sudden relief that she did not have to let go, and she tightened her hold.

'Is she sleeping?' he asked.

'I think so. She's quiet, in any case.'

'She can be a very difficult child. Always crying.'

'Perhaps she just wanted some company? It must be very lonely being a baby and no one understanding what it is that you need. Don't you think?'

Toto sat down opposite her and rested his chin on his hands, watching the two of them as Beatrice tightly gripped Emily's finger in her slumber.

'She won't let go of you.' He smiled. 'You look so natural, like she is your own.'

Emily got to her feet again and turned away from his scrutiny, towards the cot.

'I should put her down now. She needs her mother really – that's who she was crying for.'

'I didn't mean to upset you,' said Toto. He looked away for a moment and seemed to consider his next words with care.

'Tell me if I overstep. But I have always wondered why you never had children?'

Emily leant over the cot to put Beatrice down and hid her face from her brother.

'It just never happened for us,' she said simply. 'One of those regrets that one must live with.'

'You are still young, though,' he said. 'Who knows…'

'No,' she said. There was an emphasis in the way she said it, as if the decision had been made long ago. 'Don't mistake me. I'm not ungrateful for what I have. Some people choose not to have children. Some have no choice. But either way, I am much more than one thing, am I not? I am not incomplete by not being a mother.'

She turned back to register his reaction. He nodded a little in agreement, as if he almost believed her.

Having placed the baby gently into the bed, she pulled up the bedclothes and allowed Beatrice's little fingers to curl around her own once more, for just a moment, before disengaging them and returning, empty, to her chair.

Toto looked her deep in the eye before breaking away and fixing on his shoes.

'You have a bond with her, you know,' he said. 'Gabriella, well… I worry about her. She seems more angry with the world than she ever was before. It feels wrong to be so happy when she cannot feel the same. I look at my daughter and I know I love her. I know I will protect her to my last breath. But I worry.'

He bowed a little, almost as if in an act of prayer.

'Do you think it is possible that she does not wish to know her own baby? That she does not love her at all?'

'I'm not the one to ask,' Emily replied.

Not the one to ask, she might have added, *because love came so easily for me. Easy even for those souls I never got the chance to know. But all the love in the world was not enough.*

In that moment, perhaps because her thoughts tended to the same, she allowed the question she had wanted to ask her brother for so long to find form and cross her lips.

'Have you ever regretted that you married her?'

His response betrayed his shock, as the question had obviously surprised him.

'Never!' he said with a degree of irritation. But then he appeared to consider more. 'I can see why you might ask. From the outside, we argue, we fight. But I think that if I did not care for her, it would not matter, would it? Why would I care that we disagree? And in the end, we always resolve whatever it is. Even this. You think she can be unfeeling, don't you?'

Emily didn't like to contradict him, or to agree, so she seemed to nod, shake her head and shrug all at once.

'She will always fight, my wife,' he continued. 'She will fight anyone, especially those she cares about most. But I know how much she feels, though she won't show anyone else. I just have to remember that what she does, she does out of love. We don't all love in the same way, after all.'

Days passed, and after what could have been a week, or perhaps two – such was the pace of life now – Emily found herself seated on a stool, milking the goats and repeatedly wiping the sweat from the back of her neck between tugs on the udder. The heat was fearsome once again, the storm having failed to break it as expected. Any rain had evaporated so fast that the plants were now beginning to turn brown and wilt. Emily sympathised.

She allowed her eyes to droop and fantasised about lying in a hammock in the shade of the trees and sleeping the afternoon away.

'Sleeping on the job?'

She opened her eyes again to see Gabriella looking down at her. It might have been a joke. Gabriella's sense of humour was either non-existent or as dry as a desert. Emily could never decide which.

'This goat does not like me,' continued Gabriella. 'The last time I milked her, she kicked me.'

'She just likes a gentle touch, I think,' said Emily.

'I am not gentle?'

There was an awkward pause as Emily once again didn't know whether to smile or apologise. Then Gabriella poked her gently on the arm and gave her something which approximated a smile. It was the first time Emily had seen her smile, other than when she was with Toto and she thought no one was watching. Gabriella sat down on a log and became serious again.

'I wanted to thank you for looking after Beatrice today.'

'Of course,' said Emily, a little surprised. 'It was my pleasure. She is a delight. Such a happy baby.'

'She is for you.' She nodded her head slowly and Emily could see a sadness in her eyes. Just for a fleeting moment.

'Gabriella, is there something wrong?'

'No… I wanted you to know I appreciate it, that's all. All the attention you give her. It's important.'

'No thanks needed. She is my niece after all. And we all love her, don't we?'

'Yes. I suppose we do.'

Gabriella took her leave and the afternoon continued slowly. Emily finished her work and gradually made her way back up the hill. As she reached the garden, Toto came racing out of the house and down the slope towards her. He came to a halt, and she could see the look of shock and fear etched into his features. For a long moment he said nothing. Then, like an automaton, he held a letter out in front of him for her to take.

'Whatever is it?' she asked.

He simply shook his head and thrust it towards her again so that she was compelled to take the letter from him and read it herself.

The header was official-looking, and as she read the bureaucratic language, it became clear.

'It was on the wireless this morning,' said Toto, finally finding his voice.

'We have declared war on France and Britain. That is to say, Mussolini has. And this letter followed soon after, as if it were planned all along.

All reservists are being called up to fight. Including me.'

Dizzy from the heat or dazzled by the sun, Emily handed the letter back to her brother in a delirium, and, barely conscious of his voice calling her, she strode away, her pace quickening as she drove on into the olive groves and walked and walked.

In time she stopped and came again to her senses, sliding down with exhaustion beneath a tree and looking up at the birds flitting between branches. Her mind flickered back to another place and another time when she had looked up at another tree and felt the immediacy of war. The sense that an uncontrollable and malevolent force was able to reach out and drag away those she cared for, with no recourse, no debate. Except that this time it was worse. For this time, she knew what the consequences could be. Toto, whom she had only now begun to know, might return fundamentally changed. Like Richard had. Or not at all.

She couldn't escape the feeling that she had stayed too long. That the idyll she had found had in some way cocooned her from an outside world in tumult. A world that had now crashed into their lives and threatened everything in her new life. It might stop that life before it had even begun.

It occurred to her as well that she was now an enemy. A foreigner in a country that had set itself against her homeland. Set itself against her. Her throat tightened and she could feel the rising panic that she had felt once before. As she placed her head between her legs, she could recall the stuffy air and the smell of leather of the taxi so clearly. The memory was vivid. This time, though, she was prepared, and remembered the technique Toto had showed her.

Gradually, very gradually, she controlled her breathing and calmed herself. The distress subsided, but the memory remained of what had provoked it that first time.

'Are you alright?'

It was Mira, hanging on to the tree trunk with one hand and swinging around to look down at Emily. 'I've been looking for you everywhere! Toto was so worried.'

'I'm sorry. I had to find somewhere. Somewhere to think.'

Mira's open face showed all her anxiety, and she dropped down onto her knees and took Emily's hand.

'Are you scared, Emmy?'

'Of course I'm worried for him,' she said. 'But I'm sure Toto will be fine.'

'I hope so. But that's not what I meant. I meant are you scared to stay here now?'

Emily looked down at her feet. She felt an obligation to this girl. A duty to be honest with her, but also to protect her. Although at eighteen she was fully grown, she had lived little in the world and would now have no one to protect her.

'You know you don't need to worry, Emmy. We'll protect you. I'll protect you. We can hide together. You know we're used to hiding.'

Emily couldn't help but laugh a little. She pulled Mira closer to her, so that they were sitting together under the tree with their arms linked.

'I don't want to leave,' she told her. 'But I can't stay forever. If they know I'm here, they will come for me, and then... well, I don't know what will happen.'

She paused for a moment as she took notice of something Mira had said.

'What did you mean?'

'By what?'

'What did you mean when you said you are used to hiding?'

'Because of who we are,' said Mira, matter-of-factly. 'It's not like it is in Germany, but we have always had to be careful…'

She stopped as she registered the look of concern on Emily's face. She frowned in confusion.

'Toto did tell you? He told you, didn't he? He said he was going to—'

'Tell me what?' said Emily in frustration.

'I wanted to tell you for so long, but he always said it was too dangerous for you. For you or for us, I don't know which. Maybe both—'

'Mira, stop. What is it?'

Mira looked in every direction except at Emily and folded her arms tightly.

'He'll be so angry that I told you.'

'You haven't told me anything yet. But you must – please.'

Mira looked her in the eye at last.

'Emmy… we're Jewish.'

It took time for the statement to register. Emily remembered the 'feeling' that Richard had described, that all was not as it appeared. She had had it too. But she had ignored it. Supressed it even. All because she wanted this so badly. Wanted a family. She shivered involuntarily and felt a sudden and deep fear. Fear for herself. But also for her new family. To live always with the same terror of discovery. She might have been angry that they concealed it from her for so long, but what else could they have done?

'Will you go home?' asked Mira sadly.

'I'm not sure that I have one,' she admitted. 'Or that I could get there if I did.'

They sat together in silence for a while and felt the gentle breeze that was beginning to skip off the hillside. Mira tightened her grip on Emily's hand and rested her head against her shoulder.

'Are you angry?'

'No. Not angry.'

'You could write to him again,' said Mira after some time.

Emily rolled her eyes and sighed.

'Mira, what has he to do with any of it? And we've been through this. He didn't reply. He couldn't have made it any clearer. There's nothing more to be said. I don't know where you get these romantic notions. I shouldn't have given you those Jane Austen novels. He's hardly going to come riding in here to rescue me like a medieval knight. Be realistic.'

'I know you think about him, though.'

'How do you know that? Have you been studying psychiatry as well as everything else?'

Mira smiled and jabbed her gently in the ribs.

'No, but you don't talk about him, so you must be thinking about him.'

'That makes perfect sense,' teased Emily.

'You do though, don't you?'

'We were together for twenty years. So of course I do… sometimes. But it's the past. You read that book I gave you?'

Mira nodded.

'Well, it's like Mr Rochester says, the connection is snapped; he has forgotten me. I have to accept that. Nothing lasts forever, nothing can.

'Like sitting here with you…' she said, lightening the mood. 'We can't stay here all day. There are things to be done.'

They got up and shook the dust from their clothes. Just as they were turning to go back, Mira caught her hand again and looked seriously into her eyes.

'Will you promise me something, Emmy?'

'What?'

'Will you promise not to leave me? Wherever you go, you'll take me too?'

Emily tilted her head and sucked on her bottom lip while she considered. Neither answer was the right one. Part of her wondered what she owed Mira, or any of them. They had lied to her and remaining would put her in greater danger. But Mira was so insistent, and her attachment was real. It would be like rejecting a daughter's plea.

'I promise.'

Mira held tightly to her hand as they walked back up towards the house, and, as she thought about the future, unknown and unsettling, she had cause to regret the promise she had made.

As they reached the house, they found Toto and Gabriella deep in conversation at the table outside. Gabriella had a strength at times like these, and seemed determined and certain, while Toto had his head in his hands and was shaking it vigorously.

'There you are,' said Gabriella as they approached. Toto got up as he saw them and ran over. He hugged them both.

'It's alright,' he said. 'It will be alright.'

Emily didn't pull away but didn't hug him back.

'Tell me what you're thinking,' he entreated.

I don't belong here now, she thought, but when she looked at Mira, she couldn't say it.

'Why didn't you tell me?' she asked instead.

'I've only just found out myself—'

'No. Before. When you came to England. You didn't tell me everything. You didn't say you were… that I suppose *we* are…'

She found herself unable to say it, though she had never thought of herself as prejudiced before. Toto looked to Mira, whose face gave away her guilt. But before he could reply, Gabriella jumped in:

'Mira? Mira, what have you done?'

'I thought she knew…'

'You're a silly, silly girl,' said Gabriella. 'You don't think before you speak.'

'Like you?' said Mira. 'At least what I say is because I care. Because I didn't want to lie. You don't care about Emmy, or any of us… not even… not even your own baby.'

'Mira!' cried Toto.

All the colour went from Gabriella's face, as if the energy was draining away. For a moment she looked diminished, smaller, and she said nothing. Then she raised her hand, as if to strike Mira across the face. Mira flinched. But the hand fell back again

147

to her side, as though all strength had gone from it. Gabriella's eyes grew wide. She opened her mouth as if to speak, but instead she let out a shaking sigh and then turned and walked slowly away.

'Mira,' said Toto severely. 'Sometimes you need to hold your tongue.'

He hurried after Gabriella and left them standing silently together.

Time passed, and Emily and Mira found themselves at the table, talking about inconsequential things, though Mira would turn often to look in the direction that Gabriella had gone.

Toto returned at last and joined them at the table.

'She needs some time,' he said.

'I didn't mean to be cruel,' said Mira, pushing her hand across the table towards him.

Toto put his hand onto hers and stroked it gently.

'I know… Emily,' he said, turning to her, 'we should have told you. *I* should have. I'm sorry.'

She tried to smile at him in reassurance, but the fear and the uncertainty persisted.

'I know what I ask when I ask you to keep our secret,' he continued. 'But I must. If you want to go, you can. We trust you, but you cannot ever tell anyone who we are.'

'Can't we just stay here?' said Mira. 'All of us? No one will know.'

'And when I fail to report?' said Toto. 'Gabriella and I have discussed this, and she is right. They will come looking. No. No, I must go. You will have Gabriella to look after you.'

Mira's eyebrows raised as she vainly tried to conceal her thoughts. Emily avoided looking her in the eye, in apprehension of seeing her own fears reflected there. The fears she had always carried with her – of being alone and forsaken. She shifted uneasily. She needed time to think.

'I will miss you all,' said Toto. 'Even my troublesome sister.'

He touched her hand gently once again.

'And especially little Beatrice…'

Emily looked up sharply.

'Where is Beatrice?'

'In the house—'

149

'Alone?'

Emily was up and on her way inside, barely hearing her brother telling her the baby was asleep. Was it a distraction from making a decision, or something else? More and more she had been finding reasons to spend time with Beatrice. Like an addiction, each time she held her brought a surge of warmth and each time it was harder to let go.

She watched Beatrice wriggle contentedly in her sleep. It seemed impossible to leave her now, however dangerous it might be to stay. In any case, the family had lived here, undisturbed, all this time. Why should that change?

When the baby began to stir from her sleep, Emily picked her up gratefully and held her close. She heard a creak of the floorboards and turned to see Gabriella watching her. Emily moved to hand Beatrice to her mother, but Gabriella turned instead to the sideboard and poured herself some wine.

'I do trust you,' she said at last.

Emily continued to watch her while she rocked the baby, unsure what to say.

'I wasn't angry because I don't trust you. I wanted to tell you that. I was angry because… I am afraid.'

'Afraid?' said Emily. The word didn't seem to apply to the Gabriella she knew.

'Afraid for you,' said Gabriella quickly. 'Afraid for all of you.'

But there was something in her expression that betrayed her own fear too.

'When I was young, my family were very poor,' continued Gabriella. 'We learned to fight for everything. For every crumb of food. No one gave us anything.'

'I didn't know that,' said Emily. 'It was much the same for me.'

'Then you understand. We must all fight this *crapone* in whatever way we can. I won't allow him to destroy my country. Our country. Will you help me?'

'I don't think I do understand,' said Emily. 'What are you trying to say? How can I help you?'

'I cannot sit and wait. I must take action. My friends in the party are forming resistance in whatever ways they can. We campaign, we protest. Perhaps, we fight too.'

Emily looked at her in bewilderment.

'What about Beatrice?'

She placed the baby back in her crib, but as she did so, she realised her sister-in-law's intentions.

'You don't mean *me* to look after her? No, I can't!'

Gabriella pressed her hands together with Emily's and grasped them tightly.

'I will be back from time to time. I doubt she will know that I am gone,' she said, but there was little conviction in it. Almost as though she were trying to convince herself at the same time.

'Mira and I would be here on our own. I'm not a farmer. I wouldn't know what to do...'

'You know enough,' interrupted Gabriella. 'None of us is prepared for this, but we can only do what we can. What we are made to do. I know what I'm made for, and it's not this. It cannot be just this.'

'I can't think that I am made for it either,' protested Emily, breaking away from Gabriella's hold.

'You like it here, though? And you care for the baby? I can tell.'

Emily nodded reluctantly.

'If I thought it would help, I would pray to God to make me a better mother. Or to help me see another way. But there is no one there to hear. I want the best for Beatrice… but… I don't think it's me… not now, not here…'

Emily had struggled to warm to Gabriella until now. Her spikiness, which she had taken for spitefulness at times, or even arrogance, had been hard to deal with. But now she sensed a vulnerability that she understood.

'Don't say that,' she said. 'You can't mean it.'

'I envy you, Emily,' she replied. 'I really do. Because this…' She indicated the two of them together. 'This is easy for you. Give me *Das Kapital*, give me political debate, and I am at home. But otherwise it is not easy.

'I know she is my child, but it is not in here.' She thumped her heart for effect. 'You understand? It's just not there.'

If seemed impossible that Gabriella would ever cry. And yet there were tears in her eyes now.

'I haven't decided yet if I'm going to stay,' said Emily. 'It's all so much. What does it even mean to be Jewish?'

'What does it mean to be English?' said Gabriella simply. 'For most of our history, it has meant to be hated for *what* we are, not *who* we are. To be at the mercy of others.'

It could in some ways have been a description of Emily's own childhood. To be thought somehow inferior, less worthy of consideration. She had fought to leave her past behind, so that she would never again be anyone's servant. But it paled beside the fear which they must all have lived with for so many years. She could barely imagine how that would feel.

'I want to help you,' said Emily. 'I want to help Beatrice, all of you…'

'Then stay,' said Gabriella.

Emily nodded slowly. Gabriella kissed her on both cheeks, as she had on the first day they met, but this time with affection.

'You are still her mother, and you always will be.'

'You are good, Emily. Even if you aren't a communist.'

She smiled.

'Socialist?' offered Emily.

Gabriella screwed her face up and shook her head vigorously.

'As bad as the Catholics.'

Part Three

Summer 1943

Chapter 7

Hansen made a stiff bow and leaned, taking her hand in his. He brought it close to his lips, without actually going so far as to kiss it, and took in the heavy, sweet perfume on her skin. It wasn't unpleasant, but had been applied liberally, much as her make-up had been.

She smiled sweetly as he looked up at her. It was a pretty face, with slight dimples in her cheeks, and he noticed that there was a little green tint to her otherwise grey eyes.

'Would you like to sit down, Fräulein?'

They took a seat in the window so they could look out over Marienplatz, and a waiter in crisp white apron appeared promptly at his side.

'What will you have?' he asked.

'White wine,' she said, as he looked to her.

'A schnapps for me.'

The waiter bowed and left. She smoothed her blonde hair back behind her ear while studying him. It was a gesture that gave him pause.

'I was a little surprised at your invitation,' she began. 'But delighted,' she added hastily.

'Why surprised? You must have many admirers, Fräulein Giesler?'

She feigned embarrassment. Or perhaps it was genuine.

'You may call me Lieselotte if you wish,' she said. 'Or some people just call me Lotte.'

'Which people?'

'People I'm close to.'

'Well then, *Lotte*,' he said with emphasis, 'you must call me Richard. And you didn't answer my question – why was it a surprise that I should wish to have such a charming companion at dinner?'

She blushed again, and now he was sure it was real. There was an innocence to her that was undeniably attractive.

'When people hear my name, they… decide to make other arrangements. At least that's how it seems to me.'

'Forgive me. I have not been in Munich for long. But is your name one I should know, then?'

She smiled and squinted a little at him, as if trying to work out if he were teasing her.

'Genuinely? It means nothing to you?'

He shook his head. She smiled again, this time with an edge of playfulness.

'Then I'm not sure I should tell you. I'd rather you didn't know.'

'You'd rather that I didn't choose to make other arrangements?'

'Yes. At least not for tonight.'

The drinks arrived and he picked up his glass of schnapps and paused as he took it to his lips.

'As you wish. You shall remain a mystery to be discovered.'

He took a sip and flinched slightly as it stung the back of his throat. The first sip was difficult, but the second and the third by turns eased his qualms.

'I like the idea of being a mystery,' she said. 'And if I can find out more about Richard Schönfelder, I should like that too.'

'You mean you haven't already?' he teased.

She put her hands to her mouth.

'How did you know?' she said.

'I keep my ear to the ground, and I heard that you'd been asking about me.'

He relaxed and smiled, taking another sip of schnapps.

'It's alright, I don't mind. In fact it's quite flattering. I'd be interested in what you found out, though. In my position it helps to know what others are saying about you.'

'I promise you, it's all good,' she said.

'That's a shame.'

Hansen tapped his empty glass on the table and signalled to the waiter.

'No, really. They told me that you've arrived from Berlin, with a glowing recommendation from Reichsführer Himmler himself!'

She almost squealed as she said it. Hansen smiled benevolently. She leaned in conspiratorially.

'Have you met him?'

'Of course.'

Another squeal. Hansen looked with some relief at the new glass of schnapps delivered by the waiter and picked it up at once.

'What is he like?'

'I thought you were interested in me, not Herr Himmler.'

'I am, of course. Except, well, you can't blame me for being curious. Oh, your glass is empty again already?'

'It's excellent schnapps.'

He fiddled with his empty glass, looking for another refill, but wary of calling the waiter back just yet for how it might look.

'The Reichsführer was very kind towards me. I was until recently in the Ukraine, commanding a Panzergrenadier unit. He was good enough to hear some of my opinions about the campaign and make some changes as a result. But he said it was necessary to redeploy me.'

'Why?'

'Politics. What else? I am a simple soldier, but he said my determination and my experience might be useful in building the new Germany. I am happy to play the part he asks of me, of course. But until today I was a little unsure if I was in the right place.'

'What happened today?'

'I met you, of course.'

She reached across the table and touched him lightly on the hand. 'You flatter me... Richard.'

She drew back her hand, as if conscious of remaining the demure and pure Aryan woman she ought to be.

'So, aside from talking to me, what are you going to do while you are in Munich?'

'We will see. Herr Himmler suggested I find opportunities to learn the principles of government, with the aim, in time, of posting me as a Gauleiter.'

He watched her reaction carefully.

'He is going to appoint you as Gauleiter? Here?'

He took a moment and scanned the menu on the table. From the corner of his eye, he could see her twitch and fidget.

'Perhaps,' he said at last. 'He didn't specify.'

She looked eager to say something, but kept her counsel, and then smiled encouragingly.

'He must think very highly of you.'

'You'd have to ask him. But it would certainly be agreeable to have a chance to settle down somewhere.

'Now. What would you like to eat? I understand they have some *Schweinshaxe*, which would be a treat. I haven't seen any in months…'

The following morning, Hansen made his way to the Englischer Garten in the spring sunshine. The city had been largely untouched so far by raids, and, if you ignored the sandbags, you could mistake it for a city at peace.

He counted the lamp posts as he reached the path into the park. On the fourteenth, as he expected, he found a small chalk mark. He sat on the bench and took out his book. After a few moments of pretending to read, noting the people around him, he reached out one arm, as if stretching, and wiped the chalk mark off with his sleeve. He remained there for some time, and then the following morning he returned.

This time the bench was occupied, and he took out his book and sat next to the other man, who was engrossed in his newspaper.

'Anything in the news?' he asked absently.

'The usual,' said the other man. 'I notice there is a choir recital this evening, though, at Kirche St Anna. If you like music?'

'Nothing I like better.'

'Perhaps I shall see you there, then. At 7pm. I shall have a bite to eat at Zum Dürnbräu, I think, as well.'

'Good idea. Their dumplings are excellent.'

'Indeed. Well, good day to you.'

Hansen took a pew at the back of the church and found Thurso hunched at one end. His eyes were half-closed, though as he came closer it became apparent that it wasn't in reverence of the divine music, but in weariness. Nevertheless, he was aware of Hansen's approach as always.

'We should meet somewhere else next time,' he said, with one eye open.

'It was your choice.'

'It seemed like a good idea. Gestapo and Bach don't mix, at least in my mind. How did it go?'

'As planned. I played the Prussian gentleman to full effect, and I layered on the charm to such a degree that it made me nauseous.'

'Good show. And she lapped it up?'

'Sadly, I think she did. I felt like a cad throughout. You have no qualms about this?'

Thurso opened his other eye and shot him a characteristic glare.

'No. And neither should you. It's a job.'

'It's a honeytrap. And I'm not overly keen on being the honey.'

Thurso took out a packet of cigarettes and tapped one into his hand. Then he crossed his arms and held it between two fingers, pointed deliberately towards Hansen.

'You can't smoke in a church. Or is that a new code signal?'

'Read it well. And before you start to make a big moral case against…'

Hansen started to protest, but Thurso held his fingers up again to stop him.

'She is a mark. Nothing more. And most men in your position would happily pay to spend time in the company of an attractive blonde young enough to be their daughter.'

Hansen looked up at the ornate ceiling. Not for the first time, Thurso's manner repelled him, despite the charm.

'Any leads yet?'

'Not yet. Just groundwork,' said Hansen. 'She doesn't know that I know who her father is. Though it surprised me. She must think I'm a total dunce.'

'Fine if she does. As far as she should be concerned, you are nothing more than perfect Aryan bloodstock, with a chiselled jaw and a career that is sending you straight to the top. What else could she want?'

'If you have to ask, I no longer wonder why you're a bachelor. How do you suggest I proceed?'

'As you are. You need to work on being perfect marriage material, and it won't hurt to get her a bit worked up, as well... you know...'

Hansen screwed up his eyes, and Thurso mistook his revulsion for confusion.

'You know, imagine Errol Flynn in tights.'

'You're joking?'

'Not entirely. Can't you tell by now? I'm thinking a trip to the Chiemsee. A nice semi-clad day by the seaside – or inland lake, anyway.'

'You're a cheap pimp, Thurso.'

'You'll see I'm right. And remember, eyes on the objective, nothing else. If it helps, remember that you're a married man.'

Hansen nodded slowly.

'I remember.'

Hansen saw more and more of Lotte over the following days and weeks. He found that lying came easily, paying her all the attention she craved. But as he spent more time with her, he began to admire more than just her beauty. One afternoon, Hansen walked into the office on Prannerstrasse where Lotte had a secretarial position in the sprawling administrative building overseen by her father, Paul Giesler. He breezed in, secure in the authority of his black SS uniform with the collar patches of a Standartenführer, but incongruously carrying a bunch of flowers.

The receptionist took particular notice of his uniform and was quick to fetch Lotte. Having presented his flowers, he pulled rank in the most extravagant way possible, by informing her supervisor that he needed her for important work and sweeping her out of the building to his waiting car, before she or anyone else could object.

In the car she cradled the flowers in a kind of stunned silence that was half shock and half pleasure.

'Where are we going?' she asked at last.

'A little trip. Have you ever been to the Chiemsee?'

'Oh, we used to go all the time when I was a child!' she shrieked excitedly. But then considered. 'I haven't got a swimming costume.'

'On the back seat,' he replied, indicating a box tied up with a bow.

When they reached the shore, there were few other people around, and they were able to find a sheltered spot surrounded by trees where they had a perfect view of the Alps.

Hansen unpacked the picnic and self-consciously got changed into his costume, removing his shirt last of all when he was sitting opposite Lotte. He had the feeling of an artist's model, scrutinised and studied, but for baser reasons than art. Lotte at first didn't look in his direction, but gradually she became braver and then it was obvious she was regarding the scars across his chest and arm, and the mess of his knee.

'Did you get those in the war?' she asked. 'The scars, I mean,' she added unnecessarily.

'The last war,' he explained.

'It must have been painful,' she said with a grimace.

He shrugged, forcibly pushing aside the memory of the excruciating pain of that day, when he was terrified he would lose his leg, or worse.

'I'm glad you don't have to go back,' she said, handing him a drink. 'Would you go, if you could?'

'Of course,' he replied at once. It was an easy answer. No acting or deception was required. 'I owe it to my men, to my comrades. And, of course, to the Fatherland. We all fight for a greater Germany, for the better future which the Führer has promised.

'But of course I should like it if, one day, it is no longer necessary. If we can live in peace and I could have a family to come home to. A wife to look after me. Children to bounce on my knee. All of that. Isn't that what we all want?'

She started a little, surprised by the question, and busied herself with the food.

'Isn't it?' he persisted.

'What would you like me to say?' she replied, a little sorely.

'Have I offended you, Lotte?'

'No…'

'Because if I have…'

'No, of course not. It's just getting a little late. Perhaps we should head back, once we've eaten.'

'As you wish.'

They ate in silence, and in silence Hansen cursed himself. Had he not made everything perfect enough? What was missing? He was surely everything a good Nazi girl would want in a prospective husband – strong, capable, ambitious, committed to the cause and able to provide. She had seemed to like him. He had obviously been too forward. With luck, he could retrieve things. But he was uncertain how to proceed.

The silence continued for some time as they travelled back in the car, and Lotte was deep in thought. Eventually she voiced what she had been pondering.

'Do you really believe in the future you talked about? That there may be peace?'

Hansen took a moment before he replied, wary that this was a test of some sort.

'I am fully confident we will win,' he replied. 'With the Führer's guidance, it is a certainty.'

'I thought you would say that,' she replied.

She remained quiet for some minutes before she tried again.

'What about Stalingrad?' she asked. 'Or North Africa? The Americans in the war?'

Hansen was genuinely shocked. He had not expected this, and he had no answer prepared to meet it. He needed to buy himself time to understand the root of it.

'What do you mean?'

She tried and failed to suppress the anger building in her.

'Because I don't think I believe it anymore. I have friends who have lost fathers, brothers. When will it end? It's been nearly four years already. And what happens if, after everything, we lose? What will happen to all of us then?'

This was worrying, not just for the task at hand, but for Lotte herself.

'Calm yourself,' he replied, and he pulled the car over to a stop.

He leaned over and took her hands in his. She seemed to be searching his expression, and just for a second, there was a flash of recognition, almost as if she had seen something there.

'What is this about?' he asked.

'I'm worried,' she said. 'Everything I've been taught. Everything I grew up with. The life I should expect. *Kinder, Küche, Kirche*. My father always told me it was right. That Germany, after the last war, was in ruins. That Hitler rebuilt our country and made it great.'

'And?'

'And I look at you, and everything you are, and it's the same.'

'What do you mean?'

'You are perfect. Perfect like Germany is perfect. And I know you're lying.'

Chapter 8

Emily's day began the way it always did, with dawn breaking. As she warmed some milk on the stove, she mused on how things had come full circle. Once, she had been accustomed to the long hours of back-breaking toil as a maid and had fought to leave that behind. She had attained a respectable, middle-class position of comfort and intellectual challenge. And now? Long hours and hard work once again. Was there regret in that? Surely. But did regrets outweigh the dreams that she still clung to? That was less certain.

She gave Beatrice her breakfast, and they went out together to feed the animals while Mira began the housework. Beatrice followed Emily about in her meandering way, fascinated by beetles, worms and other crawling creatures all the while. Given the chance, she would spend hours with her hands in the mud, playing with any creatures she could capture.

Emily was forced to prod and cajole her at regular intervals to keep her in sight while she went about the many jobs on the farm, but she was a good-natured and curious child. It was difficult to see, sometimes, how she could be Gabriella's daughter. Though perhaps Emily had misjudged her sister-in-law.

There was always time to think. Too much time. Time to think about everything that had changed in the four years since she had left Devon. Memories of her old life, which had gradually become less painful. There was even a kind of nostalgia. Was it right to say this was a more comfortable life? No, not comfortable. Not that. But more fitting? In some sense she had felt out of place in academia. Like she might be somehow found out, discovered for the imposter she was. Richard had had a particular way to jolt her out of these crises. He would ask her to explain some obscure theory of art or describe an artist's work, and when she did so, he would simply say, 'I can't say I know what you're talking about. But that's alright, because *you* do.'

It helped. But she would still look at her colleagues, in their ease, and feel an outsider. Though she continued to miss the job itself.

By mid-morning she was in amongst the vines, tying up the new plants which Toto had planted when he was last home on leave in the spring. It seemed so long ago, and the vines had grown hugely in that time, sprawling in every direction. Ready for harvesting soon.

As they had finished the planting, there had been an odd moment between the two of them. They had discussed the future. What Mira might go on to do and what kind of world little Beatrice might inherit. Increasingly despondent, Mira had gradually put aside her books, and a realism had begun to take hold that had not been there before. Meanwhile, Beatrice hardly knew her father, and he had watched her as she pottered about in the garden.

'She is growing up so fast,' he said. 'I feel as if I've missed everything. Her first word, her first steps. And she treats me like a stranger. Wary. A little curious, but that's all.'

'She'll get to know you when you're back for good,' Emily had told him. 'She just needs time. The months when you are gone… It's a lifetime for a child.'

He had nodded in agreement. 'I just can't imagine when that will be, though. How long will she have to wait?'

'The wait always feels endless,' said Emily. 'But at least you are here now – safe. We have to hold on to the moments we have.'

Later, they had taken their leave, and Toto had pulled her close.

'*Baruch Hashem* that you are here, Emily. *Baruch Hashem.* We would be lost without you.'

It had been the oddest sensation. A premonition that there would be no reunion. That this might be the last time they were together. She didn't mention it to her brother, but the feeling lingered all through the day after he had departed, and it returned every time she thought about where he might be or what he might be doing.

There had been hope since then. The invasion of Sicily by the Allied forces. The fall of Mussolini. And, only days before, the surrender of the government. But then the Germans had arrived, and everything seemed bleaker than before.

Even so, it was not the shock it should have been when, later that day, Gabriella arrived with the news. She tried to be calm, as they sat down together in the kitchen, tried to suggest there might be room for hope, but it was obvious that she didn't believe what she was saying.

It had been garbled, she said, but there had been reports of a massacre in Cephalonia. The Germans had responded to the fall of their ally with occupation and violence. Wild with blood lust, Italian units which resisted the call to surrender were cut down. The 33rd Acqui – Toto's division – had been among them.

'I'm so sorry, Gabriella,' Emily said, reaching out to embrace her sister-in-law.

'There's nothing to be sorry about,' she said, pushing Emily away. 'We can't just believe everything we hear. It could be Nazi propaganda. It would be just like the Germans to do that. We can't fall for their lies.'

'But what if…'

'No!'

Gabriella sat heavily. She waved away any attempt to continue the conversation. Emily watched her. It was rare for Gabriella to avoid an argument.

Beatrice sensed something amiss and came over to her mother, opening her arms and pushing into Gabriella. She seemed unwilling to accept the hug, and so Beatrice ended up awkwardly holding on to her legs, the only part of Gabriella she could get hold of. Gabriella looked down at the child's round face looking up at her.

'You have his eyes,' she said finally. 'Beautiful eyes.'

'Beautiful eyes,' repeated Beatrice, practising the new words.

Gabriella stroked her hair.

'It's not your fault,' said Emily.

Her sister-in-law twisted around, pushing Beatrice away and rising from her chair. She came close, apparently on the verge of tears, but fuelled by anger too.

'No,' she agreed. 'It's not my fault.'

She paused for effect.

'It's yours. All of this.'

She looked back at Beatrice once more and then swung around to face Emily.

'None of this would have happened if you hadn't come here. If you hadn't been hiding here like a coward.' She seemed unsure, as though what she was saying was for effect. To provoke an argument and a situation she could control. She tilted her head as she scrutinised Emily's expression, puzzled by what she found there. 'This… this is all so easy for you, isn't it? Why don't you run away? Run, little rabbit!'

She put her hand to her chin and flicked it towards Emily.

'Run away!'

Then she took a bottle of wine from the sideboard and stalked off into the garden. Emily watched her go. There was as much childishness in Gabriella as in Beatrice and her moods were just as transitory. Though knowing this did little to take the sting out of the words she had used. Whether she believed she bore any blame or not, she felt responsible now for all of her family. Even Gabriella. With Toto gone, with Richard gone, there was no one to lean on. She would need to stand by herself. She had often claimed to be self-reliant, but when it came to it, others had always been there to guide her or support her. Now she must guide others.

Emily allowed her composure to break as she remembered the last moments she had shared with Toto. She raised her apron to her face to hide her tears. He had been one of the most compassionate people she had known, forever nurturing others at his own expense. Most of all she would miss his wisdom. More than once he had reminded her of Richard, and in a strange way, she still grieved for him too.

She looked back to Beatrice, who had found another beetle to study. Another child who would grow up without a father, just as she had. And she began to cry again. She took the little girl in her arms and held her tight, though Beatrice could not understand why.

As Emily walked through the garden that evening, the air, which had always seemed so sweet before, scented with lavender and honeysuckle, felt still and insipid.

She made her way automatically to the chicken coop and Beatrice, as usual, trailed behind her. But this time she was not exploring the world around her. She kept her eyes fixed on Emily and chewed on her thumb as she watched.

Emily began to scatter crumbs and seed across the ground for the chickens, who fought for every morsel. As she did so, she could hear Richard's voice in her mind. When they had been together so many years ago on another farm, he had teased that she couldn't call herself a proper Devon girl, not having set foot in a farmyard before. She smiled at the thought. On that afternoon he had shown her a little, just a fraction, of his real self. The divide between them had fallen away, and for a moment they had been just two people. It was, perhaps, the first time she had sensed that it could be more than that, though she had doubted her own feelings, and his. He had held her hand and told her of the comfort that that simple gesture brought him. But in all honesty, it meant just as much to her. Involuntarily she clasped her hand now, empty though it was.

Beatrice was crawling on her hands and knees, searching for eggs amongst the straw. Emily watched her and gradually became aware that someone was watching them both. She looked around to see Mira, her knuckles white, clasped around the fence, her eyes red, though the tears had all dried.

'Mira!' she called. 'Are you alright? Did Gabriella tell you... about Toto?'

There was no response.

They watched each other for a moment. Mira's expression was blank and lifeless. Emily offered her a reassuring smile, but to no effect. There was a tug at her skirt and Emily looked down to see Beatrice offering her a couple of eggs, grasped tightly in her little hands.

'Here you go, Mama,' she said, smiling with pride at her discovery.

There was a splutter of shock from Mira.

'Beatrice, what—' she called, but she couldn't, or wouldn't, complete the sentence. The little girl regarded her curiously for a moment, and then went back to rummaging amongst the straw.

Mira opened the gate and hurried up to Emily. The shock had been replaced by a look of fear.

'Are you not going to correct her?' said Mira at last.

'She's just confused,' said Emily quietly. 'And too little to understand.'

'She may be,' said Mira. 'But I'm not. I thought I could trust you.'

'You know you can,' said Emily.

Mira kicked the ground and spun in a circle, almost as if she were about to stamp her feet like a child in a tantrum. Like Beatrice, in fact.

'Mira, I know you're upset about Toto, but you shouldn't take it out on me. I'm only doing my best.'

'I'm not a child,' replied Mira, with a cold calm. 'Emmy, you will keep your promise, won't you?'

Mira's face began to turn bright red, sweat began to bead on her forehead and her breathing became rapid and shallow. She started to fan herself and then bent over double.

'Mira, listen, I'm not going anywhere.'

Emily dropped to her knees and took Mira by the shoulders.

'Mira, look at me. This has happened to you before, hasn't it? It's happened to me, too. You are going to be fine. Look at me. You know you're going to be fine.'

Mira looked her in the eyes and Emily nodded to her gently in reassurance.

'Count with me…'

They counted down together, and gradually Mira regained her composure, using the technique that Toto had taught them both. There was something reassuring in knowing that some part of him remained to look after them.

After a time Mira was calm again, and she threw her arms around Emily and held her tightly. It brought them both comfort, but as they held each other, Emily also felt a sense of claustrophobia. A heaviness of obligation.

Later, Emily found herself wandering in the vineyards again, and stroked one of the vines that she and Toto had planted. Though the others had flourished, this one had not grown as it should and now stood by itself. It looked weak and threadbare. But somehow it had survived.

Chapter 9

Thurso took the cigarette out of his mouth for a moment and moistened his lips. He seemed a little troubled, and Hansen wondered if he had succeeded in breaking the Scot's imperturbability at last.

'Well, that is certainly unexpected,' he said finally. 'How did you respond?'

'I can't honestly remember. I was so shocked I think I said something about her being overwrought, and that she should get some rest. Then I took her back.'

'And that was all?'

'Yes, I think so. But I was sure she'd seen through me. I should have come clean…'

'Absolutely not!' broke in Thurso.

'But surely…' continued Hansen, bit between his teeth now. 'Surely, if she is beginning to doubt what she's been taught? She's not a fool. She could be useful – more useful – as an ally.'

Thurso stubbed his cigarette aggressively into the arm of the bench.

'You will not attempt to turn her. That is an order. There's a lot more at risk here than your discomfort.'

'I don't see another option.'

'We continue with the plan. She's just having doubts. She probably thinks she'll lose you to the war. It's a good sign, really. It means she likes you enough to care what happens in the future. You need to reassure her and, if needs be, up the ante.'

'How?'

'Simple. You propose.'

Hansen struggled to contain his reaction, aware of passers-by watching. His voice dropped to an urgent whisper.

'I'm not marrying her!'

'Steady, Sir Lancelot. You don't have to. You just need to be engaged. Then he'll let you into the inner circle.'

'You mean she will.'

'He, she, it doesn't matter. It's all the same, as long as you get access.'

Hansen got to his feet and rolled up his newspaper, slapping it into his hand as if testing its strength.

'Hit me if you wish,' said Thurso, turning his head to survey the path. 'But keep me apprised.'

Hansen began to walk away, and he could see from the corner of his eye that Thurso had begun to read his own paper once again, relaxed and carefree. It infuriated him, but an order was an order.

Hansen tried to appear as discreet as he could, but his uniform drew enough attention to make his position difficult as he paced outside the offices in Prannerstrasse. He was about to leave when the doors swung open and Lotte appeared with a group of other secretaries. At first it looked like she was with them, but gradually they moved off together and left her behind. She seemed to be watching them go, but then turned away by herself and walked to a nearby bench. She sat down, took out a little package and began to unwrap bread and cheese. She was so

lost in thought that she didn't notice him
approaching until he was next to her.

'May I sit?' he asked.

She smiled awkwardly, her harsh words
during their last meeting still clearly fresh in her
mind. He took a seat, keeping his distance a little.

'They resent you, don't they?' he said after a
moment or two of silence.

'What do you mean?'

'Because of who you are.'

She looked disappointed, but continued
eating, seeming to ignore him.

'When I said I didn't recognise your name,
that wasn't entirely true. It would be foolish of me
not to know the governor's daughter...'

She stopped eating for a moment but looked
straight ahead.

'So you decided to have some fun at my
expense?' she said, in a tone that suggested as much
resignation as bitterness.

'Rather I thought I would make up my own
mind,' he continued. 'People have a way of making

assumptions about you when you have a name like yours, or wear a uniform like mine.'

'What assumptions do people make about you?' she asked.

'As a soldier, perhaps that I don't feel as others can. Because I wear this medal, that I deserve honour.'

She turned to look at him now, but it was his turn to avoid eye contact.

'If I were to tell you how I earned it, you might change your opinion of me. But you were right. I was trying to be the man I ought to be, the one you deserve. But not the one I am.'

'Tell me,' she said.

She placed her hand tentatively on top of his and, slowly, interlaced his fingers with hers. He experienced a fluttering in his chest. The power of memory. He was taking a leap of faith, but instinct told him he could trust her. If he could be certain of his instincts.

'It was in the last war,' he began. 'Towards the end. I'd been in it for three years by then, and I don't think there was anything I hadn't seen. I was commanding a battalion, attacking an enemy machine gun post. We took heavy losses. Officers who I sent forward didn't return.'

Her hand tightened in his.

'In the end I couldn't watch any more. I had somehow walked through the war unscathed…'

He looked down at his knee.

'…for the most part, at least. And all of a sudden I didn't care any longer. I didn't care if I died. So many lives were forfeit. What was another? So I just ran towards the enemy position. I pulled out a grenade, and then another. One in each hand. As I got close, and I was still alive, I hurled them, one after the other, with all my might, into the nest. I didn't even wait for the explosions. I saw a Maxim lying on the ground and I picked it up and ran to the top of the bank, firing all the way. I kept firing until the cartridge was empty, and even after that. It was only then that I came to my senses. None of them had fired back. They hadn't fired because they were all dead already. I was shooting corpses.

'Another officer came up soon after and he reported that I'd taken it single-handed. It earned me a medal. But it was a fraud. I was a fraud.

'I've never told anyone this.'

He felt unexpectedly cold and found himself shivering. Exposed. The expression on Lotte's face was hard to read, but he felt a need to press on.

'The face I show to the world is not the man I am. I just wanted you to see that what you perceived was true. There is no glamour in war, no honour. It's kill or be killed. Raw and dirty. I love this country, but when I said we would win, I'm not sure that's true either. And what's more, I'm not even sure I want us to win if it means more war.'

She started a little at this, but she didn't let go of his hand.

'Have I shocked you?'

'I don't know,' she said. 'I don't know.'

'I was worried by what you said before,' he said. 'But only because of what might happen if someone else had heard. I had to tell you that I agree. Though neither of us should say these things. I'm sure your father would not agree.'

'No,' she said. 'He definitely wouldn't.'

He gently disengaged her hand and got to his feet, though they were unsteady under him.

'I should go. You will keep this to yourself, won't you?'

She nodded. He turned to go, now horribly nauseous. It occurred to him that he might have fallen for an agent provocateur. Were she to report any of what he had said to her father or anyone else, it might be taken for sedition and questions could be asked which he did not wish to answer. Adrenaline flooded through him as he came to realise the risk he had taken, but that was not all it was.

'Richard!'

Lotte was calling after him. She hurried over to where he now stood, taught with nerves.

'I have lunch here every day. Unless you would like to make other arrangements?'

He smiled and shook his head.

'No. No other arrangements. I should like that.'

'Good,' she said. 'Good. But I should tell you something…'

'Yes?'

'That man – the one who took me to the lake – I would never marry him.'

'Oh. I see.'

'But then… you're not him.'

She gave him a knowing smile and winked.

As he walked away again, he felt the elation of achievement. Thurso had been wrong. He had trusted his instinct and it had paid off. And yet there was still some doubt. Lingering qualms. And a sense of something else – perhaps guilt. But he'd always told himself there should be no guilt when he was only playing a part. When he was not being himself.

He turned back to look at Lotte, just as she did the same.

Part Four

February 1944

Chapter 10

Emily stood back for a moment and squinted. She mixed the paint again and dabbed a little onto her brush.

'The colour isn't right,' said Mira, leaning over her shoulder.

'I realise that.'

'And I thought you were going to paint Toto?'

'What do you mean? I am painting him.'

'His eyes were brown, not blue.'

Emily looked again, and saw that Mira was right. The eyes she had painted were profoundly blue.

'Stupid of me,' she said.

'What is Beatrice painting?' said Mira, looking down at the table where her niece was busy applying green in great quantities.

'It's the cat,' said Emily. 'Though I think it's an Expressionist interpretation.'

'Is Catiline sick, Beatrice?' asked Mira.

'No!'

'Then why is she green?'

'It's the mouse she eated.'

'Eugh. Lovely.' Mira scrunched up her face and looked over at Emily. 'Did the cat really eat a mouldy mouse?'

'She's as short of food as we are, poor thing.'

'We could kill another goat?' suggested Mira.

'Then we'd have no milk for Beatrice.'

Mira sat down at the table and rested her head on her arms.

'You've lost weight, Emmy.'

'Nonsense.'

'I know you've been giving us more food than you take for yourself.'

'I get enough.'

'We could sell something?' said Mira.

'We'd have to go into the village.' Mira looked immediately worried at this idea. 'And in any case, what would we sell?'

Mira turned Emily's easel around and studied it once again.

'We could sell paintings?'

'No one's going to buy one of mine. And I don't think the Nazis would appreciate Beatrice's modern style.'

They both laughed, but Mira's started to morph into a gentle sob, and she wiped a tear from her eye. Emily put her arm around her sister.

'Mira. It's alright. We've survived this long. We'll find a way. In any case, it can't be long before the Americans get here.'

'And the British,' said Mira.

'Yes,' said Emily. 'But don't say it…'

'He will be with them.'

'I thought we'd got past your fairy tale ideas. Richard won't be coming to rescue us.'

'You'll see,' said Mira, with an attempt at a smile.

'You don't really believe that, Mira, do you?'

The smile disappeared and the tears began again, but she waved away Emily's sympathy.

'I have to believe in something, Emmy, don't I?'

She walked slowly to the door, drying her tears, and then turned back.

'I forgot. I came to tell you that the irrigation pump isn't working. I tried it this morning like you asked.'

Emily sighed heavily.

'Fine, I'll have a look later.'

Emily left Beatrice with Mira and edged slowly down the path that led to the little shed by the river, where the pump was housed. The track had become a mess of icy slush and she had to measure every step.

Things weren't helped by the feeling of atrophy in all her limbs. They seemed heavy and drained of energy as she laboured down the hill.

When she reached the shed, she checked the pump, which seemed to be iced up, but even when freed it was clear that the seals had rotted and would need to be replaced.

The walk back up the hill was even harder, and when she reached the house, she pulled out a chair and dropped heavily into it. Her head was spinning, and her eyes stung with tiredness.

'Emmy, are you alright?' said Mira, leading Beatrice by the hand. The little girl clambered up into Emily's lap and drooped her arm around her neck, contentedly sucking her thumb.

'I'm fine. Which is more than can be said for the pump. It needs new parts.'

'Oh no! What do we do now? Without the pump we'll have nothing growing by autumn.'

'We will have to get a mechanic from the village. Will you go in the morning?'

'You want me to go?'

'I can't, can I?' snapped Emily, in tiredness and frustration.

'No. I suppose.'

'That would not be a good idea.' It was Gabriella's voice. She stood in the door with the carcass of a deer slung over her shoulder. 'What's happened now?'

Emily slowly and carefully unhooked Beatrice's arm from around her neck, suddenly self-conscious. Gabriella could be so changeable that she rarely knew quite what to expect. What had passed between them might be forgotten as if it never happened, or remain an open sore. Nevertheless, there was a relief in seeing her sister-in-law again and leaning into her natural strength and assurance, when her own had been waning with the passing months.

Mira explained the situation. Gabriella took it in with a resigned nod, and then dropped the deer onto the table.

'At least we can have a decent meal. I don't suppose you've had one for a while?'

'We haven't had any meat for months!' said Mira. 'Where did you find it?'

'At the venison shop,' said Gabriella sarcastically, before grabbing Mira and giving her a forceful kiss on both cheeks. Emily held up Beatrice to her mother, who smoothed her hair and smiled, but that was as far as it went. She and Emily exchanged awkward looks and she kissed her diffidently on the cheek.

'I have had cause to regret what I said to you before,' she said, in something of a whisper.

'It's forgotten,' said Emily.

Gabriella smiled. 'Let's eat!'

Later, after they had enjoyed a sumptuous venison stew, they sat by the fire, replete. It seemed an age since they had last been able to eat like this, though as Emily watched the flames sway and jump, her mood was strangely sombre. On another cold winter night, when she had still been new to this country and this life, she remembered how Toto had sat with her, patiently teaching her Italian and keeping her mind off the wait for a letter from Richard. With each day the homesickness had grown and the hope had dwindled. She had reached her lowest point at Christmas, when her marriage seemed to have ended, not in any kind of grand symbolic moment, but with a prolonged and painful silence. She tormented herself by rationalising that the war had prevented the post. Or, in her darkest moments, that Richard had got his wish and returned to the army and a cold and lonely death. Toto had gently reassured her that if her life in England was at an end, her life in Italy was just beginning. That she was loved and appreciated by them and would come to find happiness again. And she had, at least for a time.

'Toto always enjoyed venison,' said Mira suddenly, as if she had read Emily's own thoughts. 'Which was strange, because he could never bear to shoot a wild animal.'

Gabriella looked sternly across the room at her.

'Like it says in the Talmud, he always wanted to avoid causing pain to any living creature.'

'Mira, be quiet,' cut in Gabriella tersely.

'There's no one to hear,' returned Mira. 'And I want to talk about him.'

'I don't… and there are always people listening.'

Mira folded her arms and sat quietly. Over the winter their world had shrunk down to nothing. The Nazis had spread their tentacles across the country and in November their Italian puppet state had declared Jews 'enemy aliens', with orders for their arrest and confiscation of property. They had seen German tanks in the distance, heading to Venice or Padua, and every time Mira had gone to the village, it had been in anxiety for what, or who, she might find there. For Emily, her life, as it had been for years now, was the farm, and only the farm. For now their quiet corner had remained undisturbed, but for how much longer?

In a sense, it had become a race. A race between the advance of the Allied forces, who had become bogged down south of Rome, their food supplies, and discovery. Beatrice was sound asleep, lying diplomatically between Emily and Gabriella, and she took the chance while she could to voice her thoughts to her sister-in-law. Though in fear of alarming Mira, she held back on mentioning the third possibility.

'There is a third possibility you haven't considered,' said Gabriella, nevertheless. 'Worse than the others.'

'Worse than starving?' said Mira, smiling darkly.

'It could be. The Germans have been implementing their new directive – rounding people up. You'd think they would have other concerns, but they seem set on it. Jews, communists, nationalists – they would fulfil their entire quota if they got me! It's why I came back. They were focusing on the cities, but in the last few weeks, they've been spreading out.'

'They won't come here though, will they?' said Mira. 'Not to the farm?'

Gabriella swilled the grappa around her glass, held it up to the light of the fire, and then knocked it back in one go.

'It's possible,' she said. She glanced several times at Emily, who understood her thoughts at once.

'You think I will give you away?' said Emily.

Gabriella glanced up again briefly but avoided looking at her.

'Not deliberately. But we need to be ready to leave…'

'And go where?' said Mira.

'I have a friend in Caorle,' said Gabriella. 'He has a boat. But it's small, and we'd need to go as far as Puglia to reach Allied lines. The other option is to go west and head for Switzerland.'

'On foot?' said Emily. 'It must be hundreds of miles.'

'About two hundred and fifty kilometres,' said Gabriella matter-of-factly.

'No,' said Emily, with determination. 'Surely we would do better to stay here and—'

'Hope?' said Gabriella.

'That wasn't what I was going to say. But sometimes the right choice is to choose to do nothing. And in any case, your daughter can't walk that far, even if we could.'

Gabriella had been about to reply but bit her lip at this. She pulled her knees up and folded her arms tightly around them, as if to stifle the nervous energy that was building inside her.

'What do you think, Mira?' asked Emily.

'I will stay with you, Emmy,' she replied uncertainly.

'That's not an answer,' said Gabriella testily.

'When you prescribe a medicine,' said Mira, 'it's a balance between risk and benefit to the patient. And I think the risk is too high.'

'Fine, Doctor Mira,' said Gabriella, half-joking. 'But that may change. And I may not be able to wait around for you to decide.'

Gabriella stomped up the stairs to bed and left Mira and Emily alone. Mira looked to her sister as if there were answers to be found in her thoughts, when the truth was that she was just as uncertain.

Some days passed, and it became clear that repair of the irrigation pump was beyond their capabilities. They were left with a stark choice – risk a trip to the village to seek help or risk the failure of their crops.

Mira had refused to go alone, and Gabriella stubbornly held her ground, repeating that their best option was to run. In the end there was only one solution – for Emily to go with Mira to the village, for the first time in years, but to let her sister do the talking. Old Renato, the village blacksmith, who must have been at least seventy now, was pretty much their only hope of fixing the irrigation pump, with most of the other men of fighting age gone.

It was a milder day, but with rain in the air and a gusty wind whipping up the leaves on the ground, Emily pulled the old coat up to her chin and tied a scarf around her head. Neither were hers. They had been handed on to her soon after her arrival, and, she suspected, though they had never said so explicitly, had belonged to Mira and Toto's mother.

They crossed the square in front of the church. There were few people about, but as they skirted the steps, Emily noticed for the first time a group of German soldiers milling about in front of the bar. It was what they had both feared. The only good sign was that the soldiers seemed more interested in the beer than in anyone in the square, at least for now. She did her best to appear as unobtrusive as possible, and encouraged Mira to pick up her pace slightly in the hope that they would pass unnoticed. Were they to ask for her papers, it would become obvious very quickly that she did not belong. They had almost passed out of sight when one of the soldiers called out. Emily's stomach turned over and she steeled herself, turning slowly to look at him. He seemed to be swaying slightly and called out again. This time she could just about make out what he was saying, and, thanks to years spent in Germany with Richard before the war, she understood that he was being less than polite. It wasn't, however, an official stop, and as he continued making lewd and vulgar comments, she feigned not to understand and pushed Mira on. It was clearly what he expected, and he burst into fits of laughter and pointed them out to his mates, who joined in with the barracking before they decided to retreat back inside for further refreshment.

When they were out of sight, they fell back against the wall and took a series of deep breaths. It was hardly the first time Emily had experienced such unwanted attention in her life, but for Mira it was a new and disturbing experience. Mira had been anxious in leaving the farm to begin with, and now Emily saw the first signs of panic in her once again. With the added fear of discovery, Emily drew her close and looked her in the eyes to help her through it. But this time Mira seemed able to master her own reaction and gradually calmed herself. The moment passed, but it was a reminder, if one were needed, that more than her own safety was at risk, and the danger that had once seemed remote and abstract was now immediate and real.

They continued down the street and came to the house where they knew Renato lived. Mira went first, gradually gaining in confidence, and knocked on the door gently, eager not to draw attention. There was no answer, so she knocked again, louder this time. Only on a third try, and hammering with a fist, was there a noise from inside. A short, podgy man in dirty work coat and collarless shirt answered. He seemed frail. Stooped and tired. His eyes had a warmth and he smiled wearily as he agreed to come out to the farm. Nevertheless, Emily's instincts were pricked.

'Are you sure you are well enough?' asked Mira, as Renato coughed heavily.

'I was too poor to retire before the war,' he explained between coughs. 'Now... I couldn't, even if... I wished to. There's no one else. And I'm still poor.'

He had explained that there was another errand he must run first and he would visit them later. In relief and gratitude, Emily and Mira made their way back to the farm, a task accomplished, but with a renewed sense of the threat now on their doorstep.

For the rest of the day, they went about their work on the farm. Emily had been distracted in cleaning out the chicken coop, such that when she emerged again into the dark of the evening, she didn't notice Renato until he was standing right in front of her. She cast a glance around her but remembered that Mira would be preparing their evening meal by now, with Beatrice in tow. While Gabriella was taking every chance to rest in a proper bed.

'I'm sorry to be so late,' said Renato, scraping his stubble with his hand, with a noise like sandpaper.

Emily smiled, reluctant to speak and give away her imperfect Italian.

'If you'll show me the pump, I'll take a look,' he continued, so far oblivious to her concerns.

She smiled again and guided him with a gesture towards the little shed. He seemed content to trudge behind her as she scanned for signs that Mira or Gabriella might have heard him arrive.

'Just you women now, is it?' he asked when they reached the bottom of the hill where the pump was situated.

She nodded.

'Don't you speak?' he said with a kind of crooked smile.

'Yes, When I need to,' she said at last, slurring her words as much as possible and trying to perfect her accent.

He bent down over the pump and started to fiddle with it.

'It must be hard work for you?'

'We manage,' said Emily.

'I remember Toto from when he was a little boy. But I don't remember you. He is your…?'

'Brother.'

'Em… Emilia came to live with us when my brother went away.' It was Mira, who had made her way hurriedly down the hill. 'She has been helping us.'

Renato nodded. Emily looked at him nervously, wondering what, if anything, he suspected. It was hard to read, as Renato's face showed little expression.

'How is Toto?' he asked.

'He was killed in the war,' said Mira, who was also watching Renato carefully as he fiddled with the pump. Emily frowned at her, which puzzled her sister, and she responded with a shrugged 'what?'

'I'm sorry to hear it. I liked him.' He looked towards Emily. 'It is good of you to be of help to your family. I thought you weren't from around here. I know everyone. And your accent…'

There was something in the way he said it that was alarming. Emily felt faint, as though a kind of vertigo had come upon her. She regretted not paying attention to her instincts in the village.

'Can you fix it?' she asked.

Renato got up slowly from his crouched position and bit his blackened nails as he considered.

'It'll need a part,' he said with a long breath out. 'If I can get one.'

'Fine.'

He began to walk back up the hill without saying anything more, and Emily and Mira followed, exchanging glances.

'I'll be in touch,' he said as Emily guided him to the gate. When he had disappeared out of sight, she dropped the façade and raced into the house.

'Gabriella!'

This time there was little discussion. They were all agreed that leaving was now the only choice. But the question of how remained.

'We shall need transport,' said Gabriella. 'It is the only way if the four of us are to reach Switzerland.'

'We don't have a motorcar,' said Mira.

'Then I will have to "borrow" one,' said Gabriella.

Emily regarded her doubtfully and Gabriella responded in a blaze of anger.

'I've had enough of you worrying over every detail. We need action, and if there is a risk in it, so be it. That's what happens in war. You cannot sit on your hands and pout any longer, and I won't be caught here like a peasant. Pack what you need, no more, and food and water. Be ready to go when I return this evening.'

A long night was in prospect, so they decided to try and get some sleep. Though as it was, Emily was kept awake by each creak of the house, with all her senses on alert. She told herself that Gabriella was right. The danger was real now, and risk could not be avoided. If they made good time and kept to the back roads, they might reach Switzerland in a couple of days. By travelling at night they might have a chance. She found herself shivering, though whether it was with the cold or through fear, she couldn't tell. It took all of her determination to bring it under control. She longed for a reassuring arm around her but fought in turn against her self-pitying mood. Now there were others who depended on her, and she would need all her strength and courage to find a way through.

'We are thinking to the future, not the past,' she told herself. Though it had never been as easy to let go of the past as she had wished.

They stood outside in the chill evening. The sun had long since set. Emily held her suitcase tightly in one hand and Beatrice's tiny fingers in the other. Mira stamped her feet and beat her arms to stay warm.

After some time they heard the distant clatter of a diesel engine, which gradually got louder. Then the narrow beams of headlights peeked around the bend and made their way towards the farm gate. The outline of a truck roared up the driveway. With a canvas cover over the back, it would be the perfect place to hide away in the daytime.

As the truck pulled to a stop in front of them, Emily squinted to see into the cab in the darkness. The figure in the driver's seat didn't respond when she waved.

Then the door opened, and the figure stepped down.

Chapter 11

Hansen folded his newspaper and placed the document concealed underneath it onto the bench next to him.

'I transcribed and translated it too. I know your German isn't the best.'

'Cheeking me now, are you?' said Thurso. 'Fine, be as bolshy as you like as long as you continue delivering the goods. I can't say I care for the choice of meeting place though.'

'I like the Waldfriedhof. It's quiet.'

'The quiet of the dead, perhaps.'

Thurso seemed to shiver slightly, and as he looked around it wasn't clear if he was seeking enemy tails, or ghosts. Hansen smiled to himself.

'It's an honour to be buried here. The great and the good of Munich aspire to it.'

'Perhaps. But I shouldn't wish to take up permanent residence just yet. Now, to business. We need you to find any available information on the Gustav Line, particularly around Monte Cassino. Specifically unit strengths, deployment, artillery. Anything you can get.

'And, now that you have the girl where you want her and things are moving as we'd both like…' He made the sound of creaking bed springs, accompanied by a crude gesture. Hansen rolled his eyes. 'I have another little task for you. This one is not as easy or as pleasant, I'm afraid.'

'I'd prefer you to use her name,' said Hansen.

Thurso watched him keenly.

'As you wish.'

'You have an unusual definition of "easy", in any case,' continued Hansen.

'I mean it,' said Thurso. 'This one could be a bit sticky. There's a new legend under your seat. ID card, wallet litter and so on. Just for this show. You're Kurt Hauser, an auditor from the SS-WHVA, with personal authorisation from Oswald Pohl to conduct an investigation. Details in the envelope.'

'Backstop?'

'There isn't one beyond what you have. But no one will question a WHVA auditor, and if they trace it back, you'll be gone before they get a response.'

'Gone from where? Where am I going?'

'North of the city. There's a detention camp there, near a place called Dachau. Do you know it?'

'I've heard of it.'

'We believe a new project is being run out of there, which has the codename *Ringeltaube*.'

'Wood pigeon?' replied Hansen.

'Yes. Don't read anything into the name. You will make contact with our agent and debrief them. The agent's codename is Rosenbusch, owing to their red hair.'

'Subtle.'

'I thought so. Wait for them to make contact. They will ask if you are Saxon. Your countersign is "Thuringian".'

There was a pause in Thurso's usual rapid-fire delivery.

'Is that all?' asked Hansen.

'Yes. Except…' and he put his hand out for Hansen to shake. 'Good luck.'

Hansen took the hand he offered, bemused.

'Now you have me worried.'

'Good,' said Thurso with a return to his usual bonhomie. 'Complacency is never a good thing. Dead drop on Tuesday. Usual place.'

Thurso walked away with no more consideration than if they had been strangers on a park bench.

Hansen remained for a few moments, listening to the birdsong in the trees. It was something he had learned to do since the last war, when it had been a rarity to hear, and it always brought a focus to his mind. Still and quiet. When he was sure there was no one around, he reached under the seat and pulled off the envelope taped there. He transferred it to his coat pocket in one swift movement and waited a moment more. Then casually he picked himself up and began to stroll along the path.

There had been another reason for choosing this meeting place. An idea he had circled many times since returning to the city, but he had never found the courage before. This time was different, not because he had found the strength, but because he had found a need. A need to be honest with someone, if only with himself.

He searched for it now, his eyes flicking between memorials for the name he sought. His cousin's name.

At last he stood in front of the memorial, reading the inscription:

In memory of Sebastian Hansen.
1897 – 1915. Beloved son.
'Tis not a year or two shows us a man.'

He reached out to touch the stone, as if the contact would restore the bond broken between them so long ago.

'What would you say to me now?' he whispered. 'Would you tell me I am right to do what I'm doing? What choice would you have made?'

He leaned against a tree and found himself sliding down until he reached the ground, and sat cross-legged like a child, though his knees protested against it.

He did little but trace the words again and again with his eyes. He forced himself back to that moment. The moment, now nearly thirty years before, in the trench. A trench filled with poison gas, seen through the glass of a gas helmet. He wanted more than anything to look away, but it was the moment that had defined everything else. He pulled himself back at the last second, not allowing the memory to play out, and sat with his head resting in his own arms, for want of another's. His breathing slowed and his eyes closed, and in time the birdsong faded away around him.

The question persisted in his half-waking: 'What would you have done? What would you have done with your life?'

'I would have made… a choice,' said a voice. The voice that was now only a memory. Young now, as it had been then, with the slight stammer that overtook Sebastian when he was nervous.

'I don't think either of us could have chosen differently. It was a war. We had orders.'

'I have told myself that over and over, Sebastian. I followed orders and I did my duty. But is that all? There was such possibility in your life. I was excited to see what you would do. But it was cut short. I cut it short for you. And… I think… for me, as well.

'I have become so many other people. I don't know who Richard Hansen is now, except that he is the man who fails others. The man who lies and deceives. The man who betrays. I wanted to be the perfect husband, the perfect father. And I needed to be a soldier. But I am none of those things.'

'Do you remember,' said Sebastian's voice, 'I used to worry about my exams. I would… obsess. Not about the answers I got, but the ones I did not. I always wanted to get one hundred per cent, and sometimes even then it was not enough. And you said to me, remember King Lear – "Striving to better, oft we mar what's well."'

With a sudden jerk and a sensation of falling, Hansen caught himself and rubbed his eyes. The thought, or dream, began to dissipate as soon he tried to fix it into memory, but there remained an idea. An idea of profound resonance and clarity.

'If I have a second soul, it is yours, my cousin,' he said out loud. 'And that being so, it must only contain that which is honest and true.'

At this, he staggered to his feet and turned away from the grave, with a picture of the future for perhaps the first time in years. A future in which twin duties could be fulfilled. Not perfect, but one that would be his own. That would be a future worth living, or dying, for.

Instinctively, as he turned the corner, he glanced back. For a moment, a split second, he sensed somebody there. He stopped and waited for whoever it was to pass, but no one did. Presently he continued on the path, ears pricked for the smallest sound of footsteps or breathing. But all he could hear was birdsong, and the wind in the skeletal trees.

With each step he braced himself for contact – an arm round the neck or a punch to the spine. His muscles flexed and his heart pounded. His fear of looking back was matched only by his need to see.

The path continued straight ahead, and he watched his lengthening shadow for signs of a second figure. The silhouette faded as he passed into shade, but the feeling that he was not alone did not.

All at once, legs taut with nervous energy, he darted to his left and sprinted into the cover of a mausoleum. He threw himself against the wall and waited, panting for breath. The sounds around him receded, all but the steady thump of blood in his ears, as he waited, his senses alert for any signs of approach.

Moments passed, and his muscles began to relax as his rational mind retook control and suggested that perhaps he had imagined it all. He slid back a sleeve and checked his watch. He tracked the second hand as it jerked on, one step at a time, all the while keeping one eye on the path.

This was madness. Either no one had been behind him, he reasoned, or they had realised they had been detected, and retreated.

He took out a handkerchief and dabbed his top lip, damp with sweat, despite the cold.

But as he dropped his eyes for a moment to put the handkerchief back in his pocket, there was a sudden snap in front of him, a movement in the bushes. And then, a squirrel flew up the wall and onto the roof of the mausoleum, seemingly as shocked by him as he was to see the tiny rodent.

Recovering from a heart that had missed several beats, Hansen let out a long, faltering breath and shook himself out of his absurdity.

'Bloody squirrels,' he called into the trees. 'Sebastian, if this is you, I don't find it in the least bit amusing.'

He smiled at his own idiocy. In a weak moment, perhaps he had given in to the paranoia he had been trained to resist. He hastened out of the woods and back towards the city.

He pulled his coat up tighter against the cold. Feeling in need of some warmth and, perhaps, some liquid courage, before making his way to the Giesler house for dinner, he noticed the yellow light from a bar spilling out into the street in the twilight. As he approached, the owner pulled a blackout curtain across the doorway, but made way for Hansen to pass. The bar was filled with soldiers, except for a few old men – obviously regulars – who stood by the zinc-topped counter. There were few bottles left on the shelves now, but the regulars stood there smoking and nursing their tiny glasses of beer as they always had.

'What will you have?' asked the barman.

'Schnapps?' he asked.

'Sorry. No schnapps. I have brandy?'

Hansen nodded and the barman uncorked a dusty bottle and poured a small measure.

'Six marks,' said the barman.

'How much?'

Hansen put the coins down in amazement. More than ten bob for a drink was enough to make him rethink his thirst.

'Schönfelder!' a voice called from across the room. Hansen turned and saw Giesler himself beckoning him over. He was sitting at a table with several others, some in senior uniform, some in civvies. Hansen picked up his brandy and went across to where they were sitting.

A large bottle of schnapps stood on the table in front of them, as well as a plate of fatty slices of sausage, curling at the edges. Privileges, even for the most privileged, were dwindling, it seemed.

'Gentlemen, let me introduce you to Standartenführer Richard Schönfelder. He has recently joined my office as adjutant and has been doing excellent work. But you must watch him! Not only does he want my job, but my daughter as well!'

He gave a deep and hearty laugh and the others politely smiled, or smirked.

'Sit down, Schönfelder. What are you drinking? Overpriced brandy? No, have some schnapps.'

Hansen took the glass and put it to his lips. As he went to swallow, something stopped him. A memory – a night years ago, when one drink had turned into too many. And a promise, that he was breaking again. All for this job.

But with the others around the table leading the way, and all their eyes on him, there was no room for a blurring of his past and his purpose now. He put aside his qualms and drank the glass down in one. A pleasant warmth spread through his chest.

'So, Paul,' said one of the civilians at the table, who looked like he had been enjoying the hospitality for some time. 'When is he coming?'

Giesler looked irritated, angry even, but hastily adopted a façade of nonchalance.

'What do you mean, Dieter? I don't know what you're talking about.'

The drunk man persisted, puzzled by his friend's reaction. He dropped his voice to a conspiratorial whisper, though it was loud enough nevertheless:

'Himmler.'

'Dieter, what an imagination you have. The Reichsführer is in Berlin, so far as I know. Unless you've invited him to one of your boring dinner parties? In which case, he has every reason to *stay* in Berlin.'

He laughed again, harsh and cold. Dieter was clearly humiliated.

'You should go home to your wife, Dieter, you are drunk. As should we, Schönfelder, eh? Or we shall be late for dinner, and Lieselotte will not be pleased.'

Giesler rose from the table, and Hansen followed him. Giesler excused himself for a moment and left Hansen holding their overcoats by the door. As he waited, someone entered the bar and jostled him as he came past. The man, frail and white-haired, turned briefly to see who he had knocked into.

'Excuse me, sir.'

Hansen took little notice except to accept his apology, but when he saw the man looking back again, his blood ran cold.

'Richard?'

It had been almost a decade since they had last met, but it was unmistakably his uncle. And, for his part, he was plainly astonished. In one sweeping look he took in Hansen's uniform, and his face went through contortions of confusion. He addressed his nephew, perhaps accidentally – or perhaps not – in English:

'What are you doing here?'

Hansen caught himself just in time and replied, in German, that he didn't understand. It bought him a moment of uncomfortable silence, which was interrupted in turn by the return of Giesler.

'Hansen!' he called loudly, prompting a second cold shiver to run through Hansen's body.

When Giesler slapped his uncle on the shoulder and greeted him with an insincere smile, he realised his mistake, and breathed again. But it made the situation no better.

'I must thank you for your work with the NSV, Herr Hansen. It is wonderful to see such service to our great Reich.'

'Thank you, sir,' replied his uncle meekly.

His uncle continued staring, in confusion or shock.

'Do you know each other?' asked Giesler.

'No, sir,' said Hansen quickly. 'We've just bumped into each other. Rather literally.'

'Ah, I see,' said Giesler with a bored smile. 'Well, Schönfelder, we must away. Keep up the good work, Herr Hansen.'

His uncle continued watching as they left, and Hansen could only gesture to him with raised eyebrows. A desperate signal to stay silent.

They reached the Giesler house in what seemed like moments. Hansen had turned over the options in his mind as they walked. He had grown closer to his uncle in the years since the last war, and he hoped that would count for something. But to think that he might have Nazi sympathies was a discomforting thought. How deep they ran, he could not be sure. And what of Sebastian? Was there still a part of his uncle that blamed Hansen for his son's death?

'You've been quiet this evening, Schönfelder,' said Giesler during dinner.

'Have I? I apologise. A lot on my mind, I suppose.'

'Yes, of course. But you shouldn't bring your work home with you, you know. It will only bore Lieselotte to hear about the many responsibilities of government, won't it, my dear?'

'I'm sure it should, Father,' she replied coldly.

'Too many little details to be troubled about when there are happier things to discuss. Such as where you will live when you are married, and the grandchildren you will give me! I know you want my job, but I am reluctant to give it up just yet. So perhaps another role? Though I would of course prefer that you stay close by.'

'As would we,' said Hansen. 'I can't say I've given it a great deal of thought.'

Giesler pushed his plate away and lit a large cigar, blowing out the smoke in a great cloud.

'You should. There will be plenty of opportunities, you know, when the war is over. Plenty of land and such, land stolen by the Jews in the east, that you could reclaim. Even in Austria.

Remind me again, exactly where in Austria you are from?'

'Linz.'

Giesler nodded slowly and puffed on his cigar while he fixed a relaxed yet penetrating gaze on Hansen.

'Remarkable that you should hail from the same place as our great Führer. Perhaps you will show it to me sometime.'

'I'd be delighted. It's a very beautiful city.'

'Of course,' chuckled Giesler. 'Like our wives, we all think our hometown is the most beautiful.'

Hansen forced himself to laugh.

'I don't mind where we live,' said Lotte. 'But I should like to see new places. To travel.'

'England, perhaps?' said Giesler. He showed his teeth a little, his cigar in his mouth. A smile, or a grimace. 'When we defeat them, of course. Have you seen England, Schönfelder?'

'No,' said Hansen. 'At least, not yet.'

Giesler grinned and then offered a deep chuckle.

'I shall retire, I think,' he said.

'Good night, Father.'

He kissed his daughter on the forehead and then held his hand out for Hansen to shake.

'Don't stay up too late, Schönfelder.'

'No, sir.'

He left them alone. Lotte sidled over to Hansen and took his arm.

'Shall we go into the sitting room? There's a fire lit.'

They settled on the sofa, and Lotte snuggled with him, resting her head on his shoulder.

'Why do you want to be Gauleiter?' she asked, out of the blue.

'That's a strange thing to ask,' he said.

'Is it?'

'Well, it's an important position.'

'Yes, but is that all? That can't be the only reason.'

'No.' He took a moment to consider. 'It just seemed like something I should aim for. But my father always said that power like that – position, status – it's something you should wear lightly. I think what he meant is that we all have a responsibility. That the more power you have, the more harm you can do…'

'Or the more good,' said Lotte.

'Perhaps.'

'Your father sounds wise. Mine always says the reason democracy failed is because people don't know what they want,' she replied. 'Or that what they want is inherently selfish. So we need responsible leaders who can make those decisions in our own best interests.'

'Is that what you believe?'

'I don't know. It always seemed to me that it's impossible to know what other people want. Only a god can know that for sure, so anyone who thinks they can either is one, which seems unlikely, or they must be mad.'

'Which would you say I am?' teased Hansen.

'Well, you're here with me, so it must be the latter,' she said with a chuckle.

'And what would you wish me to do with my god-like power?'

'There are so many people you could help – the poor, the old, the sick. Everyone should have a decent chance.'

Hansen couldn't help smiling. She sensed the change in expression and looked up at him.

'Why are you smiling? You think I'm being naïve, don't you? Why is that such a bad thing to want?'

'No,' he said. 'You misunderstand. It's not a bad thing at all. You just reminded me of someone, that's all. And it's not what I expected you to say.'

'You should never underestimate me.'

'Clearly.'

'Who do I remind you of?' she asked, her hand squeezing his.

'No one you know,' he said quickly, changing the subject. 'You would trust me to do all this good, would you?'

'Of course,' she replied. 'I know you well enough to know that. Though if you were to ask the people what they wanted, you'd have to start with yourself.'

'What's that supposed to mean?'

Lotte got up and went over to the fire to jab it with a poker. She started gingerly, then with gradually increasing force as she warmed to her theme.

'Is this woman I remind you of the reason why you look so worried every time I mention setting a date, or anything else wedding-related?'

'When have I looked worried?' he spluttered. 'You're being absurd.'

'Am I? Because I keep getting the "absurd" thought that I'm not quite clever enough, not quite pretty enough, not quite good enough. That perhaps you're waiting for this better version of me to come back.'

She started jabbing the fire even more fiercely.

'Have I said that?'

'I notice that you don't deny there is someone.'

He got up and put his hand out to take the poker from her grasp.

'I think you can stop now. You've killed it.'

She let go of the poker and he put it back into the stand.

'Why does it matter when we get married? Wouldn't it be better to wait until the war is over, anyway?'

'No!' she shouted, before dropping her voice again. 'No. It matters because I'm scared. I can see what's happening. You can see it too. I know you can. We're losing. And I don't want to lose you to the war, or anything else. You're the only one who sees me for anything other than just Paul Giesler's daughter. Like I'm my own person. More than the simple housewife my father wants me to be...'

'Of course you're more than that...'

'...And I love you.'

She looked at him expectantly. He'd never given her the reply she was looking for before. He'd only ever said it to one other person and meant it.

'I won't make you promises I can't keep,' he said slowly. 'You know you mean too much to me to do that.'

'I don't want a promise,' she replied. 'I just need to know you feel the same as I do.'

He cradled her face gently in his hand. She felt so fragile. So in need of protection. So like Emily.

'I do. I love you.'

She kissed him, and, as he held her in his arms, for the first time, the line between his legend and his life had become impossible to find.

Chapter 12

Emily looked up. The figure climbing down from the cab of the truck was the same German soldier she had seen earlier in the village square. Except that now he didn't leer at her. He held his gun across his chest, as if he didn't feel the need to point it at her to intimidate.

Emily tightened her grip on Beatrice's hand and looked to Mira, who held her suitcase defensively in front of herself. Neither of them spoke, afraid to give anything away, however small.

The German surveyed the house and then directed two other soldiers to go there and search.

'You – come with us,' said the soldier, in schoolboy Italian, which matched his juvenile appearance.

'No...' said Mira. Emily could see her almost shaking with nerves, but she stood her ground. 'Not until you tell us why.'

The soldier looked at her blankly, almost shocked that she should challenge him. But his eyes seemed more drawn to Emily. He gazed at her almost hungrily, before turning back to Mira to frown and point to the back of the truck.

'Get in,' he said. 'No argue.'

When Mira continued to hold her ground, he levelled his rifle and pulled back the bolt with a clunk-click to ready it for firing. Mira looked to Emily in panic, and she nodded slightly to indicate they should comply.

The soldier allowed Mira to pass and then once again looked long and hard, and longingly, at Emily, as she followed her sister, with Beatrice still clinging on.

He prodded all of them with his gun to the back of the truck, where the doors swung open.

Gabriella was inside, bound up. There was a smear of blood down the side of her face.

'I want to speak to your commander,' said Emily, in a sudden moment of inspiration. It wasn't so much what she said as the fact that she spoke to him in perfect German.

The soldier wavered, unsure of how to proceed.

'You are Italian,' he said, again in thickly accented Italian.

'No,' she said. 'I am Swiss.'

He sucked his teeth for a moment.

'I don't care,' he said at last, then jabbed her hard in the stomach with the stock of his rifle.

Emily was winded by the blow and doubled up in pain as she was shoved and manhandled by turns into the truck. Mira helped her up and crawled beside her to lend comfort as she recovered.

Beatrice was thrown to the floor and started to cry. Instinctively, Gabriella reached her hand out for the little girl, but instead Beatrice crawled to Emily and curled up in her lap. Gabriella's head fell back against the canvas and for a moment, with her teeth gritted, there was perhaps the hint of a tear in her eye.

Mira looked sideways at Emily. There was a question in the look. A desperate hope in her sister to find a way out.

'Don't worry, Mira. Everything will be alright,' she told her, though there was no conviction in it.

'I know it's just a physiological reaction, Emmy. The fight or flight response, originating in the sympathetic nervous system and caused by dopamine and adrenaline. I'm telling myself that. I keep telling myself that. But I'm scared.'

'I know.'

'Fear is good, Mira,' said Gabriella, speaking for the first time as the truck started to move off. 'We can use it. There will be a moment when we can. Watch for it. I will tell you.'

Mira nodded.

'You quiet!' shouted the guard.

Gabriella responded in a volley of expletives, which Emily, even with her now carefully practised Italian, couldn't keep pace with. The guard seemed not to understand either but recognised her tone well enough to respond with a clump across her face with his rifle.

'Big man!' said Gabriella, spitting blood onto the floor.

The journey lasted perhaps half an hour, but Emily couldn't help wishing that it would last longer. For while they were travelling, their fate was not yet determined. The options that they might have had now only came down to one possibility – the hope of rescue by the Americans, or, as Mira had pointed out, the British. They must hold on long enough and hope, whatever Gabriella might think. Thought of escape, she considered, looking down at the child in her lap, was at best unrealistic and at worst foolhardy.

When the truck stopped, the guards got out and shut the doors on them, leaving them alone while they seemed to be discussing something outside. Emily put her ear to the door to try to hear.

'What are they saying, Emmy?' asked Mira.

'I'm trying to hear,' she replied. 'It sounds like they're discussing whether to inform their officer. They're worried they'll get into trouble.'

'Maybe they believed you about being Swiss?'

'I hope so.'

Before they could continue the conversation, the doors opened and they were bundled out.

'I take you to see my boss,' said the guard, continuing in bad Italian. He guided Emily away from the others.

'Bring the others too,' she said, in German, 'please.'

'Not yet,' said the guard, now replying in his native language.

As they walked he continued to glance at her out of the corner of his eye. When they were out of sight and earshot of anyone else, he stopped for a moment and looked down at his shoes like a schoolboy overcome with shyness.

'I should like it,' he began. 'That is, perhaps... perhaps we can go out dancing sometime?'

Emily gazed at him for a moment, at first amazed, then puzzled, and finally calculating.

'If you are very lucky,' she said at last, with a little smile. 'Though am I not too old for you?'

'No,' he said sheepishly. 'I like older women. You are more experienced.'

'Are we indeed?'

'And you know, you are still very beautiful.'

'Still? You know how to give a girl a backhanded compliment, that's for sure.'

He looked a little confused.

'Never mind. But we shouldn't keep your officer waiting.'

'No.'

The guard was barely more than a boy, perhaps eighteen years old, and Emily felt oddly sorry for him. He wasn't so very different from those who had fought with Richard. Or even Richard himself, however full his head was of dogma. Though she scolded herself for indulging in these memories once again. He had been on her mind more and more in recent days.

She was marched awkwardly to the front desk in the local police station where they took fingerprints and noted her name – which she gave, almost unthinkingly, as Hansen – and other details. Then she found herself escorted to a small room and pushed into a hard wooden chair, sitting opposite the local commander. He scratched in his ledger and didn't look up.

'I am Hauptmann Weissman,' he said. 'Do you know why you have been detained?'

'No,' said Emily, in pure bluff. 'I can't imagine.'

'How is it that you find yourself on a farm in Italy with no papers?'

'I was visiting. My papers are at the house, but they took us in such a hurry.'

Weissman fiddled with his tie nervously and shuffled the papers in front of him.

'I can't see you in the records. You know you are required to register your residence?'

'I was going to. But I haven't been here long – you understand, don't you? I'm not really very good at these sorts of things.'

She smiled as innocently as she could manage, but this man was not as easily charmed.

'I don't like mysteries,' he said. 'Everything must be in order.'

'I apologise. I should have registered.'

He frowned slightly and studied her.

'Your accent. It doesn't sound like any Swiss accent I have heard before.'

Emily decided to keep her counsel, and simply shrugged a little in response, as if the idea of her being anything other than Swiss were absurd. The officer continued to twitch his tie and fidget. On one level it seemed a vain hope to try and talk her way to freedom. There were too many questions to answer, however much she might flutter her eyelashes and act the wide-eyed innocent. But what other option did she have?

'The woman…' He looked down again at his notes. 'Gabriella Portinari. You know her?'

For a moment, Emily was puzzled by the question.

'I don't understand,' she said.

'It is simple enough. Do you know her?' Before she could reply he continued. 'Because she was seen at the farm where you are "visiting". A known insurgent. A communist no less.'

Then it became clear to Emily. Renato had not given them up. It was not she who had given them away. It had been Gabriella and her determination to fight. To fight and leave her daughter behind. It had been impetuous. Reckless. And as she knew well herself, such decisions had consequences. Was there a chance now, if only a small one, to evade? To save herself, and perhaps Mira and Beatrice, by denying Gabriella?

'I'm waiting, Fräulein Hansen.'

'Frau,' she corrected.

He made a note in his file.

'And your husband?'

'Is not here,' she said simply.

'He remained in Switzerland while you travelled here?'

'Yes,' she said, feeling suddenly shamed.

'I would not allow my family to take such risks… alone. Italy is not a safe place to be. Not like Switzerland. There are insurgents for one thing.'

He picked up his pen carefully and screwed the cap onto it with deliberate precision. Then he placed it back on the desk.

'You will remain here,' he said at length.

'Why are you keeping me in this place?' she asked, feeling the situation beginning to slide out of her control.

'There are questions still to answer, Frau Hansen. We must have the complete picture, you understand. We must not… miss anything.'

He went out, locking the office door behind him.

The clock on the wall ticked on. The regular rhythm began to get under her skin and Emily found herself pacing, backwards and forwards and forwards and backwards. Her thought processes re-ran the same scenario: let Gabriella suffer alone, escape, take the others to safety. But each time she considered it, she felt sick. Gabriella might not be easy, but she was still family, and the choices she had made had been what she thought were right. Who was to say if they were or not, especially when she doubted her own decisions. The decision to give up on her own marriage, despite the love that still surged every time she thought of him. Her mother had always taught her to be practical: to choose the path to survive. But then she wondered if that had just been the easy path. The choice to run away or to do nothing. A strong person, like Gabriella, would never choose that.

She walked on and gradually she wore herself out, physically and emotionally, and laid down on the bench in the corner.

She was awakened by the door unlocking and Weissman's return, papers in hand. The clock showed almost a day had passed since she had entered the room. He threw the papers down on the desk in front of her. His demeanour had changed utterly.

'Would you like to answer the question now?' he began, with barely suppressed anger in his voice. 'Do you know the woman Gabriella Portinari?'

'Yes,' she said slowly. 'She is my sister-in-law.'

'Good,' he replied, looking down again at his papers.

'But…' she said. He looked up. 'But we weren't involved in what she was doing.'

What he did next was more than surprising. He leaned back in his chair, and he smiled.

'This,' he said, jabbing the papers with his index finger, 'this is a record of one Jacopo Portinari. It is good that our record-keeping is so efficient when we deal with such a mess of archives here. But here it is, in black and white. Jacopo Portinari changed his name in 1911. It is in the records in Mestre.'

'What has he got to do with me?' she answered, almost choking on her words.

'The farm is in his name. You – and the others – are his family. Are you not?'

A choice. To protect her own skin and deny her family. But Emily was silent.

'You have no right to silence here. You will answer.'

Still she said nothing.

'Perhaps I did not make myself clear. You will answer, or your child will not go with you.'

'Go where?'

'I will not ask again. Do you wish to stay with your child?'

'Yes,' she admitted finally. 'They are my family.'

Weissman nodded.

'You lie and you hide. You lie and you hide, and you waste my time. But the result is the same. Isn't it?'

'But what does it matter?' said Emily, though something told her she did not want to know the answer. There had been reports about the Nazis for years before the war. She had read the papers like everyone else and been chilled by what she had read. Horrified even. But she had thought little more of it. After all, she was not, she believed, Jewish. Back then, she had not even believed in God. Now, it was different. Their treatment of *people like her* was well known. Was it right to say that now? She might have the heritage, but to call herself Jewish seemed an ostentation. All the same, what would the Germans care for her ignorance of her family culture? In their eyes she would be Jewish, with all that meant to them.

'It seems the name which Jacopo was so keen to hide, which your family has successfully hidden until now… was Levi.'

Emily closed her eyes, and everything plunged into darkness.

She remembered little after that, until the young soldier returned and led her away. He walked silently next to her, holding her arm.

'When should we walk out?' she asked, with a kind of forced lightness that disguised the panic rising in her chest. 'I haven't been dancing in so long.'

'Be quiet!' he said angrily. Then, quietly, 'We can't now.'

He said it in the voice of a child, as though worried about being told off. Emily almost laughed.

They were placed in jail together, and in their cell, Mira paced backwards and forwards. Beatrice clung to Emily, shrieking every time she went to put her down. Gabriella stood staring out at the sky, barely visible through the barred window, high up on the wall.

'What time is it?' asked Mira.

'It's night,' said Gabriella. 'That's all I can tell you. What does it matter anyway?'

'They can't keep us forever, can they?' said Mira.

Emily looked up at her sadly. Why not let her hope?

'Yes, they can.' Gabriella looked grim. 'Or worse,' she said.

'But we haven't done anything wrong!'

Gabriella took her by the shoulders and Emily feared for a moment that she might be about to launch into a tirade. But instead she embraced Mira and held her tightly.

'You must be strong,' she told her. 'Stronger than you have ever been. I know you can be.'

Emily had never seen Gabriella this way with Mira before. They were opposites in so many ways, and yet as she watched her sister-in-law, she could see her hands clenched tightly, as if what she was telling Mira was as much for herself.

The door opened and three soldiers entered – the young one Emily had met before and two others. They might have been his friends from the village, but she couldn't be sure.

'Here!' said one, throwing some yellow material at Gabriella. 'Sew these on.'

Then he turned and leered at Emily, before taking her face in his hand and turning it from one side to the other to examine her.

'Get up,' he barked. 'Leave the child.'

'No!' said the young soldier, standing in front of his comrade. 'Not her. Take the other one,' he said, indicating Mira.

The soldier turned and looked Mira up and down.

'Fine. But you shouldn't be so sentimental, Hans. It's not like you're going to marry her!'

He laughed and Hans looked over to Emily sheepishly. The other two pulled Mira roughly with them towards the door. A cold shiver ran down Emily's spine and she jumped up, Beatrice clutching desperately at her leg.

'Where are you taking her?' she asked.

'We'll be back soon,' said the soldier, smirking, and lifting Mira's skirt. Mira pushed his hand away, suddenly alarmed. Gabriella ran towards them, but the third soldier clouted her across the face, sending her crashing into the wall.

'No, take me instead,' said Emily desperately.

Hans stood in front of her and held his hand up.

'You don't need to,' he said, imploring.

'Yes,' said Emily, 'I do. She's just a girl.'

'Let her, Hans. This one, that one, what does it matter? And she obviously wants to. Filthy whore.'

'Emmy?' said Mira, pleading, ashen and shaking.

Emily was stone-faced as she turned to face the soldiers. 'Look after Beatrice, Mira.'

The train was simultaneously freezing cold and stiflingly warm. Emily stood, surrounded by other bodies, swaying and falling into her at each jolt and judder. Her stomach ached with emptiness, her lips were dry, and her eyes drooped with weariness. As much as she wanted to let them close, every time she did there was a feeling of falling. Falling backwards in a darkened room, with hot breath on her neck and clammy, bony hands on her body. Hands touching and grasping. It brought her back awake with a flash of cold in her cheeks and a racing heart. She would take a moment to gather herself before the airless carriage brought the tiredness back, and with it a repeat of the same sequence. Despite the cold there was sweat dripping from her, and she longed to strip out of her clothes and throw herself into a river, as she had at San Nicolo on the hottest days of summer. She remembered those early months there, when it had all seemed so idyllic. Sunny days with bees buzzing in the lavender and the cool water on her skin. She had almost allowed it to blur in her memory. Her father's funeral had been during that time, but somehow she had attended without a distinct memory of any of it. She had wondered if she would be sad. But in the end there was nothing but indifference. It had all become the past so quickly and she did not let herself look back.

She felt a prod in her side and managed to turn enough to see Mira. There were dark red circles around her eyes, and she seemed feverish, but she was gesturing to Emily to look down at Beatrice, who was taking long, wheezing breaths. Emily pushed her arms free of those around her, and with a frantic effort grabbed Beatrice by one arm. With Mira's help she lifted her up and manoeuvred her in front of her, holding her up above the steaming bodies, and she began to breathe more easily.

Time passed slowly, and as the hours passed, Emily held Beatrice up, though her arms burned and pain spread through her back. She might have fallen but for the bodies around her preventing it. As time went on she wondered too whether those bodies were still living at all, except that the smell of so many people in one place together was unmistakable and pungent.

She allowed a tear to form in the corner of her eye, but no more. *Hold on*, she told herself, over and over. There was nothing more and nothing less to do. Simply to hold on, and, perhaps, in weak moments, she secretly hoped that Mira's fantasy would come true, and they would be delivered from this dark night.

* * *

Mira came back into the hut and sat down heavily. She still didn't look well. The fever she had been suffering from had persisted and she was struggling to keep anything down. She looked weaker by the day, but nevertheless had been once again to care for her 'patients', as she called them. In the several weeks since they had arrived at the camp, whether as a distraction from their predicament or out of an instinct to care, she had been doing her best to help others. This had all been on top of the forced labour they were required to perform. She had splinted a broken leg, dressed wounds, though there was little to dress them with, and sat by the bedsides of others sicker than herself.

Emily had tried to persuade her to rest but had met with a Mira at her most determined and stubborn.

'There is no point in what you're doing,' said Gabriella, in typically blunt fashion. 'The Nazis are like lions. They will cull the weak.'

'Mr Schweitzer is looking better today,' said Mira, ignoring Gabriella and leaning back against the wall with her eyes half-closed. 'I wish I had some medicine. I could do so much more.'

'You do plenty,' said Emily.

She took her meagre bowl of food, broke off a piece of bread and set it aside. She carefully swept up the crumbs, too, and sprinkled them on top. Then she handed the rest – a little sausage and the remaining bread – to Beatrice, who grabbed it and tore at it in a series of enormous bites, hungrily swallowing everything in a matter of seconds.

'And just because I have my eyes closed doesn't mean I don't know what you're doing,' said Mira. 'I don't want to be treating you, too.'

'I'm not hungry,' said Emily, as her stomach inconveniently growled.

'Your body doesn't lie,' said Mira.

At this moment Gabriella moved across and sat between them, dropping her voice to a whisper.

'You won't listen to me, but you will want to know this,' she said. 'I have a way out.'

'We've discussed this,' said Emily. 'It's too dangerous for Beatrice.'

'And if she stays here, she'll die like the rest of us,' said Gabriella.

'Shh!' said Emily. 'Don't talk like that when she can hear. And you can't know that.'

'Well, I don't want to stay to find out. Take the easy option if you wish, but I'm not leaving *my* daughter to rot here. There is a small gap in the fence where rabbits have been digging. In the dark, I think we can make it bigger and get through.'

Emily took a deep breath and thought again.

'The dormitory is locked at night,' she said.

'Yes, but the guards have the key and I know one who can be bribed.'

'With what?'

Gabriella held up her hand to show a lighter band of skin where her wedding ring had once been.

'We go tonight.'

The dormitory was quiet but for the occasional moan and at one point, a scream, as someone woke from one nightmare to return to another. Emily waited, wide awake, until she heard a creak in the floor next to the bunk that she shared with Mira and Beatrice. Gabriella whispered in her ear, and Emily turned to wake the others. They crept as silently as possible towards the door, and Gabriella signalled for them to wait.

She pushed the door slightly, and it opened as expected. She pushed her nose into the gap and squinted through it. A moonless night. The cold air condensed as she breathed hard.

After watching for a few moments, she turned back and nodded. Then she slid through and let Emily catch the closing door. She and Mira watched through a crack in the wood as Gabriella darted nimbly towards the fence, some twenty metres away. She reached it quickly and dropped to all fours. Watchful, she took in everything around her once more and then began quietly pulling at the soil around the hole with both hands, shifting it in big lumps. This continued for some minutes, and all they could hear was soft scratching and shallow breathing. Their own, and Gabriella's.

After a time, she stopped and waited. When she was content that all was well, she signalled to them to follow her.

Mira went to push the door open, but Emily was suddenly paralysed by an instinct not to move, and she barred the way. Mira pushed at her arm in frustration, but Emily held firm. As they wrestled, there was a sudden commotion and a spotlight flashed on, pointed directly at the fence where Gabriella was crouching.

An officer came into view and guards crowded around with rifles and dogs. The officer pointed his pistol at her, and Gabriella had no choice but to surrender.

'Is there anyone else with her?' asked the officer of one of the guards. 'I thought I saw her signal to someone.'

'I don't think so, sir. She is the only one I know about.'

The officer turned to Gabriella.

'Are you alone?'

There was a flicker of her eyes towards the dormitory, but she held it in check.

'Aren't I enough?' she said.

The officer scanned the area, paying her little attention. He very precisely replaced the pistol in his holster and secured it with a snap of its leather strap.

'Check outside the fence,' he said to the guard nearest him. 'Stand up,' he said to Gabriella, blowing languorously on his hands to warm them.

The officer paused for a moment and then in one swift motion he drew his weapon from its holster, cocked it, and shot Gabriella through the head.

Her body fell back, lifeless, into the hole she had dug out.

Emily felt a stifled shriek from Mira. She grabbed her and Beatrice and pushed them back inside the dormitory as quickly and quietly as she could. They got back to their bunk and lay down, hearts pounding.

Mira held on tightly to Emily, and Emily, in turn, drew Beatrice close to her.

Hold on, she told herself once again. *Hold on.*

Chapter 13

Dachau Concentration Camp

The car pulled up to the entrance. An enormous imperial eagle loomed from the gate as the guard approached. Hansen lounged in the back seat and waited. When the guard tapped on the window, he rolled it down without looking directly at him.

'Your papers, sir.'

Hansen handed him the ID card.

'Kurt Hauser,' he said slowly. 'SS-WHVA. I will see the commandant.'

The guard shifted uncomfortably.

'Is he expecting you, sir?'

Hansen turned towards him for the first time and fixed him with an unbroken stare. The guard tried to speak again and found his throat dry. He cleared it, then saluted nervously. He signalled for the gate to be opened and the car glided through. In the mirror Hansen saw the guard quickly pick up the telephone. He smiled. With this kind of power over others, he felt he could do anything he liked.

Inside the camp, Hansen stepped out of the car, to be greeted by the commandant, scurrying from his office and stooping all at once in reverence to his assumed identity. Hansen rather enjoyed the experience.

'Welcome, Herr Hauser. We were not expecting you.'

'Of course you weren't. If you knew I was coming, you would have had time to hide all your little… bookkeeping errors… wouldn't you?'

The commandant smiled nervously.

'Your name is Weiter.'

'Yes, sir. Eduard Weiter.'

'I know. I was stating a fact, not asking. Herr Weiter, I have *personal* authorisation from Oswald Pohl himself to conduct an investigation. It has come to our attention that some items have been going missing from shipments of prisoners' items to the

Reichsbank. That is somewhat vexing to us, you understand.'

'Yes, sir, I can see that it would be.'

'Again, not a question, Weiter. I will examine your accounts and I wish to observe your workings here. It has been my experience that where one thing is in error, there may be more… inexactitudes.'

'Of course, anything we can do to assist. But I am confident that we are scrupulous in our accounting, Herr Hauser.'

'We shall see.'

After some tedious hours poring over records of jewellery and other personal possessions taken – stolen – from inmates, Hansen was guided towards the section of the camp where prisoners were housed.

Above the gates the words *Arbeit macht frei* were formed in the metal. As he passed through them, a long line of people, bent over and shuffling, were making their way into the camp.

'Prisoners returning from their work in the munitions factories,' said Weiter.

As he said it, Hansen noticed a child pass him in the line. She was perhaps six years old.

'You employ children in munitions work?' he asked, with as blank an expression as he could find.

'They have small hands,' said Weiter.

He twitched his little moustache and picked a piece of lint from his uniform while Hansen watched the parade of prisoners. They were so thin it seemed impossible for them to be walking. Heads shaved, all had the same empty look – eyes fixed on something undefined in the distance, oblivious to anything around them. They lumbered with chains around their legs and more than one had scars or other signs of violence.

Hansen had, for a time, looked after Austrian prisoners of war in Italy in 1918. To be sure, they were lost souls, but nothing so far gone as what he saw now. Then, there had been a code. The idea that the enemy, whatever they might have done, deserved the same dignity in treatment as they would have asked for themselves. But these were not enemy soldiers, and there was little dignity.

'Where do they come from?' he asked.

'Oh, all over,' said Weiter. 'Poland, Russia. We've had a fair few from Italy in recent months.'

'Italy?'

'Yes, now we're cleaning up Il Duce's mess. These are all the dormitory blocks,' he said, waving towards lines of wooden buildings.

'How many prisoners do you have?'

'Here? About forty thousand, presently. Others in the sub-camps. More coming in all the time – several thousand every month – but of course we have… natural wastage… so our numbers remain stable.'

He offered a thin grin that showed a row of teeth yellowed by nicotine.

A group of prisoners was being herded behind them into the open area in front of what looked like the kitchens block. Hansen turned to look as the prisoners were lined up.

'Roll call?' he asked.

'Not exactly. These prisoners have been convicted of various infractions – stealing food, avoiding work, that sort of thing.'

Hansen wondered what kind of punishment might be meted out. He soon had his answer, when the soldiers lined up with rifles in firing squad formation. Before he could utter a word, the order had been given, and the prisoners fell in a massed heap.

Over in seconds. Lives that had meant something. People who would be missed. Gone in one snap of a finger. He felt momentarily faint and steadied himself. He did his best to conceal the nausea rising inside him, though his ashen white face might have given him away had Weiter been paying attention.

Another group of prisoners moved in now, under orders, and began to lift the bodies and shift them into carts.

'Justice here is swift,' said Weiter. 'Let me show you something interesting.'

With a casual swagger, he moved off towards the other end of the barracks. Hansen followed slowly, his head still swimming. They entered one of the accommodation buildings and were offered a tray of food and wine. One of those serving was the girl he had seen earlier. As he looked at her again, he was no longer so sure of her age. He guessed that she might be older – eight or nine – but for her size. She was terribly frail, and it seemed to him that he could see something of her ribcage through the thin overalls she wore. Her eyes were blue, but vacant, almost looking through him as she stood with a plate of sandwiches. Only when she looked down hungrily at the plate could he see a spark of life.

'Help yourself, Herr Hauser.'

Food was the last thing on Hansen's mind, but to be polite, if such a word had any relevance in a place like this, he took a couple of sandwiches.

'If you would like, I will show you our medical research,' continued Weiter, ignoring the prisoners in front of him. 'We are making some excellent progress.'

He took Hansen to a window, where they could observe a number of patients lying on gurneys in an adjoining room, which seemed to have been converted for medical use. One was writhing in agony, his body contorted and twisted with muscle spasms as doctors looked on, indifferent to his suffering.

'Herr Doctor Schilling hopes to make advancements in the treatment of malaria and other such tropical diseases.'

'The prisoners have volunteered for experimental treatment?' asked Hansen, dabbing his top lip with his sleeve.

Weiter chuckled lightly. A kind of low rumble like a cat purring.

'Yes, volunteered indeed.'

A soldier entered and whispered something into Weiter's ear. He nodded and then turned to leave.

'You will forgive me for a moment, sir. There is a matter I must attend to. If you will remain here?'

As the door closed behind Weiter, the room was now almost empty, except for a female guard at the far side, and the young girl who was clearing away the food that had been provided for him.

After a few moments of waiting awkwardly, Hansen strode up to the guard.

'Get me a list of the patients involved in the medical experiments,' he ordered. She looked doubtful and was about to speak when he barked: 'Now!' The guard beat a hasty retreat, and once again he found himself appreciating the power to make these people jump.

Hansen casually strolled across the now-empty room and made to pick up a glass of wine. As he drew up next to the girl, she froze.

'What is your name?' he whispered.

The girl at last made eye contact with him and she looked frightened beyond words. At last she mouthed something with a squeak that he barely heard:

'Beate,' she said.

Hansen smiled.

'I had a daughter called Beate. At least, that would have been her name.'

The words caught for a moment in his throat, and he stopped. He forced the memory from his mind.

'How old are you?'

'Eight,' she said. 'I think.'

'You don't know?' he said gently.

She shook her head. He couldn't help noticing how tiny she was. And had she lived, 'his' Beate would be the same age now.

'You know, your face is all dirty,' said Hansen. 'What would your mother say if she saw you all mucky like this, hmm?'

He took out a handkerchief and made a fuss of her, wiping her cheeks and nose. She had a pretty yellow bow tied around her wrist, which seemed somehow too bright to be real. It had, perhaps, been in her hair at one time, before it had all been cruelly shaved off. It was curious how the bow had survived. Like a remnant of the childhood that had been robbed from her.

'That's better,' he said, seeing freckles appear from behind the dirt.

She smiled for the first time, and it was worth waiting for. All the childish delight and spark was there again, just for a flickering moment.

'Here…'

He handed her the sandwiches he had been holding, though she was reluctant to take them.

'Put them in your pocket for later.'

She did as she was told, and then ran to the door. She paused and looked briefly back at him, then bolted away. Hansen followed her out of the door and saw her scurry across to another building. As he watched, there was a slight cough from behind him, and he turned to see the same female guard. She handed him the list of names he had asked for.

'Is there anything else I can help you with, Herr Hauser?'

'No, thank you. I'm just observing.'

'Very well. May I be so bold, sir, as to ask if your accent is Saxon? I have a cousin who is from there – that is why I ask.'

At this, Hansen noticed for the first time the red hair that was tightly scraped back under her cap.

'No. Actually I am Thuringian.'

She nodded and glanced around quickly.

'We don't have much time. It's too dangerous to write anything down. Can you memorise what I tell you?'

'I think so.'

'Good. *Ringeltaube* is a code name for a prototype aircraft – a fighter with jet engines. It is faster and better armed than anything you have.'

Her eyes flicked upwards, and she began to reel off information committed to memory.

'Top speed of 900km per hour, armed with four 30mm cannons, 50mm rockets and space for two 500kg bombs under the wings. They call it the ME-262.'

'When will this be ready?' asked Hansen.

'They have completed testing and it will be in production soon, if it isn't already. Do you have all that?'

'Yes.'

'Good. I must go.'

'Will you…'

'I'll be fine,' she said, stopping him, and smiling. 'Now get the information out of here.'

They parted ways without ever knowing each other's names, let alone anything else. She was clearly German, so he wondered at her reasons for working against her own people. Though, as he reminded himself, in a sense, so was he.

Weiter returned shortly afterwards and found Hansen back in the accommodation block, watching the medical experiments as before.

'Forgive me for abandoning you. There was a matter that called for me to make an immediate decision.'

'What kind of decision?' said Hansen.

'Some prisoners who have become a burden. We have arranged for them to be transferred to Hartheim. You know of it?'

'Yes,' said Hansen. In his work for Giesler, the name had cropped up. It had been designated as a euthanasia centre.

'So, problem solved,' said Weiter, rubbing his hands together.

As they continued up the avenue of barracks, there was a commotion from one of the buildings. A guard standing with his rifle by the entrance to the block caught Weiter's attention.

'Private, what is happening here?'

The soldier ran over and saluted.

'It is a small matter, Herr Commandant. We have caught one of the prisoners stealing.'

'Very well,' said Weiter. 'Deal with it.'

The soldier returned to the block and, as he reached the door, another soldier pulled a struggling figure, small enough to be a child, out of the dormitory. The soldier had his back to Hansen. There was a scream and he seemed to clamp his hand over the prisoner's mouth. Arms and legs were splayed out in a fight for freedom, but the soldier held fast. The prisoner's movements became gradually slower and jerkier until at last, with a final judder, they stopped, and the body went limp.

The soldier turned and, before he threw the figure to the ground, Hansen registered a flash of bright yellow as the child's arm fell across her body.

Hansen's soul seemed almost to stand, for a brief moment, outside his body. A soul wracked by rage and remorse, screaming into the air. All while a façade of rigid, forced calm remained in his expression.

Hansen acted the part to the end. He shook hands. He smiled. He suggested that another audit might be necessary sooner rather than later, more than anything because he wanted to see the look of fear on the face of a monster. He completed the necessary paperwork at last, and at last he left.

In the stuffy back seat of the chauffeured car, he closed his eyes and with every ounce of strength sought to hold himself together. He was fraying. Losing control. As so many times before, his palms became clammy, his heart raced, and the space seemed to close around him.

An acrid, yellow-green gas seemed to fill the car and his eyes began to burn. With gas or with tears, he was no longer sure. He found a gun in his hands and raised it. Raised it into the gas. The gas that seemed to engulf him, drown him.

And then, when the mist seemed to clear, he found himself pointing his gun into a face. The face of a child, with a yellow bow in her hair.

Chapter 14

Bolzano Transit Camp, Italy

Emily looked up at the ceiling, with the moonlight playing across the wooden slats. Her breath formed clouds which blew away up towards the light. She huddled in the thin blanket, rubbing her arms intermittently to keep the cold at bay. Sleep was impossible, with her mind re-working everything that had happened. It was true that she and Gabriella had never had a close relationship, but she had been family. It had been so fast. So sudden. So pointless. And yet she had always been so brave. Gabriella had always seen life as a battle. A fight to make things the way they needed to be. It was honest.

How many times she'd wished she could be like her, to say 'to hell with it' and seize the day, when she had always held back, too worried about what might happen or who she would hurt. Or was it rather that she was afraid? Afraid to lose those she cared for, as had happened so many times before? She instinctively tightened her arms around Mira and Beatrice, lying next to her.

'Are you awake, Emmy?' said Mira from the darkness.

'Yes.'

There was a profound pause as Mira rested her head against her.

'Are we going to die?'

'Mira, you mustn't think like that.'

'I can't help it, Emmy. I've been lying here, and I can't see a way out. Without Gabriella. She was strong. I'm not strong. And I can't seem to shake this chill. I feel worse. And I don't want to leave you alone…'

'Shh. We're going to stay together, like I promised you.'

She took Mira's hand in hers.

'I'm going to hold on tight, and you're going to do the same. We won't let go. And one day, we'll be in the sun again. Free, and safe.'

'I miss Toto. And Father.'

'I know you do.'

'Do you miss Richard?'

'Yes, sometimes. You know I do. But I remember him. And I remember the happy times. Think of those things.'

'Do you regret coming to live with us? None of this would have happened to you if you'd stayed.'

'But I wouldn't have my family,' said Emily. 'I wouldn't have you.'

It was no longer a platitude. At first she had loved the idea of a family. The one she had longed for all her life. Then she had loved feeling needed and useful again. But finally, they had become everything. Her whole world. Her whole family. Except maybe not all her family. But at least all those who loved her as much as she had come to love them. They held each other tightly.

'But why didn't you have a family in England?'

'We tried. It didn't happen for us, that's all.'

'I'm sorry.'

'So am I.'

'Father used to brush my hair. He always said it was such a tangle. And I'd sit in his lap, and he'd brush it. And then he'd put me to bed and stroke my hair until I fell asleep. Will you stroke my hair, Emmy?'

'Of course.'

In time, Emily heard Mira's breathing slow and change, until she could tell she was asleep. She held her tight. Afraid to let go. Afraid to lose again the feeling of being loved. Until the dawn broke and the reality of where they were broke in once again.

Early the next day, after a meal of lukewarm watery coffee, they were ordered out into the yard. The commander told them they would be undergoing 'routine health checks'. There was, he said, a risk of contagion, and they needed to segregate those infected to prevent it spreading.

As they lined up, men in white coats studied each of them in turn, examining their eyes, tongues and anything else that it pleased them to check. After each cursory inspection, they pushed them to the left or to the right.

Beatrice clung tightly to Emily as they moved up the line together, and Mira held her other hand. As they got close to the front, Emily looked over at one of the separated groups. Many of them were elderly, and others held on to the fencing out of fatigue or sickness. A soldier prowled the perimeter, a cigarette in his mouth. He watched them with something akin to amusement. Moving close to an elderly man holding on to the fence, Emily saw the soldier smirk. He drew his finger slowly across his throat, all the while keeping eye contact with the old man. Then he doubled over in laughter and carried on along the line.

'Next!'

Emily felt herself pushed from behind and she came face to face with one of the men in white coats.

'Open your mouth,' he ordered, and pushed her tongue down forcefully. A light was shone in her eyes and then he pulled down an eyelid.

'Very well,' he said, and nodded his head to the left. He tried at first to loosen Beatrice's grip. When she wouldn't move, he smacked her smartly across the head. Beatrice began to cry but maintained

293

her grasp. At last the doctor, exasperated, pushed them both away.

Momentarily relieved, Emily looked back to see Mira undergoing the same brief study. It was clear for all to see that she was ill, and Emily's blood ran cold when the inevitable signal was given that she should be moved to the right, where the old man, and others, were standing holding on to the fence.

'Hartheim,' said the doctor.

At first Emily didn't know whether Mira had seen the soldier and the gesture he had made, but her shriek told her at once that she had.

'Emmy!'

Emily could no longer stand by and watch, and she thrust her way back, past the guards trying to stop her.

'She's not ill,' she cried out. 'She's not ill!'

The doctor looked at her incredulously.

'Take her back.'

'It's just her time,' said Emily, in a moment of inspiration. 'Her monthly troubles.'

The doctor squirmed slightly, but doubt remained in his expression.

'She suffers for it,' continued Emily, determined now. 'But in any case, you need her. She's… she's a doctor.'

'She's too young to be a doctor,' scoffed the man.

'Nevertheless!' said Emily, and she held her ground, though a strong arm was trying to force her back.

The doctor sighed heavily and rubbed his chin.

'Oh, what does it matter in any case?' he said at last. 'What does any of this matter?'

He flicked his head back towards Emily, and the guard released Mira. She ran to Emily and hugged her, and the three of them made their way back towards the group on the left.

Over the days that followed, there was a change in Mira. With the extra food that Emily was giving her, she seemed, finally, to be recovering some strength. And there was a seriousness too. She had taken

Emily's words as a kind of commission and set out to re-double her efforts. Others in the camp had taken to calling her doctor, and in the space of only a few days, she had seemed to age by a decade. The naïve Mira was gone. This young woman, as it was right now to call her, was professional, dedicated and forceful. She begged for supplies from the infirmary, and, through her sheer persistence, was actually given some.

By contrast, after a time of such intensity, when there had seldom been time for introspection, Emily found herself with little to do but care for Beatrice. Her energy continued to ebb away. It was a struggle to move, and more than once she found herself close to fainting. At first she told herself that it was a result of the lack of food. But when she realised that it was her own monthly time, and nothing had happened, she began to worry about other possibilities.

After another week of the same relentless toil and squalor, orders were given that they should march the short distance from the camp to a railway line that ran nearby. Herded together, they were pushed and prodded into carriages, empty but for the people inside. The space around them closed and closed, until it seemed impossible for anyone else to be squeezed inside. But more continued to be added beyond that impossible point. Finally the doors closed, and they prepared themselves.

The train shook and rattled, and Emily thought back to her first experience of a train, on their journey to Cornwall so many years ago. She stowed herself inside that memory as she once again had to hold up little Beatrice for fear of her being crushed. This time the pain was agonising and there were moments when she felt she could not endure any more but for the thought of Beatrice and her future. With the light-headedness came a nausea, but with so little in her stomach, she couldn't vomit. Mira stood, flat against the door, fixed on looking through a crack in the wood.

'The sun is setting on this side,' she said. 'We're going north. To Germany.'

Chapter 15

For Hansen, all the people he saw now in the street looked different. Those who had seemed so normal before, going about their everyday business, had taken on a malevolent quality. He attributed to each base and malicious motives. The old man sitting on the bench was Gestapo, watching for signs of dissent. The mother with her child was schooling them in hate. The office worker was planning the deaths of millions. With each, the anger swelled inside him.

He reached the office and showed his identification to the security guard, complicit like the others in the crimes being carried out in his name. He took the lift to the third floor as he always did and arrived at his office. His secretary was waiting for him with a cup of coffee.

'Good morning, Herr Schönfelder.'

He took the cup and went inside without a word, closing the door on the world. He fell into his chair and felt the tension in his muscles once again. His hand started to shake, and he took it in his other to still it. He closed his eyes and focused desperately. Now was not the time to lose control.

He breathed in and out slowly, and gradually found a measure of calm. He opened his eyes again, only to see the portrait of the Führer staring out from the wall before him.

You created this, he thought to himself. How could a man who had served in the trenches, as he had, take such a different lesson from those experiences? To seek war, when he had seen the nature of it? It defied comprehension.

'People like you,' he whispered to himself, 'must never rule this world again.'

There was a knock on the door, and with the briefest of delays, it flew open. It was Giesler. Hansen felt somewhat like he had been caught with his trousers around his ankles, but Giesler seemed not to have heard him voice his thoughts.

'Schönfelder, I am going out. While I am gone, there are some files I would like your opinion on. They are on my desk. Read them and give me your recommendation.'

'Yes, sir.'

'Very good. And I've asked Lieselotte to join us for lunch later. I'm sure you'd like that.'

'Of course. I look forward to it.'

Giesler was gone, leaving the open door and only the click of typewriters to be heard outside. The gods were smiling on him, allowing the perfect opportunity to be alone in Giesler's office.

He walked as calmly as he could manage, and when he reached the office, he closed the door behind him. With filing cabinets and drawers before him, he began to rifle through them in a sudden frenzy. He passed over useful, but unrelated, information in pursuit of intelligence on Dachau and the shipments to and from the camp. There had to be a way to help – to intercept them, or re-route them.

Crawling on his hands and knees, he pored over the reports, plans, memoranda and photographs to find what he was looking for. Had he been more systematic, he might have committed more to memory or taken notes, but he was single-minded in his determination.

Finally, he raised himself up and felt a crick in his back. He'd been studying so intently he'd lost track of time. He checked his watch, which showed it was nearly noon. Giesler would be back soon.

Hastily, he began shoving documents back in their drawers, and was nearly finished when he heard the door open behind him. He froze. He had his hands in a filing cabinet that he had no business being in.

'What are you doing?' said a voice – but not the one he had expected.

He turned to find Lotte staring at him, open-mouthed. Her forehead creased, and the look of suspicion grew.

'Oh, it's you, my love,' he said, as lightly as he could manage. 'Your father asked me to look for some papers.'

'On his desk,' she said slowly. 'He told me. But not in there.'

'I was looking forward to having lunch with you,' he offered. But it was no good. The expression on her face read of only one thing: betrayal.

'No,' she said at last. 'No! I knew something wasn't right. But this isn't who you are. It can't be.'

'Lotte,' he said, with pleading in his voice.

'You can't call me that,' she said, tears beginning to run down her face. 'Only people who care for me call me that. Who *are* you?'

'I am who you think I am.'

'A man who lies. A man who uses people to get… here. You always knew who I was. You just told me everything you thought I wanted to hear, and when that didn't work you told me something else. Something else that ended with "I love you". And poor, ridiculous, desperate person that I am, I believed it. I actually thought you could see the real me, and wanted me for me. I should have known better.'

'It wasn't a lie.'

'Which part?'

'That I liked you.'

'Liked. But not loved?'

'Lotte, I'm sorry. But this is important. You don't know what they're doing. If you did, you'd want to stop them too.'

'Are you even Austrian?' she asked.

He couldn't lie to her any more, and simply tilted his head to one side.

'I see.'

'Lotte, they're killing people.'

'It's a war.'

'Not in the war. What they're doing is not war. They're murdering people. Thousands of them. Old people, women… children.'

He stopped, unable to continue. Her expression softened a little for the first time and she stepped towards him.

'Are you crying?' she asked.

He wiped his eyes quickly, ashamed of the suddenness with which it had come upon him.

'You have to help me,' he said.

She shook her head slowly.

'I can't even tell if you're acting. You could be on the stage. Laurence Olivier – he is your great actor, isn't he? Or, no… Maybe you are more familiar with Orson Welles? I realise I know nothing about you – not even where you're from.'

'I'm half-German.'

'And the other half?'

'British.'

'You think that makes it better?'

'I don't care what you think of me…'

'Clearly you don't.'

'…but this is important. There's a place called Dachau. And other places. That's where all these people are being sent. Innocent people.'

'Enemies of the state,' she said unconvincingly. 'It's necessary to arrest those who would threaten us – communists, Jews…'

'You don't believe that.'

Her face told him he was right.

'You have to leave,' she said finally, moving towards the door.

'I can't. What about lunch?'

She let out a burst of laughter, mixed with tears.

'Not today. Today I will make other arrangements. I will eat lunch as I always have – on my own.'

She slammed the door.

After a few moments, he gathered up the files from the desk and tidied everything that remained. He went back to his own desk and began to work on the proposals. He made his excuses for lunch, and at the end of the day, he returned to his apartment.

He sat on the settee and waited. His instinct had always been to trust her, but what now?

He watched streams of rain trickling down the window pane and wiped the condensation away with the back of his hand to allow a view of the street below. All the while he drowned his sorrows in a bottle. His word was clearly worth nothing now, so why hold to an old promise to Emily, who must feel the same way about him as Lotte did now. It was taking more and more schnapps to quiet the thoughts in his head.

At last, when the clock reached eleven, there was a knock at the door. He straightened his tie. If he were to be taken, it would be with dignity.

He opened the door to find Lotte, her hair wet and, without a raincoat, her clothes soaked. She was visibly shivering. His protective instinct kicked in, and he guided her quickly inside.

'You poor thing, you're soaked through,' he said. 'Come and sit by the fire.'

He took her hands in his and warmed them in front of the fireplace, much as he had done for the young Emily on their first meeting so many years before.

'I wanted to prove you wrong,' she said, taking the brandy he offered her.

'Whatever illusions I had left about this country,' she continued. 'I wanted to preserve them.'

'I understand.'

'So I searched my father's briefcase. The one he always brings home with him. And I found these.'

She handed him some papers.

'It talks about using poison gas to execute whole groups of prisoners,' she began. Hansen's hands clenched involuntarily at the mention of the word. 'And how they should dispose of bodies… It's monstrous!'

She stopped and put her head in her hands.

'I didn't want to believe it. To believe that my father could have anything to do with this. But he does, doesn't he?'

'I'm sorry.'

'What do I do now?' she asked. 'I don't know who I'm supposed to be if everything is a lie.'

She took to pacing the room. Hansen studied the documents. They were plans that detailed an acceleration of operations. The last document was a list of names – a manifest of prisoner shipments to Dachau, with dates and times. Exactly what he had been looking for! But his exultation was short-lived when he began to read down the list of names and came upon one that was more than familiar.

'What is it?' asked Lotte, noticing his change of expression.

'Nothing.'

'Is it someone you know?'

'You must get back,' he said, taking an umbrella from its hook. 'You'll be missed, and so will these.'

They went to the door, and as he handed her the umbrella, he took her hand for a moment.

'Will you tell him?' he asked.

'I don't know.'

Chapter 16

Emily drifted in and out of a kind of half-consciousness. Not really asleep, and not really waking. Her arms had lost all feeling, and breathing in the stifling, airless carriage had become a deliberate effort.

In this dreamlike state, with the rock and clatter of the train, it took some moments to register when the movement came to a sudden and screeching halt. There was a piercing whine as the wheels locked and skidded on the icy track, and had there been space for anyone to fall, they would have been thrown forward. As it was, there were shrieks and groans as those at the end of the carriage were crushed by the mass of people.

Then everything became still. There was a momentary silence as everyone waited and watched.

'Mira, can you see what's happening?' asked Emily.

'I'm not sure. There's a lot of snow. Wait, there's some men coming over the bank. They've got guns.'

There was a crackle of gunfire, followed by a lot of shouting, and then more gunshots. They felt the thud of an explosion, before vibrations rocked the carriage. There was a hum of chatter in the group. The idea that this might be an attempt at rescue. Hope, that rarest of commodities before now, was faintly alive again.

The firing continued for some minutes, but it was impossible to know what was happening outside. Then there was a shake at the door. Then the thud of another explosion, much closer this time. And then with a final rattle the locks broke, and the carriage door slid open with a roar in front of Mira. She had to steady herself to avoid falling out. Fresh, cold air rushed in, and it stung the back of Emily's throat as she gulped at it.

As their eyes accustomed again to the bright sunshine, they found a group of partisans outside, their backs to the train, desperately firing back at

German troops. One of them signalled at Mira and waved his arm.

'Get out – run!' he shouted, in German.

Two people next to Mira jumped onto the ground and started to run but were hit in the crossfire almost immediately. Mira looked around at Emily.

'What should we do?'

'Stay here,' called Emily, as more people made a break, with the same result.

The partisans seemed to be losing ground. One was shot in the head, and another took several shots to the chest and fell back. When the leader, who had been calling to them, was hit in the leg, his comrades helped him away, and the group began to retreat.

As the partisans fell back, the Germans advanced, and soon came in line with the open door. One was ordered to watch them while the others pursued the partisans. He held his rifle towards them, but when a stray bullet hit him in the neck, Emily saw a chance. With the other Germans chasing their attackers, no one was watching the open door, and the firing had moved away from them. It was now or never.

Emily pushed her way free, lowering Beatrice to the floor and willing her aching, stiff joints to function after so long pinned in one place.

'Come on!' she shouted.

She limped to the door and flung herself out into the unknown. It was higher than she had expected, and she landed heavily on her hip and rolled awkwardly in the snow until she recovered her balance. The dying German reached out for his gun, but could do nothing as his life ebbed away, the ice around him turning a blood red.

'Beatrice, come on, sweetheart!'

The little girl leapt from the carriage and into Emily's arms, and Mira quickly followed. They ran for their lives, hand in hand, down the bank of snow. Every second she expected a shot to ring out, but they went on, running, sliding, careering down the slope. She was filled with an unexpected energy, adrenaline surging through her chest.

At the bottom of the snow bank, perhaps a hundred metres from the railway line, was a conifer forest. Beyond the tree line, the forest darkened. Intimidating yet inviting. If they could only reach the trees, it might be possible to hide amongst them.

What would come next, she had no idea, but for now, it would be enough. Enough to be free, and away.

'Get to the trees,' she told them. 'Get to the trees!'

She had no desire to look back, though she feared what might be behind them. They went headlong for the safety of the forest. As her lungs burned and her legs went to jelly beneath her, they felt the snow give way to soft pine needles, and the ground almost bounced them forward. A delightful, all-concealing darkness closed around them. They had made it!

When they had gone some way into the forest, Emily turned round for the first time to look behind them. She saw a glorious sight: a canopy of trees cloaking the snow beyond, and no sign of pursuit. Whether others had braved the dash and made it, she could not tell. But they were clear – at least for now.

'Emmy, you did it!'

Mira hugged her, and Beatrice held her arms out too, and they all collapsed in a circle, holding each other.

Emily took a moment to breathe in the fresh air and recover. The sudden stop cleared her mind, and inevitably the question arose of what would come next. They had perhaps minutes before they were discovered.

'Mr Rubin. He was shot,' said Mira. 'And Mrs Bassano.'

'I saw.'

'So many bodies…'

She tried to haul them up again, though her own head spun, but Beatrice resisted.

'I know you're tired, sweetheart, but we need to keep going.'

Mira took a long breath and picked herself up, too, and she caught hold of Beatrice's hand. 'You know how to play hide and seek, Bea, don't you? We have to hide from the bad men. You don't want them to catch us, do you?'

The little girl shook her head vigorously, and they moved off together at the best pace they could muster, which was not much.

After what must have been hours of walking, though they had no way to tell, it became apparent

that the winter sun was dropping in the sky, and it
would soon be dark.

'Emmy, we should stop soon. I can't carry
Beatrice anymore.'

Emily nodded. She was so tired she could
barely think, and if she had been offered the chance
to collapse on the mossy ground and curl up, she
would have done so right there. But there appeared
to be a clearing ahead, where the sun was brighter
than elsewhere, and she was keen to reach it.

'We'll stop soon, but I want to get to that
clearing. We might be able to see where we are.'

As they reached the edge of the clearing, it
became apparent that it was not a clearing after all,
but a hillside where the trees opened out. The views
were wide, and on a promontory some distance
away, Emily could see the towers of a castle. Her
mind, fogged as it was, nevertheless responded well
enough to recall a memory. Some ten years ago,
perhaps, they had been to that castle on an excursion.
A day trip from Richard's aunt and uncle's nearby
farm, which they visited many times in the years
before the war. She tried to draw out all the memory
she had. It was strangely vivid. They had stood
looking out at just this view, and she had leaned in to

whisper in Richard's ear that she was pregnant. It had been the first time. As she closed her eyes now, she could almost feel his embrace, the joy they had shared in that moment, and their hopes for the future.

'Emmy, we should make a fire.'

She was brought abruptly back to the present. 'Yes. We should. You can do that?'

'Of course. Are you alright?'

She smiled.

'Yes. I am now. I know where we are. That castle is about thirty miles from the farm that belongs to Richard's aunt and uncle. We can go there.'

Mira frowned.

'That's a long way. Are you sure it's safe?'

'They were always kind to me.'

Mira's frown remained while she scanned the ground. 'There are some dry sticks around here. I'll make a fire. See what you can find to eat.'

Soon after, with the sun dropping out of sight, the three of them were sitting around the fire, warming their hands, and sharing out the results of the forage. It was meagre enough – some chestnuts, dandelions and a few mushrooms. But compared to the food they had been given in the camp, it was a feast. Meanwhile, they melted some snow in a leaf and took the first drink they had had all day. They made up a little bed for Beatrice from some moss and fir branches. She curled up and was soon fast asleep.

'I'm glad she can sleep so easily,' said Mira, as they watched her chest gently rise and fall. 'How much of this do you think she'll remember?'

'None of it, I hope,' said Emily firmly. 'I know what it is to start life in fear. But I want her to know that she is safe. And that she is loved, whatever happens.'

Emily carefully laid some moss and bracken across the sleeping Beatrice to keep her warm.

'You know, I was wrong…' began Mira.

'About what?'

'That you should put her right about being her mother.'

'I'll never be that,' said Emily. 'But…'

'Not everyone has the chance to know the mother they were born to,' said Mira, interrupting. 'But some of us are lucky enough to find another.'

She reached out to gently touch Emily's hand.

There was a sense of profound responsibility in realising what she had come to mean for Mira. But most of all a great warmth. A great warmth and protectiveness. As she looked at her, and at the little sleeping girl, the void that had remained in her heart seemed filled at last. So she contented herself with just 'Thank you.'

They sat in silence for some moments, Emily's eyes drooping once again, but this time in contentment.

'Will it be difficult to go there?' asked Mira.

'It's a long walk, for sure.'

'No, I mean, to see the place again, and see his uncle and aunt? Won't it bring back memories for you?'

'Memories aren't always a bad thing.'

Even in the firelight, Emily could see a cheeky little smile on Mira's face.

'Stop it, Mira.'

'What? I didn't say anything. Except… what would you do if he were there?'

'Don't be ridiculous! How could he be?'

'But if he were…?'

'He won't be, so there's no point speculating. Why do you keep on with this notion?'

Mira stayed quiet for a full minute, but then pushed again, to Emily's irritation.

'I will stop asking, I promise. But I know you're still in love with him…'

'Mira…'

'It's so obvious that you are. So I don't understand why…'

'Because he didn't love *me* anymore!' said Emily, in exasperation, loud enough that Beatrice began to stir. She dropped her voice again to a whisper.

'Because he blamed me for everything that happened. I couldn't give him the family we wanted, and every time… every time we tried, he pulled further away. He used to tell me everything. And then he just stopped. In books, it's always the end of the story, to be happy. Maybe for some people it is happy ever after. But not us. And when it ends, it just dies away, slowly. Painfully. Like the cord of communion is broken, and you are bleeding. Bleeding to death.

'There was part of me that didn't want him to follow me to Italy. Because I couldn't have borne it, to be like that again. Someone to love, and someone to love you, that's what I always thought I wanted. And it's what we had, for a while. But half of that is worse than none at all. So it was better, in the end, that he didn't come. That it ended.'

Mira's hand reached out across the darkness, and Emily took it.

'I love you, Emmy.'

'I love you too, Mira.'

When Emily opened her eyes, the sun was already peeking over the hillside. She was stiff with cold, and the fire was now only a smouldering heap of ash.

As she looked about her, she could see that Mira and Beatrice were still sleeping. She poked at the fire and tried to coax it back into life with some twigs. In that moment she heard voices, and, faintly, a dog barking. In a hurry, she picked herself up and shook the others awake.

'Mira! Mira, wake up. We have to go. Beatrice, wake up, sweetheart.'

They stirred and stretched, and, rubbing the sleep from their eyes, they made off along the ridge towards the place where the woods began again. But as they started down the path, a soldier emerged from the trees and trained his rifle on them.

'*Halt!* Stay where you are!'

It seemed that he was on his own. He came closer and took Mira by the chin, turning her head to one side and then the other, looking her over.

'Don't touch her!' shouted Emily.

His hand on Mira's face brought a feeling of revulsion. A memory that she tried to push aside. The young soldier, Hans, who had tried to be so gentle, and yet in doing so had somehow made it so much worse.

Emily threw his hand away and stood between the soldier and Mira.

'Perhaps I should just shoot you here,' said the soldier, raising his rifle again. 'Filthy Jewess!'

He shoved Emily backwards and she lost her balance, falling into the undergrowth. The soldier bent over to pull her up by the arm and, as he did so, Emily called up all her strength and yanked him downwards. The move was so unexpected that he fell to the ground, and she clambered on top of him, trying to pin down his arms.

He laughed at her efforts, and it made her all the more angry. He shook one of his arms free and took her by the throat, choking her. Mira tried to intervene, but he pushed her away and intensified his grip on Emily's throat. She tried to breathe in but found no air reaching her lungs. She felt herself getting weaker, and daylight seemed to fade around her.

In a last, desperate effort, she circled with her hands on the ground, grasping for anything she could find. Finally, she caught hold of something firm. A branch, she thought. She brought it down hard, as hard as her remaining strength allowed, onto his head.

His movements stopped. She fought to release herself from his grasp, collapsing onto the

ground, gasping for air. As she gradually recovered,
Mira was bending over the man.

'I think he's dead, Emmy.'

Mira raised his arms above his head and
began to pump them up and down to stimulate
breathing, her doctor's instincts kicking in. Then she
placed her hands on his chest and began rhythmically
pushing downwards, counting as she did so.

Emily crawled over to where she was. The
man was staring upwards, unmoving, blood dripping
from a great gash across the side of his head. On the
ground next to him was a stone, marked with his
blood.

As Mira struggled to save him, Emily heard
other voices in the distance, and the faint barking of
dogs.

'Mira, we have to go,' said Emily, unable to
look away from the rock and the blood. She was
desperate to leave this thing behind, but still drawn
to look. This body that was now empty of the
essence of humanity. Though it seemed strange to
think of that word belonging to this man.

'I can save him.'

'He's the enemy!' she hissed.

Emily's instincts told her to run, *now*, even if it meant leaving them behind. Mira turned to her, shocked.

'He's a human being,' she said.

Emily could only shake her head.

'Mira, please!'

Mira felt for a pulse and found none.

'I think… I think he's gone.'

Emily's muscles quickened and she shivered with nervous energy, which she displaced by pacing back and forth. She looked nervously back down the track, which still seemed mercifully clear.

'It's time to go. Come on.'

They set a path in the opposite direction, and the distant voices gradually faded away entirely as they walked. The expression of pity on Mira's face made Emily mad.

'Don't look at me like that! I had no choice!'

'Oh, Emmy. I'm sorry for you, that's all. Can't I feel sorry for you?'

'No!' she said sternly. 'No. Never that.'

They stomped on, in silence, for hours. Several times Mira came close and seemed to want to take her hand or put an arm around her. But each time she moved away. She felt unworthy of comfort. And the more she tried to think of other things, the more the stone and the blood came into her mind's eye.

Beatrice cried with hunger, and, short on temper, Emily scolded her. She began to cry, so Mira took her by the hand and distracted the little girl by showing her the different trees in the forest and trying to spot birds in the branches.

As the sun reached high in the sky, they came to a river and stopped to drink. Though it was cold to the touch and made their teeth ache, they drank deeply. When they had had their fill, Mira looked around.

'We should find a place to cross.'

'No,' said Emily. 'We should swim through it.'

'What! Are you mad? We'll get hypothermia.'

'It will put the dogs off our scent.'

Mira wrinkled her nose and pouted.

'I'm fairly sure that's just something you've seen at the pictures.'

'Come on!'

Emily took them both by the hand and plunged into the river, which was far deeper, and far colder, than she had expected. It was such intense cold that it was painful, and she quickly lost all feeling in her hands and feet. Nevertheless she dragged them through in a kind of doggy paddle, and out onto the far bank.

'Holy Mary, mother of God!' hissed Emily through chattering teeth as she clutched her arms to herself and tried to get warm, while rubbing Beatrice's little arms too.

'And I'm fairly sure,' said Mira, between shivers, 'that that's not a phrase a good Jewish girl should use.'

She began to laugh, and so did Emily. But as they laughed together, Emily's giggles morphed into slow sobs. The worst weeks and months of her whole life had left her drained of everything, and now, through her own recklessness, she had invited hypothermia on them all too. The dam burst and it all became too much. Then the sobs became stuck in her throat, and she found she was struggling to breathe. She could feel her face flush hot, and for a moment, a dreadful moment, she could feel his hands on her throat again, and she wondered if she would ever find another breath.

Then she felt Mira take her by the shoulders and call to her. She made her count with her. Slowly, from twenty. And by focusing on her voice and the words, she found herself again.

'I'm sorry,' she said, as she released a long breath. 'That was so foolish. I don't know what I was thinking.'

'You weren't,' said Mira. 'I think maybe you should let me do the thinking for a while.'

Emily nodded.

'When did you become so wise?'

'Well, I am a doctor now.'

'You are,' said Emily.

'I'll make a fire.'

Sometime later Emily woke to find herself wrapped in soft foliage. Her clothes hung from branches stuck into the ground over a blazing fire. And mixed with the wood smoke, which was pleasant enough, was the much more pleasant smell of roasting meat.

'Is that a rabbit?' she asked, peering up from her cosy huddle.

'I caught it,' said Mira. 'Do you want some?'

She took a piece and chewed at it with no regard for manners, sucking the bones clean.

'Father taught me to hunt and trap. Years ago. I was never interested. But it's funny how you remember these things.

'When you've eaten, I saw a shepherd's hut over that way. One they use when they bring the animals up in the summer. I think we should go there. It's better than being outdoors.'

The little hut contained a stove, blankets and cooking utensils. It was dusty and neglected, but dry. And once they got a new fire going in the stove, they were properly warm for the first time in days. Perhaps even since they left the farm. They ate some fruit and nuts they had collected and wrapped themselves up in the blankets. Mira had done most of the work and she insisted that Emily rest in the single bed, with Beatrice curled up at the foot of it.

'We could stay here,' said Mira, as she looked up at her sister from the floor. 'It's not bad. We could just hide here until they stop looking?'

'I don't know,' said Emily doubtfully.

'You said sometimes the best option is to do nothing,' said Mira.

'How would we survive? There's not enough to eat here. And what if they find us?' Mira shivered noticeably at this, and Emily smiled warmly in reassurance. 'I think you and I both know what Gabriella would have said. And she would be right. We must go on.'

Mira pouted, in an expression which Emily had come to know meant that she was holding something back. A rare occurrence.

'What is it, Mira?'

Mira put her hands to her mouth, as if to hide the words that would follow.

'How…' she began diffidently. 'How do you know you can trust them? I mean… I mean they're Germans…'

'So is Richard,' said Emily.

'I know,' said Mira. 'But he wouldn't hurt you.'

Now it was Emily's turn to hold back.

'I trust them,' she said at last.

Mira looked down at the yellow Star of David that was still stitched to her clothes. 'With our lives? With Beatrice's life?'

'We have to.'

In the morning they turned the blankets into makeshift clothes, filled their thin shoes with soft moss and packed whatever food they could find into an old milk churn, which they took it in turns to carry. They began to make their way down from the hills into a river valley where it was a little warmer. They followed the water for the next two days, resting where they could and eating whatever they could find. Mira carried Beatrice on her shoulders for much of the time, until the river came alongside a road that Emily recognised. They continued along the road, dropping into the drainage ditch every time they saw anyone. At last, with blistered feet, skin red raw from cold and empty stomachs, they came upon the village of Peterhausen, and the entrance that Emily recognised. There was the long driveway. The line of trees, and the house with its yellow walls and terracotta roof. It was at once a reassuring and a disquieting sight.

Emily pulled her blanket down to conceal the yellow star, and they began to walk towards the house.

Chapter 17

Hansen went ahead into the little chapel and peered into the darkness. He could only see a few candles flickering as he stepped across the threshold and into the centre aisle.

Without warning, he felt himself grabbed by the lapels and pushed back into the corner of the building, up against the wall.

'What the bloody hell did you think you were bloody doing, you bloody fool,' said Thurso, his gentle Scottish accent roughened with his lost temper.

'God damn you!'

He let go of Hansen, who lost his balance and scraped down the wall and onto the floor with a thud. Thurso paced in front of him.

'I'd have you up on charges if we weren't in the middle of fucking Nazi Germany.'

'Is this about the train?' asked Hansen.

'Of course it's about the bloody train! You go behind my back to authorise an attack on a prisoner transport. An attack which cost lives. And worse – which failed!'

'I had intelligence.'

'I know. And it's only because of that fact that I'm not bouncing your head on the bloody stone floor and making a bloody mess.'

Thurso drew a deep breath. He had never lost his cool in this way before. He had feigned anger for effect many times, but this was genuine. Nevertheless, there was always something in his manner that made it seem like he was joking.

'I wanted to save lives,' said Hansen. 'If you'd been to that place, you'd feel the same.'

Thurso fixed him with a stare. Not his usual penetrating gaze, looking for weaknesses, but with wide eyes. Wide, sad eyes.

'You think I would have sent you if I could bear to go there again myself?'

Thurso looked down for a moment, searching for control over his temper. When he looked up again, it was with a long, deep breath.

'You thought you were doing a noble thing, I know. But if the enemy guesses that we have intelligence on their prisoner movements, and intercept them, what do you think they'll do, hmm?'

'Those people!' said Hansen. 'When I saw what they were doing, I was ashamed, Tony. Ashamed to be what I am. I've never been ashamed before. I fought for Britain, but I could always look at my enemy, and know my duty, and respect him. To know that it was only by chance that I wasn't fighting for them. But when I saw that place, it made me hate myself. Hate all those parts of me that belong here. They have taken my country and brought it to its knees. And none of us is clean of this. We will all come out of this war dishonoured.'

Thurso sat down at last on a pew, his rage exhausted, and lit a cigarette at the third attempt.

'Look, I understand,' he said. 'I do. But we're here to do a job, as I've always told you. We're not heroes. We're not soldiers. We can't afford pride, or honour, or dignity. We find information to win the war, that's all. And if that means we swim in filth, then we do it. And we do it gladly. You said Lotte got you the information. Do you think she can provide more?'

'I think it's unlikely.'

Thurso tilted his head questioningly.

'There's a chance Lotte may have blown my cover,' said Hansen slowly, forming each word carefully.

Thurso simply closed his eyes and rubbed his forehead as if to relieve a sudden headache.

'And you think this because...?'

'I told her what I am.'

'Marvellous,' said Thurso, stubbing his cigarette out fiercely. 'Bloody marvellous. Well, that's it then. We'll have to pull you out. All that work...'

'But...' said Hansen, 'I feel like I can trust her. She gave me the intel, after all. And I'm still here.'

Thurso looked him up and down slowly.

'Sadly, you are.'

He took a moment to consider, seemingly running the possibilities through his mind and reaching the same conclusion.

'You could be right. Maybe you got under her skin more than we thought. The Hansen charm… Or they could just be letting you run on to see where you go.'

'There's something else I haven't told you…'

'There's more?'

'Himmler is coming.'

Thurso let out a single guffaw, like laughter caught in mid-flow, and rubbed his eyes once more, as if to confirm he was not waking from a dream.

'Heinrich Himmler? Little man, glasses, silly moustache?'

'The same.'

'Coming here?' he continued, half-believing. 'When?'

'I don't know. But soon.'

Thurso got to his feet again, brushed down his clothes and straightened his tie.

'Alright, I've clearly lost all sense, so I'll let you continue. But no risks. That information could be a plant. Do what you normally do. Let it play out. Get what you can and get out. And be sure to let me know if anyone other than me tries to kill you, won't you? Unless of course they are successful. What about Lotte?'

'I haven't seen her.'

'Keep it that way.'

On his return to the office, Hansen walked calmly through the lobby, aware of everyone around him, looking out for whispers or sidelong glances. He continued on into the lift. He half expected to be stopped at any moment and escorted to some dark room for interrogation. A place where he would be forced to tell the truth at last. The thought almost made him smile.

As he approached his office, Giesler stood in his path, arms folded. The smile that had been on his lips dropped away in an instant.

'Schönfelder. My office, if you please.'

Hansen followed meekly, and Giesler closed the door behind him as Hansen surveyed the room, looking for signs he might have left of his previous visit.

Giesler walked around him, in a move calculated to intimidate. Then he rounded his desk and dropped into the chair.

'I'm concerned, Schönfelder.'

'Oh. Why so, sir?' he asked, as if he needed to.

'Lieselotte. I am worried about her.'

He paused a moment, but Hansen waited too. They sized each other up a little, looking for clues as to the other's thoughts.

'Have you noticed anything?'

'I can't say, sir. She seemed herself when I saw her last, but that was a few days ago.'

'Indeed, that's the thing. You haven't been to see her, and she has been withdrawn. Keeping to her room. You see how I might think the two things are connected?'

'I can see how you might, sir,' said Hansen, doing his best to maintain eye contact. 'But I have been working late, that's all. If Lotte feels neglected,

I am sorry for it, and I shall make amends, of course. But she has not said anything to me.'

'No, well, you know how women are. She won't.'

He stood up again and subjected Hansen to one of his forensic glares. At length he broke off but seemed unconvinced.

'Very well. I shall hope to see you for dinner soon.'

Hansen turned to go, but Giesler called after him.

'The latest from the Russian front is not good, I hear. Reinforcements may be needed.'

He said no more, and Hansen left, fully understanding the barely veiled threat.

After a day of pointless paper shuffling, during which he struggled to focus on any one task for more than a few minutes, Hansen left for home on foot. His temporary home, as he kept telling himself, though it begged the question of where his real home was now.

His thoughts were so occupied that he had gone half a mile before he thought to look behind him, change direction or backtrack, as he had been taught to do. He passed a bakery, stopped abruptly, then pivoted on the spot back to the shop.

As he stood looking at the few loaves in the window, he caught a glimpse of a figure on the other side of the street. The man appeared to be studying newspapers on a stand, but his furtive glances gave away another purpose.

Hansen continued on his way home, and in the next window he stole a glance and saw that the man was now moving in the same direction on the other side of the road. Hansen increased his pace and, when he passed a narrow alleyway, darted swiftly into it and lengthened his stride. His knee twinged sharply at the sudden exertion, but he did his best to ignore it and half-ran, half-limped to the end of the alley and out into a side street. He turned into another alleyway and had to shuffle around boxes and crates as he worked his way parallel to the main street. At last, after a wide loop, he found his way back to the main street. He drew level with it and checked to the right and left. There was no sign of his pursuer. In relief, he made his way gradually back to his apartment building and climbed the stairs.

When he reached his flat, he went inside, dropped the keys on the side and made himself some ersatz coffee, which had little to commend it save for its warmth. He kicked his shoes off and went to close the curtains on the cold night outside. As he did so, he chanced to see a figure in a doorway opposite. It was hard to tell in the darkness, but it seemed to Hansen that it was the same man he had seen earlier. The same stocky build, the same beige coat.

Had the man seen through his ruse? Or had he been there for days or weeks without his having seen him before?

The next morning Hansen was at the office early. On his walk in he had seen no sign of his companion, or anyone else. He began to question whether it was his paranoid imagination after all, or whether they were cleverer than he thought.

Inside there was a buzz of activity, with clerks and secretaries running hither and thither. He made his way calmly through this feverish tumult and came upon Giesler, who waved at him frantically.

'Schönfelder! I need you!'

344

He didn't need to go over, for Giesler was already on his way to him. He took Hansen by the arm and guided him into the nearest office, which was Hansen's own.

'What's going on, sir?' he asked.

'We have had communication only this morning. The night porter took it and shook me out of bed. Rightly so. While you lay slumbering, I have been here preparing...'

'For what?'

'For what, he asks. For the Reichsführer. He is expected within the hour.'

'Why did we have no warning?'

'Security. He is scheduled to stop here on his way to see Generalfeldmarschall Kesselring at Monte Cassino. He wants an update on our progress. I shall need you to sit in on the meeting to take notes.'

'Yes, sir.'

'Order some coffee. Real coffee. And cake. He has a sweet tooth.'

Giesler flew out again, issuing more orders as he strode off down the corridor. He was in his element.

Hansen did as he was instructed, but as he made arrangements he couldn't help repeating it to himself. Himmler. Himmler was coming, and he would be but feet away from him. There was no time to seek instruction from Thurso, but he sensed he knew what he would say. Observe, note everything and report. If he was on his way to Monte Cassino, he might be carrying orders for the Italian front. But as he considered, the memories of Dachau and what he had seen invaded his thoughts. The skeletons showing through the skin of the prisoners. The beatings. The squalor. The deaths. And this man, the man who would be standing so close, was responsible.

The time passed quickly, and he found himself standing to attention as the door to the meeting room opened and Giesler walked in, closely followed by a small man. Surprisingly small. A black SS uniform, his hair closely cropped, a tightly trimmed moustache and round glasses. There was no mistaking Hitler's closest ally.

Himmler nodded brusquely to him, or rather at him, as Giesler introduced them, and then Hansen took his seat and busied himself with his pen.

'I am glad to see you again, Giesler. I think the last time was at Posen last year, was it not?'

'Yes, Herr Reichsführer. A day never to be forgotten. The power of your speech was extraordinary. You held us all in the palm of your hand.'

'You flatter me, Giesler. Sadly I do not see the progress I would like. But it is only a matter of time, after all. The work we are doing will be seen as so important by future generations. I am determined to see it through, come what may.'

'I wholeheartedly agree, sir. We cannot turn back now when we have made such progress. Only when every Jew and Jewess on this continent is swept away can we secure the future. It is, as you said then, the solution to our struggle. The final solution.'

'You are a party loyalist to the core, Giesler. The Führer would be proud to hear it. And that is why I need you here. Now, tell me how things are progressing.'

Hansen wrote down what he heard. And what he heard turned his stomach. Over coffee and French cigarettes, these men casually discussed the euthanasia of thousands. Strategies for driving prisoners to their deaths through overwork or starvation. The means by which they could carry out summary justice. It was calculated, cold-blooded murder. And on unimaginable scale. What made it intolerable to hear was the manner in which it was discussed. Not with hate or anger. But with simple, logistical calculation. And Himmler even joked while they did so. The thin, tooth-clenched smile between drags on his cigarette.

Hansen's head began to spin. The oppressive heat in the room, the stale smoke in the air and the words he was scratching onto his notebook made him nauseous. Finally, when he could feel it welling up in his throat and he knew he could no longer suppress it, he stood up in a sudden movement that made Giesler and Himmler freeze and look at him.

'Are you quite well?' said Himmler, the smile sliced across his lips once more.

With a muttered apology, Hansen ran out. Into the corridor. Into his office. He slammed the door, threw open the window and gulped at the cold air rushing in.

He took some moments to steady himself. Whichever way he looked now, he could see the girl's face. Beate.

It has to mean something, he thought to himself. *That life. That short life.*

He fell into his chair and instinctively his hand went to his heart, where he carried the small folding picture in his jacket pocket. He had concealed it from Thurso. The one link to who he had been before he became Schönfelder. He felt compelled to help all those Himmler would hurt. But would he have ordered the attack on the train if it had just been about that?

He got to his feet again and, in doing so, his hand went to his holster. He had never imagined himself using a gun again. His hand could barely touch it. And yet…

Hansen returned to the meeting room and found Himmler alone. He was leafing through documents. Lists of people.

'Ah, feeling better?'

The smile again.

'Herr Giesler has had to attend to an urgent matter. While we are waiting, would you be so kind as to get me some coffee and another slice of that delicious Prinzregententorte.'

Hansen stepped across to the table, his back to Himmler, and poured the coffee. His hand began to shake as he contemplated what he might do. What he surely must do.

'Try not to spill any,' chuckled Himmler.

Hansen placed the cup and plate down and backed away. His hand brushed his holster again, and he tensed. What would come next? Panic. He would be detained. Shot, probably.

'Shall we have some music?'

Himmler had moved to the gramophone in the corner, and shortly afterwards came the strains of Schubert. Symphony No. 4. It had always been a favourite of Sebastian's, and of his father.

Himmler had returned to the table and was humming along as he scratched through the names on his list and added amendments in blood-red ink.

Time was running out. Hansen released the strap on the holster and gripped the stock. He curled his fingers around it, but his muscles tightened and burned. As he tried to grip it, his fingers became numb. He found he couldn't even detach them from the weapon, and at last he had to shake his hand clear. It was impossible.

Himmler continued writing, unknowing.

Sweat trickled down Hansen's back and he leafed through his notes as a distraction, wiping the perspiration from his top lip. His eyes cast around the room, flicking from vases to bronze sculptures, to the poker by the fire. Himmler's neck was now bent over the table as he scrutinised the document. It would be so easy to strike it, or to put his hands around it and squeeze. Perhaps there would be time to leave the building? To run and hide, and live. But what did it matter? The world would be served better by trading his life for this man. Like an exchange in a game of chess. A pawn for a queen.

He had almost made up his mind when his hand went again to the portrait photo in his pocket. He inhaled deeply. If there were the remotest chance that she had escaped. The slightest hope that she might make her way there, to the only place she would know. The only place she would be safe. Then there would be a need. A need to stay free, and to stay alive.

And as he thought about Emily, the time to act trickled away. Giesler returned, and the meeting went on as before.

With Himmler safely on his way to Italy, Hansen considered his actions. A chance had been lost. A chance to make a difference to the war. He had no wish to take a life, any life. Perhaps now he was incapable of it. But he could not regret his choice. As he settled into the driver's seat and turned towards the Peterhausen road, all he could picture was the summer's day, so many years ago, when she had followed him to Germany. To see her smiling, understanding face then had been the most wonderful, the most unexpected, but the most perfect thing. It had been the moment when he could no longer imagine life without her.

As he made the turn past the Englischer Garten, a Daimler was visible in the wing mirror, keeping close behind.

Chapter 18

Emily knocked hesitantly at the door. After some moments there were footsteps on the wooden floor and the door was flung open. A plump, grey-haired woman beamed at her, without the least suggestion of surprise in her expression. Emily had come to know Gerda well during their visits over the years, and to admire Richard's aunt profoundly. She had a warmth and a love for all that had remained unchanged despite the challenges of life.

Wrapped in filthy blankets and wearing nothing but soggy slippers on her feet, Emily was all too aware of how she must appear. Though Gerda, as ever, feigned not to notice.

'My dear, come inside. All of you.'

She did seem a little surprised that Emily was not alone, but again, she hid it well.

'Sit by the fire. You must be frozen.'

Emily translated for Mira, and the three of them seated themselves in front of the roaring log fire. The warmth of it was glorious, and Emily's hands stung as the numbness began to recede.

'Are you Italian?' said Gerda, switching to that language as she spoke to Mira, who nodded.

'Richard told me you might come,' she continued. 'He asked that I take care of you if you did. Not that he had to ask, of course!'

'You've seen him?' said Emily.

'Yes. He's been here.'

'How did he know I would come?'

Gerda seemed not to hear the question and went towards the kitchen.

'I imagine you're pretty hungry. I shall bring some food. One of the benefits of living on a farm – there's plenty to eat!'

In moments she had returned with a tray full of food. There was a jug of fresh milk, bread, cheese, sausage, a rich potato salad and sauerkraut. Emily had never got the taste for this last item, but she was so hungry, and they fell ravenously upon the food.

There was silence for some minutes, with only the sound of chewing. But even though she was famished, it quickly became difficult to eat more, and Emily sat back, satisfied. Sometime later Mira did the same, though Beatrice continued picking at the food while they watched.

'Thank you,' said Emily.

'A pleasure, my dear. It's so good to be able to share what we have.'

Emily felt her eyelids grow heavy and, though she knew it was impolite, she leaned back in the chair and rested her head on the wing back.

'Now, little one…' said Gerda.

'Beatrice,' explained Mira.

'Little Beatrice,' continued Gerda. 'Would you like to help me feed the animals? There are ducks and hens and cows.'

Beatrice looked a little nervous, but after some reassurance from Mira, she agreed to go, if they went together. Mira turned to Emily.

'I think I shall stay here and rest, if you don't mind,' she said. 'You two go with Gerda. Have fun.'

As the door closed behind them, Emily allowed her eyes to close. Just for a moment, she told herself. Just for a moment.

When she opened them again, it was dark, and Gerda was sitting in the chair opposite, her fingers moving quickly with a click-clack sound as she knitted. Emily raised herself, stiff, but warm, finding a blanket laid carefully over her. The dirty rag which had been wrapped around her, concealing the yellow badge, was gone.

'Hello, my dear,' said Gerda, peering over her glasses. 'The others have gone to bed. We didn't like to wake you. I am making some mittens for little Beatrice. She told me she doesn't have any. I will make some other things for you as well. It gets so cold here at this time of year.'

She had made no mention of their prisoner uniforms, the yellow Stars of David, or their sudden arrival.

'You must be wondering at our appearance,' said Emily. 'And who Mira and Beatrice are.'

'I must admit that I am curious,' said Gerda. 'Though first, you must know that you are welcome here. We will conceal you for as long as you need. You are family. So there is no need to explain anything if you don't wish to.'

Emily related, as briefly as she could, the story of the last few years. How she came to be in Italy, their capture and escape. Although it was not the whole story. When she was finished, Gerda got up slowly and came over to her. She bent down and embraced Emily warmly.

'I remember when we first met,' she said. 'You came here to find Richard. The day he told us about Sebastian. Not a day I shall ever forget.

'You were here in a foreign country, because you knew it was the right thing. To be here for him. It was so brave. And now, again. A strength I know I don't have.'

Perhaps it was the exhaustion, or the comfortable position she was in, but Emily felt the need to confide.

'I don't feel it,' she said. 'All I know is that no matter how much I try, I have failed. I tried to hold my family together, and here we are, broken. I've given everything I can, given up my own needs, but everything I've fought for is lost.

'My brother is lost. I could never give back all the support and love he showed me. Gabriella, who gave her life to protect us, while I only watched. And my father, who tried to make amends, when I could only hold on to the anger I had for him. And Richard...

'It feels so pointless. I'm so tired of trying, so tired of failing. And mostly I'm just tired. And...'

She paused, unsure whether to go on.

'And... and I have been sick. I have felt sick every day, lately...'

Gerda looked at her quizzically.

'You're not well?'

'No, I'm well enough.'

'Oh, I see,' said Gerda.

She held her close again.

'You know. You say you are not strong. But I think those two upstairs would disagree. And I have always thought strength is not in the success we have, is it? But in the persistence to try. And sometimes, to just hold on. We never know what will happen then.

'After Sebastian died, I felt like giving in, but if I had, I would never have seen Richard again, or met you. You have always been like a daughter to me, and that won't change.'

'Thank you, Gerda,' said Emily, burying her face in her shoulder. 'I've felt so alone. But you are kind. You always have been. Though you must know what happened between me and Richard. We will leave before he returns, I promise.'

'Don't make any hasty decisions, my dear,' said Gerda. 'Things look different in the morning. Why don't you come upstairs, and I'll find you a room?'

Emily agreed, and they went up together. As they passed along the hall, she pointed to the room where Mira and Beatrice were sleeping. Then she indicated another room and pushed the door open.

As Emily went inside ahead of Gerda, she noticed a case on the side and some other things that clearly belonged to a man. She went to the wardrobe and opened the door to find suits hanging. As she drew close to the clothes, she smelled a warm, familiar, reassuring scent that excited and saddened her in equal measure.

'I can't stay here,' said Emily, turning round. 'I don't mean to be ungrateful…'

'Now, Richard isn't going to mind,' said Gerda. 'And there aren't any other rooms.'

Emily sat down reluctantly on the bed. Gerda went to the door, but before she closed it, she turned back.

'Not that it is my place to interfere,' she said, with a sapient little smile. 'But if you were to open that case, you might be surprised by what you find. And if he asks, you can always blame me.'

'No, I can't,' said Emily.

Gerda simply gave a meaningful nod and then closed the door. But it felt now like an intrusion, however close they had once been, to go through his things.

Emily pulled back the bedclothes, and as she climbed in, for a moment it was like being back in their shared bedroom. Not in Exeter, where the memories were too raw, but in Oxford, where they were of contentment. A closeness she had never known before or since.

She glanced across at the case. Without Gerda, she would have left it untouched, but now curiosity began to overpower her. She lay back on the pillow, but the more she tried not to, the more she pondered on what could be in there. At last, she gave in, swung out of bed and went across to the dresser. After a moment's hesitation she flicked the catches and opened it.

Inside, tucked into the lid and the pockets around the sides, were dozens – no, hundreds – of letters. They were bound up with ribbon. She picked one at random. On the envelope, unmistakably in Richard's writing, was her name. Nothing more. No address, just her name.

Emily pushed the letters back and returned to the bed. It was surely an invasion of privacy to go on. But, she thought, they were addressed to her.

She sat for a moment just looking at the case. Weighing the possibilities. Remembering. Several times she reached out but pulled back once again.

Then, finally, curiosity overcame her qualms, and she pulled out a package of letters.

I'll just have a look at one, she told herself. *Otherwise I shall never sleep.*

She took the first letter and opened the envelope. The letter inside was written in carefully formed script – not his hurried work writing, but something much more considered. It was dated 24 January 1941. Her birthday.

Dearest Emily,

I thought so much about you today, on your special day. I wondered how you might be celebrating. Hoping you are enjoying every moment. Today I completed my training. I am both anxious and excited for my first assignment. Anxious because of what it means to go to serve my country again, and the importance of what we must do, but excited because it brings me a step closer to you. Whether you will ever forgive me, I do not know. I pray that you will (and you know I am not religious, so it is as much a surprise to me to write that as I'm sure it is to you – and God, should he exist). I have no expectation that we will be reunited. To tell you the wish I made on my own birthday would prevent it coming true. But if I could hear you say that you forgive me, even if that were all you should say, then all would be well.

And know that I shall always love you.

Richard

Emily let the letter drop from her fingers. She put a hand to her chest and felt for her heartbeat, which began to race. She felt like screaming, though from joy or frustration, it was difficult to know. She caught herself and stifled the noise with a hand over her mouth.

Greedily she looked for more letters and began to order them by date. Then she read, and read, and read. It was impossible to stop. With each letter she looked for more reassurance. She still doubted his feelings. But most of all, she wanted to hear his thoughts again for the first time in uncounted years. His honesty on paper was what she had been longing for, though it was painful too, to know that he had kept all this from her.

The date of the letters jumped. A period in September 1939 was missing. When she read on, it became clear why. While she had been waiting for him to come, he had been languishing in the place he had most feared he would end up. And all the time unaware of her own letter. She wrenched at the bedclothes in frustration and sorrow, remembering how Mira had pleaded with her to write again.

With each page she felt closer and closer to him. There he was once more – the man she had known, open again and full of love. Love, and regret.

At last she reached the most recent letter, containing descriptions of a place that he would not name.

> *In seeing her I felt everything again that I had experienced before, each time we lost our child. That shock, that utter desolation. And again I was powerless. Powerless then to help you, to take away your grief. And powerless to help her now. And for fear of hurting you more, I let go of you.*

Emily lay down on the bed, clutching the letters, as the pale dawn approached beyond the window. Amongst the joy and the sadness was still anger, and one question above all others. Why? Why hadn't he told her then? Why had he allowed her to leave?

As she lay in a storm of conflicting emotion, there was a gentle knock on the door.

'Good morning!' said Gerda brightly. Then, with a concerned look, 'Have you been up all night?'

Emily could do little more than nod slightly.

'I don't know what's in those letters,' said Gerda. 'But I know some of what Richard told me. How do you feel?'

'I don't know,' said Emily, with all honesty. 'I think I understand… but so much time has passed. I don't even know what I would say to him if I saw him again. And with everything that has happened…'

'Why don't you come down and have some breakfast? And we ought to find you some new clothes. Let's take one thing at a time.'

Emily agreed, and after a quick wash she joined Mira and Beatrice at the kitchen table. Mira gave her a sideways look as she helped Beatrice to some bread and honey.

'Are you alright, Emmy? Did you sleep?'

'Not really,' she said, making light of it. 'I think I had too long a nap yesterday.'

'I think you are all tired,' said Gerda. 'You can rest here for as long as you wish. Have plenty to eat, get some warm clothes. It's just what you need.'

'It's very kind of you,' said Mira.

'Not at all. It's nice to have a full house again. Normally it is just my husband and me. He is on one of his fishing trips. I never know where he gets to, leaving me here to look after things on the farm.'

'We can help now,' said Mira. 'We have a farm… or… *had* a farm, I suppose.'

'Thank you,' said Gerda.

'I miss it,' continued Mira, with a dreamy kind of look coming over her. 'I know I complained, but it was a beautiful place, wasn't it? I used to roll down the hill in the orchard when I was little. And Father would tell me off for getting all muddy. Or Toto would… I'm sorry.' She wiped a tear from her cheek. 'Silly of me. But I haven't known anything else. And I miss it.

'I would go back, you know… if I could. I would milk the goat that always kicks me. I would clean out the chickens. I'd stop all my foolish dreams of being a doctor… I would. If I could go back there. Go back there and be safe.'

'Farming is a good life,' said Gerda kindly. 'But there is a world beyond, you know. One which I care not to look at for now. But one day perhaps it will be worth seeking again, especially for young people like you. And there will be plenty of help needed then, that's for sure. And they will need doctors. And I have an idea that you will do much more good there than in a place like this.'

'Maybe one day I can do that,' said Mira. 'If we get to England. But in any case there are always other ways to help people.'

She smiled at Emily and then went back to her breakfast. Emily sat next to her quietly and put her arm around her sister.

'Why do you say that we're going to England?' asked Emily after a time.

'I don't know, I just assumed,' said Mira. 'You know, because of Richard…'

'Don't assume!' said Emily suddenly, feeling the weariness and the anxiety return. 'We can't just click our heels.'

She got up from the table and went to the stove to fetch some coffee, feeling Mira's confusion as she did so. She regretted snapping at her, when dreams were so important to Mira – the fragile hopes and silly fantasies that sustained her. Silly fantasies like reuniting with Richard. They couldn't fly away from all their problems on the wings of those dreams.

Later, after they finished eating, Emily dried the dishes, lost in her thoughts, as Gerda washed up.

'Oh!' said Gerda in surprise. 'There's someone coming down the driveway.'

Emily broke out of her thoughts and craned to look at where Gerda was pointing. A figure was walking determinedly down the long track towards the house. 'Are you expecting anyone else?' she asked, peering at the figure to try and make him out.

'No,' said Gerda. 'I'm not expecting anyone. The only person it could be is Richard.'

Emily began to fidget and pace around the kitchen. She had hoped to have more time. More time, as though five years were not enough. She wanted so much to see him again. But there was fear too. A fear that perhaps she had changed. Changed so much that he would regret everything he had written. Gerda guided her into the sitting room to the others.

'What's going on?' asked Mira, noting Emily's agitation.

'My nephew is coming down the driveway,' said Gerda.

'Go out and meet him, Emmy,' Mira said gently, taking her sister's hand. 'We'll stay here. It's alright, Bea,' she whispered to her niece, who had begun to fidget at Emily's departure. Emmy will be back soon.' Emily turned to go out into the garden alone, when she realised with a jolt that she was still wearing her prison uniform. She looked down at herself and then at Gerda in horror.

'It will be alright, my dear,' said Gerda. 'The garden is hidden. And he will understand.'

Gerda guided her firmly out of the door, and as she paced anxiously on the path, she squinted at the trees that concealed the driveway from the garden. It was these trees that had hidden Richard from her so many years ago as, their places reversed, she had been making her way up the driveway. Then, she had been running as fast as she could, fearful of what she would find.

She considered twenty different ways to greet him – from a simple hello to a kiss, and everything in between – but nothing seemed right. It felt as awkward, after all this time, as the meeting with her father had been. The two things were more similar than she liked to think. Being left alone in the world to fight for herself had been the pattern of her life. Like the trees, she had grown and endured, but there was something, too, in their bare branches that felt kindred. Bitterness and anger were real, though she tried to suppress them. And there were other factors now too. How would she explain everything that had happened… and what might yet happen? At last she heard footsteps on the gravel and turned to look. Gradually, a figure dressed in black rounded the tree line. Emily noted the Nazi uniform and insignia of the SS. She had suspected from his letters – as much from what he had not said as what he had – that he was involved in something dangerous and covert. Nevertheless, the uniform made her uneasy. He seemed to be scanning his surroundings, perhaps for signs of being followed.

In her nervousness Emily almost called out to him, but then, as he turned back to face her for the first time, she saw with a shock that it was not Richard at all. Similarly blonde-haired, this man had a sharper, more weaselish look about him.

On seeing her, and the dirty prisoner uniform she was still wearing, with a half-hidden star of David, he ran towards her and drew his gun.

'Who are you?' he asked, in German. 'What are you doing here, Jew?'

Emily froze with fear, unable to move or speak, the barrel of the gun coming closer and closer. He was within a yard or two now. His eyes narrowed.

'You are one of those who escaped from the train. What is your name?'

Emily opened her mouth, but as she began to steady herself, she decided the only option was to buy time for the others to run. She would wait it out and give nothing away. Though she knew what would happen. Gerda would get Mira and Beatrice to safety – she hoped – if they were watching. But one more thought ran through her mind, that she would never get to say goodbye – to them, or to Richard.

'I will ask one more time,' said the man, growing frustrated.

Then, with still no answer, he raised his gun and cocked it.

As he levelled it to aim at her head, Emily held her breath, waiting for the inevitable.

Then a shot rang out.

Emily flinched, her eyes closed tight, waiting for the end.

But it didn't come. Emily found her breath caught in her throat, and, with difficulty, she made herself gulp the air, the moment broken. Her head pounded with the thumping of her heart, and it took all her strength to open her eyes. Once she had, she could not draw them away from the body now lying sprawled across the ground, blood pooling around the gaping hole in his head, shards of skull and flesh spattered across the muddy earth.

She heard a sound and looked around. There, another figure – dressed in the same black uniform, dark like the souls of those who wore them – pointing his gun at her, or rather, past her. This time it was the face she expected. He gripped his gun in both hands, which were shaking uncontrollably. He dropped his arms and let the gun fall to the ground with a clatter.

Richard was translucently pale, such that the veins seemed to show in his cheeks. His eyes were fixed on the man on the ground in the way hers had been. It was a look she had seen before, after the last war. But now she understood that feeling, and shared it.

He looked up at her at last and gazed, without speaking, for some moments. He studied her face, and as he did so, a memory seemed to play across his mind, which gave rise to the flicker of a smile. Was it, she wondered, the same memory as hers – the moment, in this place, so many years before, when they had known each other's feelings for the first time. Neither of them seemed to want to break the spell.

After what might have been minutes, or only seconds, they were finally interrupted by Beatrice, who had appeared from the house and now ran to Emily, throwing her arms around her legs and holding on tightly.

'Mama!' she cried, burying her head in Emily's thin dress.

Richard looked from Emily to Beatrice and back again. He looked confused. Scared, even. Emily began to form the explanation in her mind, but something stopped her. Instead she remained silent, and simply put her arm around Beatrice to calm her.

Richard stooped for a moment to pick up his gun and, with an automatic movement, put it away in his holster, his eyes looking to the sky. She fancied she saw him close them briefly and take a deep breath before he turned back to her and walked towards them.

Richard held his hand out, and she took it unthinkingly. As on that cold day when they had first met, when her hands were chilled to the bone, the warmth of him shocked her. And as it was then, the reassurance in such a small gesture was enormous.

He smiled, though she could tell it was forced, and bent down to Beatrice.

'Hello there,' he said, in English.

To hear his voice again, so soft and warm, was almost painful. Beatrice backed away behind her and lost herself in the folds of her skirt.

'No! You're a bad man!' said Beatrice.

Mira came running out and took the child's hand.

'He's not a bad man, Bea,' she said. 'You mustn't be afraid. He's the knight. You remember? The one I said would come to rescue us.'

Emily winced to hear it, and hoped Richard would not understand what she was saying. Mira brought Beatrice out from under her skirts and held her hand out for Richard to shake.

'I am Mira,' she said, now in English. 'I am Emmy's sister. Half-sister, that is.'

'Richard,' he replied. He added no more. What had she expected him to say?

He and Mira chatted lightly, though Emily heard no more. She continued to glance at him, and he at her, as Mira guided them all inside, away from the brutal scene on the lawn.

Inside, Richard embraced his aunt warmly and they exchanged a few quiet words. Richard looked back out of the window and paced uneasily. Emily scrutinised his hands and found no ring on his finger. Hers, too, was gone, but for different reasons. They all sat down as they had the evening before, and Gerda took Richard by the hand and made him sit, too.

'It's not so surprising that Beatrice was afraid of you,' said Emily at last. 'Wearing that uniform.'

As she heard herself speak, she wondered at her own coldness. The part of her that wished only to embrace and kiss him was put aside, and it was a part of herself that she hardly recognised that came to the fore now.

He looked down at his uniform, almost shamefully.

'It's not what you think,' he said.

'How did you know we would be here?' she cut in, not allowing him to continue.

'I can't tell you,' he replied.

'No,' she replied. 'As ever.'

For his part, he kept looking down at her clothes. It made her self-conscious.

'The attack on the train? That was you, wasn't it?' said Mira, jumping in on the awkward silence.

'Friends of mine,' said Richard, smiling. 'I'm only glad it worked. Are you…' He glanced across at Emily. 'Are you alright?'

'We are,' said Mira, though with a significant pause as she tried not to look across at her sister. 'I think we are.'

'Good,' said Richard. 'Good. But now I must go. And so must you. I will make arrangements.'

'Go where?' said Mira.

'Switzerland. There are people who can take you there and get you across the border. It won't be safe here now. They will be looking for… him.'

Richard stood again and looked out of the window. Emily saw the look in his eyes again and wanted more than anything to hold him and bring him comfort. But she held back once more.

Richard took his leave and went outside. Mira looked over, her jaw hanging, and mouthed 'go after him' at Emily. Emily followed, though with each step it was as if a weight were holding her down.

She could see Richard struggling to lift the body. The thought of going near it repelled her, but she went to help him anyway. They lifted it together and took it to the barn, where they dropped it onto a pile of hay and covered it.

'Thank you,' he said.

After a moment he took out his gun and laid it on a straw bale.

'Take this. In case you need it. I will ask some people to meet you – at the church in the village. They'll use a code word: broadsword. Then you'll know you can trust them.'

He nodded slowly and meaningfully.

'Take care.'

At this he turned to go.

'Are you coming back?' said Emily, softly now, experiencing an unexpected wave of tenderness.

'No. I can't. There's still work to do. And I must make sure of your escape.'

His blue eyes glistened as he looked, and he edged towards her. All the love she still felt for him came bubbling up again and she almost trembled in anticipation. He reached out gently to caress her cheek.

Suddenly, any momentary tenderness was gone, and she found herself reeling away, a darkness filling her thoughts with unasked-for memories of a dank, putrid Italian cell and a sickeningly gentle Nazi soldier. She shivered with a clamminess that filled all her veins. Dirty, squalid and soiled. She couldn't help it. Involuntarily she squirmed away, and as she looked back at him, Richard was in shock.

Reassurance was there for the taking, in those arms. She wished she knew how to open up to him, but in her shame she rejected it all. Rejected him.

'I'm sorry,' he said, embarrassed. 'I don't know what I was thinking.'

He turned again to go, and, dizzy with the volatility of her emotions, she was furious again.

'That's it?!' she cried. 'After all this. After all this time, you're just going to leave?'

'What do you expect me to do, Emily?'

'I want to know why.'

'You have your family. You need to look after them. And I... I have my duty to do.'

'Then why come here at all?'

'Because I wanted to protect you. I always have, from the moment we met. You know that. And because—'

But she cut across him. 'When I was little more than a child. I told you then, I've always looked after myself, because that's all there was. You don't need to protect me from the world. You can't.'

The memories of the cell came again, fresh and vivid.

'Would you rather I let you suffer?'

'How would I know the difference?'

Richard's eyes shone again, as if holding back a flood, and he nodded sadly.

'You're right. Of course you are.' He nodded again and tried to smile. 'So this is for the best.'

As Richard closed the barn door behind him, Emily felt a wave of grief, for all that had happened to her – to them both – and all that was left unsaid, that she couldn't say. She fell onto the bale and clutched it in a desperate embrace, her hands gripping the straw and squeezing until she had no more strength to give.

Chapter 19

Hansen let the barn door fall closed behind him and shuffled away towards the farmhouse. Whatever he had expected – a reunion, an understanding, a reconciliation – in his mind's eye, it had not been like this.

Gerda was outside, spraying the garden with a hose, but not to water the plants – to wash away the consequences of what he had done.

'Richard, my dear. How is she?'

'Angry.'

She dropped the hose and took his hands.

'I'm sorry.'

'Will you go with them to the village?' he asked. 'My people will meet them there. They need to leave here…'

'Of course I will.'

'And so do you, though I know you will say no.'

'I'm too old. They won't touch me. What have they to accuse me of?'

'They don't need a reason, Auntie.'

'Your uncle is respected hereabouts. They won't hurt us.'

He took hold of her arms and looked with meaning into her eyes.

'I can't be sure it wasn't him.'

'What do you mean?'

'I can't be sure that it wasn't him who had them follow me.'

'Your uncle doesn't know you're here.'

'Yes. Yes, he does.'

'Well, even so. How can you think he would do that? You are his nephew…'

'And perhaps he has never really forgiven me. Or perhaps it's just the disease that is infecting this country –perhaps it has infected him too.'

'You're not making any sense, Richard. You know he loves you, though he may not show it. I know him – there is no anger left there.'

'I've seen what is happening…'

He told her, sparing the details as much as he could. What he had seen and heard at Dachau, and from Himmler. She dropped onto a garden chair and put her apron to her face.

'I'm sorry. I didn't want to tell you.'

'Poor Emily. To think she might have gone there. To that place.'

He bowed his head. 'Wear it lightly.'

She looked at him questioningly.

'Something Papa always said. When we have power, we have a duty to others. To use it with care. To use strength as a shield, not a sword. And then I see what is happening here. I loved this country, once…'

'And you must not stop,' she said, hugging him tightly. 'Never stop. You saw it back then, after everything that happened in the first war. We were grieving and suffering, and looking for someone or something to rescue us. It is a kind of madness.'

She gently prodded him with one finger.

'People who are hurting can do the wrong things for the right reasons. It will pass. And there is only one thing that will heal all of this hurt in the end.' She placed her hand over her heart.

'I must go,' he said finally.

'Will they not be looking for you now?'

'Probably.'

In the village he placed a telephone call from the café while the proprietor watched him. The arrangements were made. Then, in the car, Hansen busied himself in copying out all of his notes from the meeting with Himmler and every other piece of information he had gleaned, including what had happened at the farm. He parcelled them up and was about to leave them in the usual way when it occurred to him that it may no longer be secure. Instead, he took a chance. He scrawled an address on the envelope, stamped it and left it in a remote post box. Not for the first time, he was gambling with his life, and others'.

In Munich he made his way back to the office, but before he entered, he took the folded photo frame from his pocket. He kissed it gently. 'I'm sorry,' he whispered, and then dropped the photograph into a litter bin.

He looked up at the office building and took a deep breath. Then, with a confident stride, he made his way in. As the doors opened he could see whispered conversations at the desk, and then a guard stood before him.

'One moment, please, sir.'

'What is this?'

'Herr Giesler wishes to see you.'

'Very well.'

He turned in the direction of the lifts, but the guard stopped him.

'Not that way, sir.'

As he wheeled around, he found another guard behind him, and his arm was crushed forcefully against his back.

He was pushed through a door he had never noticed before, and then down drab corridors. It seemed to get colder as they continued downwards into a basement, and finally he was led into a small room with only a table and two chairs. He was pushed into one of the chairs and his hands were handcuffed behind him. Then he was left alone.

After some time the door opened again and Giesler came in, alone. He sat down in the chair opposite and pulled out some cigarettes. He lit one, then pushed the pack towards Hansen.

'Would you like one?'

'I am a little tied up at the moment,' he replied.

Giesler did not smile.

'I will remove the cuffs, and give you a cigarette, if you tell me your name.'

'What do you mean?' said Hansen, attempting to bluff it out. 'You know my name, sir.'

Giesler drew on his cigarette and blew a line of smoke gently in the air. Then, in a sudden movement, the smoke dissipated as he spat into Hansen's face. His control broke and he slammed his hands down onto the table, pushing his face close to Hansen.

'Tell me your name!'

Hansen remained still and waited. Giesler regained his temper and sat back again.

'I have suspected you for some time, *Schönfelder*,' he said pointedly. 'But only of cheating on my daughter. For that I would have cut your throat, of course, but then you were seen. Not only with another woman, but in the act of murdering one of my men. This is not something an adulterer does, Schönfelder, is it?'

Hansen again said nothing.

'But it *is* something a spy does. So, you see, I know what you are – and, in time, I will know who you are. And we will have your accomplice too. I have ordered her to be detained at once. And she will talk, even if you will not. I'm sure you would wish no more harm to come to her than is absolutely necessary, and I am a gentleman, as you know. But, of course, things do happen, especially when soldiers are bored and away from home.' He paused ominously. 'So, I ask you again: what is your name?'

Hansen looked around him at the room, which was without windows or any other features, except for the one door. He decided on another strategy. To stonewall. To give away nothing at first, then only useless and out of date information. They would break him eventually, he knew that, but whatever time he could buy – hours, minutes even – would help Emily and the others to get away.

'Richard Hansen,' he said at last. 'Lieutenant-Colonel. Service number 5661789.'

Giesler flicked ash from his cigarette.

'You are British?'

'Richard Hansen. Lieutenant-Colonel. Service number 5661789.'

'You are a spy, Colonel… Hansen. You are not entitled to the provisions of the Geneva Convention.'

Giesler got up from his chair and went over to open the door. A huge army sergeant came in. He had to bow his head as he passed through the doorway and dragged his arms in a fashion that reminded Hansen of a gorilla.

'I will see you again when we have your associate in custody.'

He nodded to the sergeant and left the room. The soldier pulled out a knuckle duster from his pocket and placed it very particularly on one hand. He drew the arm back so that Hansen could see. With careful misdirection, he swung his other, unseen, hand and smashed him around the side of the head.

It was so unexpected that Hansen took his eye off the sergeant's other hand, such that when it caught him on the cheekbone, it came as a second shock. His head jerked back, and his chair almost toppled over backwards. His skull pounded and a burning pain spread across the side of his face.

As he regained some awareness, he could see the big man simply watching him, expressionless.

'I am an officer,' he told him, his mouth already numb.

Then he felt his head being taken between two huge hands and pulled towards the desk. There was nothing he could do to stop it, and with a horrible inevitability he braced for the impact across his face.

The pain came in the aftermath of the impact, as the hands let go again and he raised his head gingerly. He felt blood flowing across his lips and tasted the ferric bitterness of it. A piece of tooth dislodged in his mouth, and he spat it out onto the table.

His head was wrenched back again, and a fist caught him now in the stomach, driving all breath from his lungs. Then came a second, and a third, this time into the centre of his chest, at the bottom of his ribcage. He heard an audible crack, and he doubled up in pain, the heat of it seeping out across his torso. He caught breath in time to see a swinging arm arch towards his head once again…

When he opened his eyes, he could see nothing. The room was completely black, save for a tiny chink of light at the bottom of the door. The gorilla was gone. His head still ached and as he tried to shift position, a searing pain shot through his chest. His mouth was swollen, and he caught his lips on his teeth as he tried to close it.

The door opened and the light came on once more. Giesler entered and again sat in front of him. He didn't look at him, merely at the papers he was carrying. After a pause of some minutes, he spoke without raising his eyes.

'We shall be able to end this soon, I think. We will have little more use for you, as your comrade has told us everything we need to know.

We had to use some unpleasant methods, of course. I did warn you…'

Hansen's heart pounded and he wanted more than anything to be able to free his hands. They tensed with the anger that flowed through him, but to no avail.

'The only thing we do not know is who else you passed the information on to. If you tell us this, we will allow her some treatment.'

Hansen wrenched the cuffs once more, but this time, as he exerted what was left of his energy, his mind worked. He forced his swollen mouth into a sickly smile.

'You have rather spoiled the peace of our Sunday,' said Hansen. 'We were due to go to church. Perhaps you should go, to repent of your sins.'

'My conscience is clear, Colonel. But is yours?'

Hansen lifted his head once more. He was certain now that this was all an extravagant bluff. If they really did have Emily, they would have seen the Star of David, the little girl too, and her sister – Mira, was it? And yet there was no flicker of reaction at the mention of church.

'You are entitled to know my name, my rank, and my service number,' said Hansen. 'Nothing more.'

'As you wish, Colonel.'

As Giesler got up to go to the door once more and the gorilla returned, Hansen could hear the chime of the church bells. They sounded one o'clock. His weary brain allowed a quick calculation. If everything went to plan, they would need perhaps another eight or nine hours to be over the border. Ten o'clock, then. Hold on until ten o'clock and they would be safe. Emily would be safe. One last duty, and he was determined that he would see it through.

Then the blows came again and he clenched his teeth, trying to take his thoughts away from the pain and the blood that streamed down his face. He fixed on a poem that he had read once. It had been one that Emily had come upon after her first miscarriage. She had found something in it, and though she had tried to hide the book from him, he had read it secretly. He repeated it to himself now, over and over.

Though they go mad they shall be sane,

Though they sink through the sea they shall rise again;

Though lovers be lost love shall not;

And death shall have no dominion.

When he raised his head again, it was to the sound of the church bells chiming three. There were two soldiers there now. One held him down onto the table while the other crossed behind him. They had stripped his shirt away, and he could feel the cold of the air on his bruised and broken skin. The pain had been constant but bearable, but now came something new.

The soldier behind him was holding something, something that sizzled and smoked. Then he felt it make contact with the base of his spine, and it burned, burned like his whole body was on fire. It overtook everything and left him quivering and limp. An inconceivable, overwhelming agony that didn't allow for any thought or any feeling but pain. Then the heat was removed, but the burning remained. He raised himself slowly and looked the soldier in the eye. He was searching for something. Some sign that these were men who thought and felt as he did. He told himself it was to find weakness, to build rapport, as he had been taught. But really he was looking for hope. Then the light faded, and everything was black once more.

When he came to, he was again held back by arms of iron, but this time it was to inject him with a hypodermic syringe.

'What are you giving me?' he tried to ask, though his words were muffled and indistinct.

'Don't worry, Colonel. This is just a little something to make you more cooperative,' said Giesler. He took his seat opposite and signalled for the others to leave.

'You know, I did like you,' he continued.

Hansen watched him, his face a blank but for the occasional shiver, as he tried desperately to hold the agony in check.

'You must be in a lot of pain.' There was almost sympathy in his expression, though it rang exceedingly hollow.

'You did persuade me, I'll admit it. You were good at your job, and I had *almost* decided that you would be a good husband for Lieselotte. So you should be proud to have got that far. Now, though, you really needn't carry on. It's all a grand game. There doesn't have to be any malice in it, does there? You did what you were required to do, and I am doing the same.

'We can make things easier for you. But only if you tell us what we need to know. I know you want to tell us. To get it off your chest. It is hard work to lie so much, isn't it? To know that you are lying to everyone, even those who care for you.'

A feeling of light-headedness began to overtake Hansen. Almost as if he were drunk. He felt compelled to share all the thoughts in his mind. Unchecked. Unfiltered. He balled his hands into fists. No matter the temptation to speak, he stopped himself.

Time ticked by, and he heard the clock outside strike again. Eight, this time.

It was not in character for Giesler to show such patience, and at last he gave up the pretence.

'When Lieselotte learns what you are, she will grow to despise you.'

Hansen watched him, unmoving.

'Or… perhaps I will have to teach her a lesson too. For collaborating with an enemy agent.'

Hansen smiled.

'She knew,' he replied, in a hoarse whisper. 'She knew who I was. And she would have done anything for me. Anything at all…'

He wanted the focus on him. He wanted Giesler to care only about him.

With a surge of anger, Giesler threw the table and kicked it to pieces. He picked up a table leg and brought it down hard on Hansen's shoulder. Again and again he hit him – possessed, manic. It continued until at last the table leg broke, smashed across Hansen's arm with a splintering crack of wood and bone.

Giesler stood back, his rage ebbing. He wiped the sweat from his brow and went to the door. He gave orders, and shortly afterwards they brought in a piece of equipment that looked like a large wooden ring with wire attached to it. They put it around Hansen's neck, then removed the light bulb and plugged the apparatus into the fitting.

'My own invention,' said Giesler. 'If you touch the wire, you will receive a shock of mains electricity. So… as you English say: "chin up, old boy".'

He went out, laughing, and shut the door.

In the darkness of the room, cold and clinical, there was no concept of day or night. Hansen held his head as straight as he was able, though it seemed to spin and droop. He craned to hear the clock strike. He focused everything on that. He tried to lick his lips, cracked and dry, and he could feel his mouth, thick and swollen, though it no longer hurt. Pain was so dispersed now around his body that it had all become one. A throbbing, burning sensation that spread from his arms to the top of his skull. A cold trickle of sweat – or blood – across his forehead.

He took to counting the time as best he could. It was something to occupy his mind. But his eyes were heavy, and a drowsiness overtook him. For a moment he fancied he could see Emily's face, clearly, in front of him.

'I'm sorry,' he heard himself say. 'I'm sorry.'

'We look to the future. Not the past.'

He moved to embrace her, but was ripped bodily back to reality…

His whole torso went taut and his muscles convulsed with the shock that was coursing through him. At last, with supreme effort, he managed to break the connection. He twitched and shivered as the shock died away, feeling at once burning hot and freezing cold.

He focused all his energy on keeping his head up, to stop it touching the wire once more. He pricked his ears for the sound of the clock chimes.

Oh, why wouldn't it strike?

To hear the bells ring out and to know it could be over. He ached to sleep, to lie down, but most of all to hear that sound.

Then – half through a dream, muffled – he heard the chime. He snapped awake, all senses tingling, and he counted. One, or had it been two? Three, four… and on. At last, he counted ten. Or it might have been eleven. But whatever, it was enough. Then, silently, a shaking started through his chest, and slowly, gradually, it erupted into a dry laugh. Almost a cough. And he couldn't stop himself. With each exhalation his ribs ached and his arm throbbed. He had hardly enough voice to be audible, but yet he laughed.

There was the mechanical sound of the door once more, and a light that dazzled his eyes. Giesler stood in front of him, close enough for Hansen to feel his hot breath.

'Colonel,' he said coldly. 'The game is nearly over. Time has run out.'

Hansen merely smiled and nodded.

'It is a shame,' said Giesler. 'To lose.'

'No…' said Hansen, in barely a croak. 'I… am the… shield… not… the… sword.'

Giesler pulled something from his pocket, and when he turned his hands into the light, Hansen could see a thin wire, like a cheese cutter. He held it taut between his hands for a moment, and then he opened it out and Hansen could feel his hands on the back of his neck. The cold of something metallic on his throat. Giesler looked him in the eye for the first time, and then with a flicker of his eyelids, he signalled to an unseen comrade to one side.

There was the scratch of the hypodermic syringe in his arm again.

'We'll give it a moment to take effect,' said Giesler to the other man. 'And then it's all over.'

Chapter 20

Emily fell back onto the bed. The mattress, deep and soft, seemed to envelop her. It was a feeling of utter comfort and, as she lay still, watching the rain stream down the window, there was the sense of a great weight lifted. But nevertheless, though she told herself that she was finally safe, the feeling of fear lingered.

Twice she had reassured herself that the door was locked. But still she found her gaze drawn to it, subconsciously expecting an unknown assailant to enter at any moment. She actively tried to relax but found her muscles tense and her breath caught in her throat.

While Beatrice slept peacefully, Emily paced. Her wakefulness saw the night pass almost unnoticed, though she hardly knew what she had been thinking or feeling during that time.

As she sprinkled some water onto her face, she surveyed the view of mountains from the window, surroundings which made everything doubly unreal. A ski resort, closed due to lack of tourists, reclaimed for refugees like her. The three of them had been given a comfortable, almost luxurious room to share, with the first bath she had seen in months. At any other time it might have been a pleasant holiday.

The future was waiting to be considered, but at this moment, in this peculiar place, it was difficult to imagine what it might look like. A place to live, to work. School for Beatrice in time. Perhaps for Mira, the career she had dreamed of. But there was so much to consider it was overwhelming. And there again was the weight of responsibility. Fear for her life might be in the past, but a fear for their lives would be the future.

Down in the restaurant, Emily sat with Mira as they ate breakfast. Rationed though it was, the food was still more than they had seen, other than at Peterhausen, in ages.

'You look tired, Emmy,' said Mira, when they had finished eating.

'I'm fine. Did you sleep?'

'Not really.'

Mira took Beatrice for a walk. Neither of them seemed to want to break the strange trance that had come upon them since they had arrived. Mira had known better than to ask Emily about the events at the farm, but the glances she continued to make towards her sister on the journey told their own story.

Emily sat by the fire in the lounge and watched the flames dance and jump. She found herself flinching with each crack of the wood and each time she closed her eyes in weariness, she opened them again, afraid of what she might see in her mind's eye.

She had been sitting there for an hour or more when a familiar figure opened the door and came in, scanning the room as if looking for someone. When the little man saw her, his head tilted a touch to one side, and he pushed his round glasses up on his nose. He smiled broadly and came over to her. Crosse put his hand out, and when Emily stood to take it, he pulled her into a warm embrace. She squirmed a little, and, sensing her discomfort, Crosse gently helped her back to her chair.

'I am so glad to see you, Emily,'

'As I am you, Ernie,' she replied. 'And surprised. How is it you come to be here?'

'Oh, well, I'm doing my bit to support the British Embassy here, and when I saw your name, I had to come and find you.'

There seemed a great deal more to it than that, but Emily decided to take his answer at face value.

'They're looking after you?'

'Oh yes. We're very comfortable, thank you.'

Crosse watched her intently, and after a few moments, he removed his glasses to clean them in the way she had seen him do so many times in years gone by. It made her smile.

'I'm glad to see that smile again,' he said. 'I dare say there has been little cause to smile recently?'

Emily drew her legs up onto the chair and wrapped her arms around them.

'You should see the doctor,' he continued. 'Just as a precaution, you understand. It's normal for all new arrivals here. Many of them have had a rough time of it, you know, and it's always good to take care.'

He continued to watch her.

'I'll be around if you need anything.'

He got up to go, but as he put his gloves on, he turned back to her.

'You should talk to someone.'

'About what?' she asked defensively.

'Whatever you wish. You forget, I have seen the difference it can make. And so have you.'

Crosse left her where she was, and the numbness that had suffocated her for the last day or more began to dissipate. Replaced with a powerful regret. There had only been one person in whom she had confided in that way, as Crosse knew well. And any hope that they could speak again had been lost with their parting at the farm. She was reminded again of the proverb Toto had told her. For if it was a sign of age and a weariness with life for regrets to outweigh dreams, then today she felt as old as the world. It seemed hard to think of a future with nowhere to go, no belongings but her borrowed clothes. Whatever strength had carried her through seemed to have vanished, and she could scarcely find the energy to move from her seat.

In time, with no thought or direction, she found her way back to her room and lay down. Mira came in with Beatrice and they sat for a time together.

'What are you thinking about, Emmy?'

'Things I don't want to think about,' she replied, almost absently.

Mira bit her lip and hugged a pillow to herself.

'I know it must be horrible for you,' she said. 'To think of what happened. But you know you couldn't have done anything differently…'

'I could have done everything differently… Everything…'

'He was the enemy,' continued Mira.

Emily looked at her, half-confused, and then realised the misunderstanding. There was so much to regret, but it was the meeting with Richard that she regretted most of all.

'Yes,' said Emily in a flat tone, the emotion gone once again.

Her sister tried to engage her in small talk, but to no avail. At last, Mira went to the door again.

'It's dinnertime, Emmy,' she said.

Emily noticed for the first time that it was dark outside. A whole day had passed without notice.

'I'm not hungry. Can you take Beatrice down?' she asked.

'Of course. I'll bring you something back. Oh, and Emmy…' She looked down at her quickly and then away again. 'You should probably change your clothes. I will find you some towels.'

Mira and Beatrice left their room and as Emily glanced down to where her sister had been looking, she saw a patch of red on the counterpane beneath her. With a shudder there was a sudden explosion of laughter and relief. Not since she was twelve and her mother had explained to her that first time had she been so shocked by it, or so relieved. She wished she could weep with joy, but something stopped her. Her eyes began to sting, but that was all.

She went into the bathroom to clean herself and, as she studied her thin, grey face in the mirror, she wondered again at her reaction. Only so few years ago, it would have been the very opposite of what she had wanted. Was it this that had held her back at the farm? Shame at what had happened? Or fear? Fear of being with child, or that once again it wouldn't last?

As she sat down again with a glass of water, trying to steady herself, there was a sudden knock at the door which made her flinch violently. She had to let her heart return to a normal beat for several moments before she could get up to open it.

Crosse was standing there, sucking nervously on his pipe. She had seldom seen him so worried.

'Emily. Can I come in?'

Emily looked back at the stain on the bed and made an excuse.

'I was just about to go to bed.'

'Oh, I see,' he said, clearly not altogether believing her. 'Well, I'm afraid this won't help your sleep.'

'What is it, Ernie?' she asked, more and more nervous now.

The little man shuffled a little and removed and replaced his spectacles several times.

'I've just heard from our people in Germany.'

She understood his meaning through the pause and held her breath.

'Richard has been captured. He's being held by the Gestapo.'

'I see.'

Emily could feel the tension close her throat and the rising sense of panic that she had come to know. But with it came an embarrassment. She knew only that she wanted to close the door and be alone.

'I would like to offer some cause for optimism,' continued Crosse, oblivious. 'And, of course, we'll do everything we can. But I'm afraid, in these situations… well, it's not looking good. He won't be treated as an enemy combatant, but as a spy, and that only means one thing…'

Emily closed her eyes, desperately trying to maintain some control.

'He did know the risks, and as he always does, he went anyway. I'm so sorry, Emily.'

'Thank you for telling me, Ernie,' she said, barely getting the words out. 'Good night.'

She closed the door on him, trying to block out the world. Light-headedness drove her to the floor, and she let her head fall between her knees as she began to shake. In a cold sweat, she had to let the first waves pass before she could even try to focus on counting. She began to worry that the technique would not work as she started again for the third time with no success. When, finally, she got control of herself, she collapsed to the floor, soaked with perspiration.

In a way, she had grieved for him for the last five years, and now there was no more left to feel. She had lost half a family in that time. Half a marriage. And half of herself.

When she woke the next morning in bed, where she must have been carried, she got dressed straight away and went to the door. Mira climbed out of her own bed and stopped her.

'Emmy, wait, let me come with you.'

'It's fine, Mira,' she said, feigning brightness. 'I have to go to the consulate and sort out our passports. And I must write to the Ashmolean. I think it's unlikely they will still have a job for me after all this time, but, well, I can ask. There's so much to do. Have you thought about what you will do when we get to England?'

'No,' said Mira.

'Well, you should give it some thought. We can't sit around here forever. Will you look after Beatrice?'

'Yes. But Emmy, what about Richard? That man said... I'm worried—'

'Don't be,' she snapped back. 'These things happen. And you have to go on. That's what I'm doing. I'm looking to the future, because we don't think about the past.'

During the day, Emily busied herself in making arrangements. She spoke to the consul about their passports, she wrote numerous letters enquiring for work or about places to stay, and even wrote to their old bank manager.

In the afternoon, she walked around the grounds of the resort. It was pretty, and the sun was shining for the first time since their arrival. The air was cold and crisp, but it was the kind of day she would have relished. Being outside in the cool air

411

had always been a comfort. A place to think and find equilibrium. But now that calm was missing. Instead there was an ongoing agitation, though she fought, as ever, to stay focused on practical things.

Inside she found a few shelves of books in one of the sitting rooms. They included several of her favourite novels, and she did her best to distract herself. Jane Austen had always been a place of comfort and cosiness for her, but she found herself reading and re-reading the same pages over and over, without taking in any of the meaning. Finally, she cast the book aside.

At dinner, Mira watched her carefully as she tried to encourage Beatrice to eat. The little girl was quiet too and could no longer be left to wander happily on her own as she once had. Now she was in constant need of reassurance, something Emily found it hard to give.

'Emmy, I know you're worried. But he will be alright,' she said, though her eyes betrayed her uncertainty.

'We need to get some new clothes, you know,' said Emily, looking sharply at Mira. 'We can't wear the same things Gerda gave us forever. I could make some. I used to do that.'

'Emmy—'

'Mira, don't…'

She looked her in the eye. Emily could feel the tears welling, and were she to continue, it would be impossible to hold back. So she simply shook her head. There was nothing to be gained by falling to pieces now. Not when they were depending on her.

Another day passed in the same way. And then another. And just when Emily felt that perhaps she had control over herself at last, the telephone rang in the evening. It was Ernie.

As she replaced the receiver heavily, she let out the breath she had been holding in a long sigh. This place, the past few days, had been a haze, dreamlike and illusory. Nothing seemed quite real.

The future, she told herself. *Now it is all about the future. Away from this place and everything that has happened.*

Chapter 21

There was a hum at first. A low drone. Then something that sounded like a roar. He felt his body shift a little, pulled by an unseen force. It was at this movement that the pain was ignited once more, down his arm and across his chest. He opened his eyes, and they were stung at once by the bright sunshine. He shut them again instantly. His hands were free now, but on moving his right arm, a shiver of excruciating pain ran down it. He must have cried out, for a voice answered him.

'Alright, old man?'

It was a voice he recognised, but as if calling from another room.

'Tony?'

'You should address me as Oberführer Konrad von Tüllman, special representative of the Führer himself. Or simply "sir" will do.'

He tried to look once more and saw, through watering eyes, the back seat of a car. The voice was coming from the front passenger seat. Thurso twisted around to look at him.

'Do you know how hard it was to get you out of there? But fortunately, it seems you are of personal interest to Hitler. Or so it says here on this complete work of fiction.'

He held out an official-looking letter for Hansen to see. It bore the stamps of German High Command, asking the recipient to render any and all assistance to the bearer of the letter. Signed, *Adolf Hitler*.

'I think I caught the way he does his "f"s rather well, don't you think?'

'How did you know?' said Hansen.

'That you were there? Well, it was certainly a masterstroke on my part, but you did help yourself too. Rather a clever idea, posting everything you knew to Lotte.'

'She told you?'

'Yes. But I think you should ask her yourself.'

When Hansen looked more closely at the driver, she turned back to look at him and smiled.

Hansen started to laugh, but regretted it immediately, as his whole chest burned and throbbed all at once.

'Steady. You've got broken ribs, I'd warrant. I'd say, well… all of them. Arm, too. And as for your face, well, let's just say I won't be using you for any more honeytraps any time soon.'

'You've blown your cover,' said Hansen, feeling every word in his swollen mouth.

'Oh, well and truly. It will take one telephone call to break open my legend like an oyster. I've never liked shellfish, incidentally. So I'm afraid you might have done better staying where you were.'

'I'm sorry.'

'You do have a unique way of persuading other people to do things for you, Richard. And, strangely, not to resent you for it. It must be that Hansen charm. If we had time, I might ask you to have a go at turning Eva Braun.'

'Nothing to do with me. I've just learned not to underestimate certain people,' he said, looking pointedly at Lotte.

'Indeed,' said Thurso. 'It seems she knew where to find me, in any case. A happy by-product of following you, not that you noticed. But if we do make it…' Thurso's voice dropped and he continued in a grave tone, 'I do believe your greatest challenge lies ahead.'

'What do you mean?'

'Well, as we always used to toast in the navy: "to wives and sweethearts – may they never meet!"'

He chuckled to himself. Hansen looked at Lotte, who appeared not to have understood. Hansen tried to take in what Thurso was saying.

'Emily… Emily is safe?'

'Oh yes, safely across the border with her sister and her niece three days ago.'

Hansen wasn't sure if he had understood any of what he had just heard. Not for the first time since waking, he wondered if it was all a dream. Certainly his head still felt full of cotton wool and his limbs as if they belonged to anyone but him.

'Did you say… three days?' he asked.

'Yes. More or less, give or take a few hours.'

'Why didn't you just leave?'

'Well, I had assumed you'd give me up inside ten minutes, so I didn't think there was any point. I was just waiting around for Johnny Gestapo to come and collar me. But then I remembered that promise I made you, fool that I am…' Hansen looked blank. 'To help you rescue Emily? Goodness, I could have saved myself the trouble. And, you know, doing the impossible takes just that bit longer.'

'There is a heart inside the tin man after all.'

'Purely pragmatic.'

'It wasn't only Lotte following me.'

'You shock me.'

'I think it was my uncle who gave me away.'

'Why would he do that?'

'I met him by chance.'

'Yes, he mentioned it. Nearly gave the old man a heart attack. You weren't supposed to know about each other. But in any case, he's safe now too, with his wife.'

'Safe?'

'Who do you think took Emily across? He's been running our lines into Switzerland for the last two years, getting prisoners and information across. It obviously runs in the family. Although *he* does at least notice when he's being followed.'

Thurso continued in rapid fire, though what came next seemed unimportant to Hansen compared to the safety of his family. He rested his eyes again and tried to blot out the pain. Consciously and unconsciously, a weight had been with him since the war began. Now it was eased for the first time. To know that Emily was finally out of danger. At the farm he'd had so many questions. And she had had the same hollow expression that he had seen on the faces of prisoners at Dachau. He feared to know but was also desperate to know. And to find a way to comfort her.

Sleep must have come on again, for when he opened his eyes once more, the rocking of the car had stopped. He shuffled himself gradually into a sitting position, intense pain in every tiny movement. He took a breath as he rested his head against the seat. The leather was pleasantly cool against his skin, which now felt warm to the touch.

The back door opened, and Lotte leaned in.

'Can I get you anything? Coffee? I have a little bread and cheese.'

'Thank you.'

He found himself ravenously hungry. He had eaten nothing since his capture. They had allowed him merely a little water. However, as he tried to eat now, he found each bite was an ordeal, and he could hardly hold the bread in his hand. In frustration he threw it down, feeling utterly helpless.

'I'll help you,' Lotte said kindly, and began breaking off small pieces and soaking them in the coffee so he could chew them more easily.

'I don't deserve your kindness,' he said, between mouthfuls.

She looked down, brushing it off.

'Nevertheless. I can't watch you suffer.'

As he ate, she watched him, as though she wanted to say more but was holding back.

'I was worried he would hurt you,' Hansen said, breaking the silence.

'My father? He would never do that.' There was deliberate emphasis on the *he*.

'But you can't go back?'

'Not now. And I don't wish to. I wanted to be someone else. I still do, even if it's not...'

Though she didn't finish the sentence, he could fill in the gap for himself well enough. And he understood how he had hurt her. Arguments of necessity or the requirements of the job were inadequate when he could see the effects in her eyes.

'What I promised to you...' he began uncertainly. 'I will honour—'

'Stop!' she said. 'Do you think I want that? I won't be your obligation.'

'It's not an obligation...'

'Then can you tell me that you love me?'

She studied his face, and for a moment there seemed to be just a glimmer of hope there, before his silence made her head fall again. She shook it sadly.

'My English is not the best, but I understood you well enough before,' she said. 'You want to be with your wife.

'No, you really shouldn't underestimate me.' She smiled a little at his obvious embarrassment.

'I did think... I mean, I thought, perhaps... I do care for you. But any love there was, I now realise, was a memory. A memory of my love for Emily. Because you remind me so much of her... before.'

'I should take that as a compliment, I think,' said Lotte.

'In another time and place...'

'No. Let us not play that game. I won't spend any more time hoping for things to be different. I have a choice. To resent you and hate you, and carry that bitterness around with me. Or to remember the times we had, and how you made me feel, as a good thing. I wanted to have choices, and I believe memory is as much a choice as any other. So I'm not going to be angry. I can't look at you now and want to hurt you. I can't.'

In great pain, and with every ounce of strength he possessed, Hansen leant towards her and gently caressed her face, allowing his forehead to gently rest against hers.

'If you will let me, I should always like to call you Lotte.'

'Always.'

They continued on their journey, keeping to back roads and tracks. Thurso took the wheel, and Lotte sat with Hansen on the back seat. Gradually drowsiness overtook him, and, increasingly clouded by sleep, he found himself resting his head in her lap. She would stroke his hair tenderly and he would drift away, only to be wakened again by a movement of the car, bringing a renewed wave of pain.

As the light of the day faded, the car pulled to a stop. With a gentle tap on the shoulder, he found Thurso leaning across him.

'Hello, old man. We're near the border now. I have diplomatic papers for myself and my wife here, but I'm afraid we'll have more of a challenge explaining your presence, especially since you look like you've been ten rounds with Joe Louis.'

Hansen wanted to reply but found himself barely able to keep his eyes open.

'He doesn't look well,' he heard Thurso say under his breath to Lotte.

'He has a fever,' said Lotte. 'He's burning up.'

'Well, it won't be long now. Take care of him,' Thurso replied in hushed tones. Then to Hansen again:

'We're going to have to cover you with some coats and luggage, old man. Can you slide into the footwell? I'm sorry to have to do this, but you'll need to stay as still as you can. We can only hope they don't look too closely. I know this crossing and they rarely do.'

'What happens if they do?' he heard Lotte whisper. Hansen did not hear Thurso's reply.

He lay as still as he could manage, his body shivering cold though he was sweating with heat. They laid blankets across him and then stacked heavy objects – the suitcases, he guessed – on top. They pressed into his ribs and the pain was excruciating, but he bit his lip and waited.

He felt the car move off, lurching from side to side and bumping down the rough road. Each jolt brought new agony. At last, they began to slow down.

'We're at the checkpoint, old man,' he heard Thurso call. 'Stay as quiet as the proverbial church mouse now.'

There was little Hansen could do but concentrate on remaining silent, though he was slick with perspiration and struggling to breathe under the thick blankets. He searched for something to focus on, and only one image came to mind. Though she might never want to see him again, he thought of Emily and how it would be to hold her again. She was so clear in his mind's eye, but there was a nagging doubt, too, that it was all hopeless. He could feel himself drifting away through this infection, if that's what it was, and ending any chance of a second reunion. Nevertheless, there was comfort in feeling close to her, and he held to the image as intensely as he could manage, thinking of what he would say to her that might heal the rift between them.

'Papers, please,' he heard someone say, as if from a great distance.

'My name is Friedrich Herrmann. This is my wife Elsa.'

'What is your business in Switzerland?'

'I am procuring automobile parts.'

'You take your wife with you on business trips?'

'What can I say? She likes to ski. Don't tell my boss!'

There was no response from the guard. Then: 'One moment.'

There was quiet for some minutes. Hansen could only hear the sound of his own breathing, slow and laboured.

'What is he doing?' he heard Lotte whisper.

'I'm not sure.'

'Is he speaking on the telephone?' she hissed again.

'Stay calm. It may be nothing. A routine call. A wrong number…'

There was quiet again. Prolonged quiet. It was maddening not to know what was happening. And harder still to keep his mind focused. He seemed to be drifting in a fog, at some moments spinning, at others falling.

Then, in his delirium, he thought he heard the sound of a car door opening. Something shifted in the weight on top of him.

'Specifications and blueprints,' he heard Thurso say. 'And bearer bonds for the transaction.'

'And these other cases?'

'My wife's things. She will always overpack.'

Hansen felt other cases move for a moment and held his breath.

After a wait that seemed interminable, there was another clunk as the door shut.

'Alright. Move along,' he heard the guard say at last.

The car began to move again, and Hansen breathed once more. Emily was safe. Lotte was safe. His mind drifted again and the world around him faded away.

Chapter 22

Mira curled up and rested her head. Beatrice had fallen asleep, though it was difficult to say how long that would last. Each night since their arrival in Switzerland, she had woken with bad dreams and Mira had done her best to soothe and reassure her. It was something she felt sure Emily would have done, had Mira not taken care to prevent her. Emily needed the rest more than she did. More than any of them. Her sister had tossed and turned as well, but now seemed to have settled, finally.

She wondered what it was in Emily's thoughts that kept her awake. She kept so much to herself. It was habit, perhaps, or a way of protecting them and herself. Mira felt as close to her sister as anyone, and yet there was still much she didn't know. Her constant prodding to reveal more was an irritation, she knew, but she couldn't help herself. And most insistent was her curiosity about Richard.

When she asked herself why this was of such importance, why it should matter to her who her sister loved, it had become increasingly clear to her. It was vicarious. She longed for a connection just as profound with someone of her own. There had been more to her dreams of rescue, which she had known to be a fantasy, than simple hope. There was a passion there too.

For a while, it had seemed that all hope for the future – for that intimacy, for a career, for a life of any kind – would be lost. When she considered how close they had come, she shivered. And she knew all that Emily had sacrificed to keep her safe. The guards in the prison cell. Emily thought to hide what had happened, but she knew. And there was the food she had given to Mira and Beatrice, when she was starving herself. Mira knew. And the guilt she bore for defending them and doing what was necessary. The guilt for ending a life. She knew that, too.

If only I could take all that from you, Emmy, she thought to herself. *To help you forget.*

And now, misery heaped on misery, there was the waiting. The waiting for news, good or bad.

She thought of the promise she'd asked Emily to make her: to always keep her with her wherever she went. It had been years ago, and to Mira it seemed as though it had been another person entirely who had asked it. The Mira who had believed in a world that was wondrous and shining. A child. She looked around her now and saw a world that was nothing of the kind. It was cruel and malign. And yet, there was life. And she had learned that she could stand on her own two feet. She had helped people, and not just accepted help. And she could fight, like her father had, like Toto and Gabriella had. And like Emily always would. Maybe the dream of being a doctor was not so foolish. When she looked back, she had found the strength to do what she had done in the camp, with nothing. How much more could she do? If strength was enough to earn a better future, then there was no one who deserved it more than her sister. She would pray for it. To conjure up the ending that Jane Austen would have written for her, where hope would be rewarded with happiness.

The next evening, the telephone rang. Emily picked it up and spoke in English. It was a short conversation, and at the end she replaced the receiver and let out a deep sigh.

'Who was that, Emmy?' Mira asked. 'Is there news?'

'Yes,' said Emily slowly. She put her hands to her temples and seemed, finally, to relax. 'There is news.'

Mira watched Emily cross the room. She was calmer than she had been for days. Calmer since the telephone call. And almost happy since the events of that morning. Something of her old spirit was returned. A sense of purpose and a dignity.

She went to the dresser and opened the suitcase she had brought from Germany. The case she had been determined not to leave behind, despite everything. The case which she had only said was 'important'.

She took out what appeared to be a letter and sat down on the bed with her back to Mira. She studied it quietly. Touching, almost caressing, the paper.

Then she turned, and with a wan smile, she beckoned to Beatrice. The little girl crawled across to where she was and climbed into her lap, happily sucking her thumb and cuddling the teddy bear which Mr Crosse had got for her. Mira watched them play together. Beatrice giggled as Emily tickled her. Mira smiled to see the difference in her. The little girl responding naturally to the change in her mother. She paused at that thought. She wondered if it was wrong to think in those terms. Except it felt natural to think it. She went across and sat next to them.

'Do you like your teddy, Bea?' she asked. Her niece nodded decisively. 'Does he have a name?'

'Mmm,' she considered. 'Bear Bear.'

'Ah, that's a nice name. What does Mama think, is that a good name?'

Emily nodded. 'Yes, it's...' Then she realised what Mira had said. '...a good name.'

'Yes,' said Mira. 'I think it's the right name.'

Emily looked at her inquisitively. Mira nodded to her with determination.

'If that's your choice?' she asked.

'Yes, it's his name,' said Beatrice simply.

'Of course,' said Mira. Then she looked at Emily again. 'I know it's your choice, Bea. It couldn't be otherwise.'

Emily reached out and gently stroked her sister's arm. 'Are you sure?' she whispered.

'Gabriella would have chosen you. And I'm not ready, not yet.' She paused. 'I need to follow my dreams. And so do you. And…' she began, mischievously, 'it's the pragmatic choice.'

Emily smiled. Then she seemed to become thoughtful. She picked up the letter once again and held it close to her heart.

'Beatrice,' she said at last, 'I would like to introduce you to someone. Someone very important to me. Someone I love. And I hope you will come to love him too, in time.'

Chapter 23

Hansen stretched out his arms and, in the darkness, shadows of imagined enemies seemed to rise and morph back into the furniture when he turned to look again.

Always in the corner of his eye, always out of reach. He wasn't sure whether he was awake or dreaming. His limbs were sluggish, as in a nightmare – rigid and slow to respond. And he seemed to spin and whirl through everything, unable to focus, unable to stop himself. But then, in the darkness and the uncertainty, he felt a warmth. A reassuring presence. He reached out for it and, it seemed, felt a connection. A spark or a shiver of something real. Someone real. Just for a moment, in a sea of chaos, heat and pain. Like a drowning man, he struggled to regain the security of what he had touched, just for a moment, but the connection was lost, and the room of phantoms and illusion seemed to close around him again.

With a glare of bright light, he found his eyes open. He breathed steadily and took in the unmoving room, nondescript and dull now in the light of day. He pulled himself up in the bed to look more closely at the place. He had no memory of how he had come to be where he was. And something else was missing. Pain. That companion which had travelled with him from the moment of his capture was, it seemed, gone.

'Hello?' he called out. 'Hello!'

There were a few moments' delay before the door opened and a nurse walked in, followed by, if his eyes did not deceive him, Ernest Crosse.

'Awake, I see?' he said, stowing his pipe in his pocket at the insistence of the nurse.

'With you here, I'm not certain if I am or not,' said Hansen.

'No, well, the morphine won't help with that. But I am certainly not a figment of your imagination, and you're safe, in Switzerland. Time to rest now.'

'Is everyone safe?'

'If by "everyone" you mean Emily, then yes. You may not have noticed, but she was here. She sat with you all night, as she has for the last week.'

He couldn't help but smile.

'I never dared hope that she would want to see me again.'

'Of course she wants to see you,' said the nurse rather pointedly.

He recognised her face now, though his memory was still fogged. Not a nurse as he had first taken her to be.

'You are…'

'Mira,' she said. 'Emmy's sister.'

'Of course. I'm glad to see you safe as well.'

She smiled warmly and fluffed his pillow so he could sit up properly.

'This is all hard to believe,' he said. 'To be here.'

'It was a near thing, old chap,' said Crosse. 'They banged you up pretty thoroughly. Something of a miracle to get you out.' He grasped the crucifix which hung around his neck. 'But thanks to the care you've had here, you're going to be fine.'

'We should let him rest now,' said Mira.

'Of course,' said Crosse. 'I'll be back later. I'll have a word with the powers that be to make sure you get everything you need. By the by, when you see Emily, perhaps you could tell her that I have arranged a passport for her and little Beatrice. In the name she requested – Hansen.'

He gave a wink and took his leave, and Hansen was left alone with his thoughts. Half agony, half hope. That such precious feelings might not be gone forever. In the days since, he had had time enough to consider what he would say. He rehearsed it all again in his mind as Mira left the room, and within only a few minutes she returned, with her sister this time.

'I'll leave you,' she said.

She closed the door and left the two of them alone. Emily hesitated for a moment, but then, in a sudden burst, was at his side. She took his hands without a word and held them close, caressing the scars on his wrists.

'There was something I should have said before,' he said. 'Something I ought to have said before all this began, to prevent it ever happening.'

She looked at him enquiringly, continuing to clutch his hands as if they were locked together.

He paused, gathering his thoughts and his resolution.

'I'm sorry,' he said at last. 'I'm sorry, I'm sorry, I'm sorry…'

She grasped his hands more tightly and lifted them to her lips, kissing them tenderly. Then she shook her head vigorously.

'No apologies,' she said. 'I forgive you.'

Slowly, he disengaged his hand from hers and put it gently to her face. She edged away a little, and he could hear her breath quicken, but she allowed him to caress it.

'They hurt you, didn't they?'

Her instinct was to back away, but he stopped her, taking back her hand. He realised now, he couldn't always protect her. He couldn't always stop her getting hurt. And he had to allow her to hurt in her own way. But his duty was to be there by her side, to help her through.

'It's alright,' he said. 'No words are needed. It's enough that I know. Your strength and your love were mine when I needed them. Even when I felt I didn't deserve them. But you don't need to be strong now. You don't need to hold on anymore. Let me hold *you*.'

They grasped for each other, feeling every one of the many months they had been apart. His embrace surrounded and sheltered her and, like letting go of a weight held taut for the longest time, she fell limp, the tears flowing in a way they had not done since she had first left. She shook uncontrollably, but she was safe. Vulnerable. Human. Loved.

When at last she felt calm, she turned back to him and just gazed, trying to re-remember everything.

'Do you remember, we used to say we think to the future, not the past?' he said. 'But it can't be like that. The past matters, however painful, however imperfect.

'I want to talk about it. I want to talk about it all. And I want to talk about our family. Our children. All of them.'

She took his hand again.

'You always had your duty. But now I have a duty too. I would like for you to share it with me. Would you like to say hello? To Beatrice? To… our daughter?'

Postscript

*Being a transcript taken from Hansard, 13 July
1972, of a speech given by the Honourable Member
for Oxford, Miss Beatrice Portinari-Hansen, during
the third reading of the European Communities Bill.*

'Mr Speaker, I am thankful for being afforded the
chance to speak in this debate today, as it has
personal interest for me. My right honourable friend
the Member for Wolverhampton South West may
disagree with me. Indeed, I'm sure he does, but
today could mark a watershed in the history of this
country.

'Honourable members may know that I am
proud to call myself a "mongrel". Through my
adoptive parents – and I am pleased to say my
mother is here in the visitors' gallery today – I am
British, but also Italian and German. Italian by birth,
I am Jewish by culture and British by upbringing.
This country afforded me – indeed, all of us – a
home at different times. I am an immigrant. But, as
my mother is fond of saying, we are all of us
immigrants; we only need to go back far enough to
discover it.

'My family knows well what can happen when we forget the ties that bind us and focus instead on those things that divide us. My mother, who gave birth to me, fought fascism all her life and died in a concentration camp doing exactly that. She never gave up the fight. But as honourable members on the benches opposite will remember, it was Sir Winston Churchill himself who told us that "to Jaw-Jaw is better than to War-War". My family, through their work at the United Nations for the last quarter of a century – and my aunt prominently at the World Health Organization – have sought to work for peace, understanding and care for all. To make friends of those we once called enemies.

'My father saw a world war that promised an end to all war, only for there to be another twenty years later. We have come a long way in a short time, and I hope that, if we do our duty and pass this bill tonight, we will take a step further on that road – to join the European family, and to be able to say, finally, and this time with certainty: "never again".'